The Me I Meant to Be

The Me I Meant to Be

SOPHIE JORDAN

HOUGHTON MIFFLIN HARCOURT
BOSTON NEW YORK

hmhco.com

The text was set in Palatino.

Library of Congress Cataloging-in-Publication Data
Names: Jordan, Sophie, author.
Title: The me I meant to be / by Sophie Jordan.
Description: Boston ; New York : Houghton Mifflin Harcourt , [2019] |
Summary: Told from separate viewpoints, best friends Willa and Flor are
tempted by love that would violate the Girl Code when Willa's long-term crush,
Zach, breaks up with Flor, who is fighting her own crush on her math tutor.
Identifiers: LCCN 2018007164 | ISBN 9781328977069 (hardback)
Subjects: | CYAC: Best friends—Fiction. | Friendship—Fiction. |
Dating (Social customs)—Fiction. | Love—Fiction. | Family problems—Fiction. |
High schools—Fiction. | Schools—Fiction.
Classification: LCC PZ7.J76845 Me 2019 | DDC [Fic]—dc23
LC record available at https://lccn.loc.gov/2018007164

Printed in the United States of America
DOC 10 9 8 7 6 5 4 3 2 1
4500744074

For all the girls out there:
May your journey be full of highs and lows (but mostly highs),
and may there be good friends, first kisses, and plenty of
chocolate to sustain you along the way.

The Me I Meant to Be

GIRL CODE #1:

Never date a friend's ex or a guy your friend is really into.

Willa

"WHAT ever happened to girl code?" Jenna asked, sitting cross-legged in the center of my bed, nodding grimly as her teeth savagely tore at a Twizzler.

"Yeah, well, Ava isn't a believer," Flor muttered as she crouched in front of my window, peering between the open blinds like this was some kind of stakeout.

Sadly, it was not an unfamiliar scenario. Girls had been looking out my blinds to the house next door for years.

I lived next door to my best friend's infatuation. In fact, he was most girls' infatuation, but at the moment I only had Flor to contend with. Trust me, she was more than enough.

For ten plus years, I'd had a bird's-eye view into Zach Tucker's life—a fact that made me the envy of every girl at Madison High. It also made me the supreme authority on all things Zach Tucker. It wasn't a designation I wanted, but it was mine nonetheless. Perhaps the thing I was *best* known for. Yeah. Not something to be proud of.

Complete strangers—girls, naturally—would approach me in the halls just to ask if I really lived next door to Zach Tucker.

I needed to move.

"Remember when Ava moved here in seventh grade and I invited her to sit with us at lunch? Our fathers golf together." Flor looked back at me, outrage brimming in her eyes. "I gave her a ride all last year so she didn't have to take the bus."

"No loyalty," Jenna agreed, not helping. I sent her a look. She shrugged and took another vicious bite from the long rope of red.

I was all about *not* fanning the flames of Flor's indignation, but Jenna didn't seem to get that.

Flor looked back out the blinds with a frustrated sigh, bending at the waist and propping her hands on shapely hips. Hours of soccer per week gave her a body I could only dream about. In fact, that was what most guys did—dream about Flor Hidalgo's body. Except Zach Tucker.

Unfathomable as it seemed, he had held that dream in the palm of his hand and he didn't want it anymore. But then he was Zach Tucker. A dream in his own right. He could have any girl he wanted.

I opened my mouth to defend Ava, but then I didn't know if I should . . . or *could*. I didn't exactly know what was right here. I only knew that *I* would never make a play for Zach.

Even if I thought I had a chance.

Even if I hadn't been friend-zoned since we were eight and riding our bikes around the neighborhood.

Flor had had him first. Always and forever. He was her ex-boyfriend. Bottom line. I knew that. Ava should have known it too.

Flor faced me again. "Have you seen him today?" Her dark eyes searched mine. "Is he even home?" Hair in a ponytail, makeup long sweated off from running up and down a soccer field, she was still prettier than any girl had a right to be.

Jenna stared at me too, waiting and sucking on her Twizzler until it resembled a disgusting red antenna.

Spinning around in my swivel chair, I looked at Zach's window directly across from mine and felt the familiar ache in my chest.

Ivy draped the entire side of his house. Only his window was spared the tangle of green. The devouring mass of vines and leaves had mesmerized me over the years, growing and expanding before my very gaze—just like my infatuation with Zach Tucker.

Once a year, Mrs. Tucker hired someone to trim back the ivy and keep it from swallowing his window. As a little kid, I would always breathe a little easier then. As though Zach were saved from being consumed.

Motioning in the general direction of Zach's driveway, I pointed out, "His car's here."

Flor looked back at me, sinking her perfect white teeth deep into her bottom lip. "But he could have gone somewhere with his mom or a friend or something. Did you see someone pick him up?"

"No, but I haven't been watching his house all afternoon."

"You know, you could just text him," Jenna suggested, dropping flat on her back on my bed, her hair fanning out around her head in a golden pool.

I glanced back at my laptop. Mr. Martinez had posted practice questions for tomorrow's test. We were supposed to be studying, but I should have known we weren't going to get any work done. An hour in and we hadn't even made it through two problems. And I still needed to practice my cello. Ms. Rivela had assigned a new arrangement, and I was really struggling with it.

Flor shot Jenna a quick glare. "I have texted him. He hasn't replied yet."

"Maybe he's too busy with Ava."

I shot Jenna a death look. Did she really have to go there? Speculation was already ripe at school ever since Ava had sat with Zach at lunch this afternoon and not us like she did every day. It was a bold move. The kind of move someone only made when they had a sudden change in relationship status. Everyone gawked as she plopped herself down beside him. Laughing, flirting. Touching his arm every chance she got.

Jenna shrugged back at me.

"You think he's with her now?" Flor demanded, her velvety eyes wide with alarm. And that was strange. Flor Hidalgo was many things, but never insecure. If this was what happened when a guy dumped you, no thanks. Single sounded just right to me.

Zach had broken up with her nine days ago. Nine endless days ago. They had been together for three months. The longest three months of my life. A month ago I'd sensed that Zach wanted out.

There were all the little signs. Easy to catch if you knew him. His eyes strayed from Flor's face when she was talking. When they touched or kissed, he pulled away first. He missed a couple of her soccer games even when I knew he didn't have anywhere else to be. And then there was the night when Flor got stupid drunk.

4

Something went down between them that night, because he broke it off the next day.

It was like watching a car crash about to happen. Everything dragged to slow motion. I knew it was coming, but I wasn't able to do anything except brace for the impact.

Still, I didn't think he would hook up with another girl so soon. But this was high school, and hot, popular guys didn't stay alone for long. I knew that. I had just hoped Flor would be over him before then. Or it would be summer and I'd be busy working and able to escape the ensuing drama.

Flor sank down on the foot of my bed, her face screwed tight with emotion. Clearly, she was far from over him. She pulled her knees up to her chest. She was still wearing her shin guards and socks, dirty and grass-stained from practice. "Friends don't do this to friends."

I glanced back at my laptop, tapping my fingers nervously on my desk. The guilt was there, even though I didn't act on it.

"Willa?" Flor stared at me in an expectant way. "Can you believe Ava is doing this to me?"

"Yeah. It's . . . wrong."

"Wrong?" Her beautiful eyes blinked. "It's more than *wrong*. It goes against girl code. We might not be best friends, but we're tight."

"There should be an official girl-code manual given out the first day of freshman year," Jenna declared. "It would make girls think twice before they betray their friends. At least there wouldn't be any confusion." She stabbed a finger in the air. "You break girl code and everyone knows you're a traitor."

"For real." Flor fell back on the bed beside Jenna and took a Twizzler from the bag Jenna held out to her. A moment of silence fell.

I turned back to my laptop, looking at the long-neglected math problem but failing to see it.

The Twizzler bag crinkled as they continued to eat.

The numbers blurred and danced. I side-eyed the window of Zach's room. There were no blinds. Just curtains, and they were drawn, revealing a neat sliver of his navy blue bedspread. His mom always made his bed for him. She doted on him—even though he valiantly resisted her efforts.

Somewhere inside my house my sister's child started crying.

"Chloe!" Mom's voice rang out from downstairs.

I squeezed the bridge of my nose. My sister didn't answer, but I didn't expect she would. She was conveniently in the shower. She'd been in the bathroom for two hours. Ever since my brother-in-law dumped Chloe for another woman and she moved back home, she'd been spending a lot of time in the shower. I think she thought no one could hear her crying over the running water. The water bill was getting out of hand, if the increase of ramen on the menu was any indication.

"That's it," Flor suddenly announced. She sat up, waving a floppy Twizzler, her face alight with inspiration. "We need to write it."

"Write what?" I asked.

She waved her hand in a little circle. "An official girl-code manual. We'll write one and distribute it. Just like Jenna said." A militant gleam entered her eyes. "All the Avas of the world will know their betrayals aren't okay, and everyone will see them for the back-stabbers they really are."

"Yeah." Jenna propped herself up on her elbows. "Right on."

I stared at them both, my stomach twisting into knots. They were serious.

"Quick." Flor motioned to my laptop. "Start a file in Google Docs. That way we can edit and add to it as we go."

Stifling a sigh, I opened up a document and titled it: *The Official Guide to Girl Code*. Staring at those words on the screen, I felt a strange sense of foreboding sweep over me, and those knots just twisted tighter.

Flor leaned over my shoulder. "Nice. All right. I think we can all agree on the first rule." For a moment I didn't move, simply gazed at the blank screen, my fingers poised over the keyboard. The toddler was full-on wailing now, and I knew I should get up and go hold her. Mom was too tense. It was like Mia could sense that and cried harder.

"Come on, Willa," Jenna pressured. "Type."

Nodding, I started typing.

Flor cast a heavy shadow over me as she read my words aloud. "'Girl Code Number One: Never date a friend's ex or a guy your friend is really into.'"

GIRL CODE #2:

If your dog hates him, you should rethink whether the guy needs to be in your house.

Flor

A beat-up Honda was parked out front when I got home. A shadow sat behind the wheel, and I remembered with a jolt that I was supposed to be here at seven.

"Great." I sighed and bumped the steering wheel with my fist. I'd been so distracted with everything else that I'd forgotten my tutoring session. Not good. I'd practically had to beg the guy to give me even an hour of his time. Without Mr. Martinez's encouragement, he wouldn't have agreed at all.

For whatever reason, Grayson O'Malley, National Merit Scholar, this year's likely valedictorian, president of the robotics club, didn't *want* to tutor me. It didn't even matter that he charged thirty an hour and I could pay him. Apparently he was very in demand and had his pick of clients, and he didn't *want* to make room for me. It had taken considerable begging.

And I'd kept him waiting.

I guess it was a lucky thing he was still even here.

Guilt gnawed at me as I parked in the driveway and stepped out of my car. The evening air was dense and sat on my skin like a fine vapor. I inhaled a thick breath.

When I turned around, he'd already emerged from his vehicle. His long legs carried him up the driveway.

"Hey," I greeted him, pasting a smile on my face, hoping that would encourage the flat, unbending line of his mouth to curve upward. "Sorry."

He glanced at his phone. "You're eighteen minutes late." Still no smile.

I clung to mine, using that hundred-watt grin that usually got me most anything. I wasn't sure what else to say. I'd already apologized.

He looked notably unimpressed, staring down at me through his black-framed glasses. Like I wasn't anyone special. Like I wasn't . . . anyone. "I get paid by the hour. I started charging you eighteen minutes ago."

"Of course you did." I dropped the smile. It had been failing me lately anyway. First Tucker. Now Tutor Guy. Maybe I needed to buy some teeth whitener or something. Or just accept I wasn't as cute as I thought I was. Clearly, I was infinitely resistible. Actually, the first person to prove this fact had been my mother. Otherwise she would never have left.

"I have to leave at eight. I have another client."

Client. He was such a nerd.

"C'mon." I led him through the wrought-iron patio gate. He caught it, stopping it from clanging loudly behind him. Most of my friends didn't bother to catch it and just let it crash shut.

The pool waterfall gurgled as I stopped in front of the back door. Inside, Rowdy was barking, his nails scratching madly on the wood floor. When I glanced back at Grayson, he was surveying the backyard. My gaze swept over it all: the pool with the rock waterfall, the outdoor kitchen, the colossal rock fireplace surrounded by plush couches. It was like something out of a home-and-outdoor magazine.

I looked at it all from his eyes. A boy who drove a beat-up car and tutored struggling kids like me for thirty bucks an hour. It was impressive. Decadent, even. He glanced at me and I read his expression clearly. He thought I was a spoiled brat, and I guess I was. I was the picture of privilege. I'd done nothing to earn any of this, but I had it nonetheless.

After unlocking the door, I went inside, telling myself that it didn't matter what he thought of me and it shouldn't bug me.

Rowdy charged out, burying his nose directly in Grayson's crotch. I grinned as he hopped and danced on his feet, shoving at Rowdy's nose.

Grabbing Rowdy's collar, I dragged him off the guy. "C'mon, boy." I shoved him out onto the back porch. Moving an overweight Labrador wasn't an easy feat. I blew out a breath as I shut the door behind him.

"Thanks." Grayson shook a leg as though needing to adjust his jeans after Rowdy's vigorous greeting.

"We can sit here." I motioned to the kitchen table. It was big, with eight chairs surrounding it. A waste considering Dad and I never even sat down together for a meal anymore. Even when Mom had been here it was just the three of us.

"Want a drink? I'm thirsty." I dropped my backpack on the table. His eyes flicked to his phone, clearly checking the time. "I know, I know. I'm on the clock."

He shrugged. "It's your hour. Get your drink. I'm fine."

I moved into the kitchen and poured a glass of juice, looking up when I heard the back door open. I watched as Grayson let the dog back inside.

When I returned, he was already sitting in his chair with Rowdy panting dotingly between his feet, getting his ears scratched.

"I let him in," he unnecessarily explained. "He was whining."

My opinion of him adjusted slightly. If he was a dog person, he couldn't be all that bad.

I took the seat beside him and opened my laptop to the online practice problems.

"The test is tomorrow . . ." I started to say.

"So you thought you'd start reviewing tonight?" His eyes were gleaming dark and full of derision behind the lenses of his glasses. *Derision.* See. There was an SAT word. I wasn't terrible at every subject.

"If you must know, I tried this on my own at first. I've never needed a tutor before."

"Okay," he said, the single word full of skepticism.

For the next twenty minutes, he watched me go through the practice problems, interjecting only when he saw me making a mistake—which was more often than not. He never did the work for me. Annoying at first, even though I realized that was the whole point. Me figuring it out for myself.

He was quiet, patiently watching me work, his voice deep and steady beside me when he did speak.

I watched him under my lashes as he explained how to break down inverse functions in an easy manner. Well, easy for him. He acted like it was as simple as making a peanut butter sandwich. That must be nice: being so smart that the things that stumped the majority of people came easy to you.

I guess he was attractive. In a nerd way. Some girls would go for him. Probably Willa. But totally not my taste. I preferred athletes. Football players. Soccer players. Throw in the occasional wrestler. I liked a guy who could carry me out of a burning building if need be and not break a sweat.

He was wearing a henley shirt, long sleeves pushed up to his elbows, but his forearms looked strong.

"You work out?" I asked abruptly.

He looked up and blinked, his brown eyes confused. "What?"

I shook my head, mentally kicking myself. "Nothing."

We spent another five minutes with our heads down, working.

The flash of headlights streaking across the patio broke my concentration. A car door slammed shut, followed by another.

Voices drifted from the driveway. Dad was home. And he wasn't alone. As usual.

I felt Grayson's stare on the side of my face.

"My dad," I explained.

The outside gate opened. Dad and Dana passed in front of the blinds, carrying Whole Foods bags.

They entered the doorway laughing, so caught up in each other they didn't even notice us sitting at the table. Dad ushered her ahead of him, his hand on the small of her back.

"And you're going to be the man to teach me to love chicken mole?" Dana teased, tossing a head full of perfectly color-treated blond hair.

"The way I prepare it? It will melt in your mouth. Trust me. It's better than s—"

"Oh!" Dana's gaze landed on me. "Flor." She said my name like she was surprised to see me. Like I didn't live here. So annoying.

But then lately she had been here enough that she might as well live here too.

Her beautifully manicured hand fluttered to the front of my father's shirt with practiced ease. She looked up at him as though they shared some inside joke. I could just imagine. Gross.

"Flor, princess. You're home." Dad shifted the bags in his hands.

"Yeah. I live here."

He chuckled, sharing a long glance with Dana. "We just thought you were out with your friends tonight."

Dad didn't really know what I was doing these days. The first six months after Mom left, he wallowed in wine and work and overparented me. He started making sure I drank milk with every meal and packing my lunches for school. Elaborate bento boxes that he learned how to do online. No one had made my lunch since the fourth grade. And he cared about things like curfew and who I was dating and how short my skirts were. I was actually glad when he joined a dating service. I even encouraged him to do it! I wanted him distracted and a little less involved in my life.

You know the adage "Be careful what you wish for"? Yeah. That.

I never expected him to so fully throw himself into the dating scene. Or for the women he dated to be so young.

I never expected that he would settle on one of them so soon or that she would only be eight years older than me. It was pretty gross.

"It's a school night." I motioned to the laptop in front of me. "Got a test tomorrow."

"And who's your friend?" he asked, but the question was more obligatory than interested. His gaze was already following Dana in her skinny jeans as she moved into the kitchen, her high-heeled boots clacking on the tile floor.

"This is Grayson, my tutor."

"I didn't know you needed a tutor." Dad frowned, and I resisted pointing out that there was a lot going on in my life that he didn't know about these days.

Dana angled her head. "But your dad said you're so smart."

Subtle. I smiled brightly at her, tapping my pencil on the table. "Guess he was wrong about that."

Dad cleared his throat. Slid another glance at Dana. Looking back at me, he lifted a grocery bag. "We were just going to make some dinner. Did you eat?"

We again. When exactly did they become a *we*? Dana looked like she should be clubbing with other twenty-somethings rather than dating my fifty-year-old father.

"I'm not hungry."

"Ah." He nodded and moved into the kitchen, his manner

much more subdued. Because I was here. He couldn't be himself around me anymore. The himself that suddenly had a twenty-five-year-old girlfriend. My father had become a cliché. Who knew it could happen to him? To me?

"What about your friend?" Dad looked at Grayson. "Are you hungry, Mason?"

"Grayson," I corrected.

"No, thank you, sir."

"Such pretty manners." Dana hummed in approval as she turned and opened a cabinet, stretching on her tiptoes, her ass on full display as she reached for wine glasses. Settling back down on her heels, she turned and bestowed her glossy-lipped smile over her shoulder at all of us . . . lingering, I couldn't help noticing, on Grayson. "Whatcha working on?"

I shot a look at Grayson, scowling. He didn't seem affected by the ass flaunting. At least there was that. Not many eighteen-year-old guys could stand up to such enticement. I mean, my own father couldn't, and he was fifty.

"Math," I supplied, trying to hide my irritability. I didn't want her talking to my friends. Especially guy friends. Not that Grayson was a friend, exactly. But still.

"Oh, I was never good with numbers," she commented with an airy laugh.

"Big shock," I muttered under my voice.

Grayson made a slight sound that could have been laughter. When I glanced at him, however, his expression was as bland as ever, focused on the screen of my laptop and the problem we'd been working on when Dad and Dana had walked in the door.

Dad pulled up his playlist on the Bluetooth speaker and then started washing off the vegetables as Michael Bublé crooned on the air. I sighed.

"Cab or chardonnay?" Dana asked, holding up two bottles.

"The cab, please."

So they were pretty much going to conduct their date like we weren't even in the room. Perfect.

Grayson watched my father and Dana in the kitchen, and his expression cracked slightly, revealing the first hint of . . . something. Compassion, maybe, because he'd glimpsed the suck that was my home life. Even Willa didn't get to see this. I didn't bring her around anymore. I didn't bring *any* of my friends around. None of them knew the truth of my reality . . . that I was alone all the time and Lean Cuisine and I were on a first-name basis. That home equaled loneliness.

I felt Dana's gaze intent on me before her voice rang out across the kitchen. "So, Flor. Is this your *new* boyfriend?"

Once. One time she met Zach, and she still mentioned him every time I saw her.

"No. Grayson is only helping me study."

"Is that what you call it these days?" She giggled over her glass of wine and sent a coy look to Dad.

I rolled my eyes. We were sitting at a table with an open laptop and pages of math work in front of us. She was awful, but Dad doted on her in her Forever 21 clothes and Louboutin knockoffs.

I glanced at the time on my phone. Five more minutes.

"We'll just stop for tonight." I closed my laptop and reached for my bag on the chair beside me, taking out some money to pay him.

"You sure?" He glanced at my father and Dana. "We can go into another room—"

"For five minutes?" By the time we got settled in another room it'd be time for him to leave.

"I can run a little late."

I stared at him for a long moment. Now he wanted to be nice to me? Heat crept up my face. It wasn't compassion. He felt sorry for me. Pitied me. Because of my father and his jailbait girlfriend. He probably had great parents who did the whole home-cooked meal thing every night and attended all his award ceremonies.

"That's okay. I think I got this," I lied.

I grasped the material enough not to fail. Maybe. My stomach knotted. I needed to do a lot better than "not fail" considering I had a 64 average right now. I'd let things slide for too long. But shame and pride had me ready to show him the door even under threat of failing.

There was a strict no-pass-no-play rule at school. If I failed, then I couldn't play school soccer next month, and that would suck. Sure, I'd still have year-round club ball outside of school, and recruiters scouted there, but I was slated for captain this year. I had wanted to be captain of my varsity high school team since forever. I had to pass.

We both stood.

Dad and Dana were laughing as he chopped up some garlic —but not nearly as oblivious as I thought, because right when we were about to step outside the door, Dana called out, "Bye-bye! It was nice meeting you, Gray! Looking forward to seeing you again."

Because she was so comfortable in her place in Dad's life that she assumed she would see him again.

"His name is Grayson," I said before stepping out after him and shutting the door. I followed him through the gate. Mostly because I just needed to get out of the house for a few minutes and breathe air that Dad and Dana didn't occupy. I walked with him down the driveway.

"I have time Sunday afternoon," he said.

I nodded, relieved. We had weekly quizzes. It would be helpful. "That would be great. Thanks."

"Was that your stepmom?"

"Dana?" I blew out a snorting laugh. "God, no."

"She seems . . . young."

"She's twenty-five. My dad is fifty. Such a cliché, right?"

He glanced at my house. Those glasses on his face actually suited him. Not everyone could pull off that look. "Guess clichés exist for a reason, right?"

"Right." I followed his gaze to my house. The oversize sconces lit the front of the rock edifice. "Think if my dad was a janitor she would be interested in him?"

Grayson was quiet for a moment. "I don't know. My dad is a janitor." He shrugged one shoulder. "My mom fell in love with him."

I closed my eyes in a long, pained blink. Well, I'd really stepped in it now. When would this night end? "God, Grayson. I'm sorry. I didn't mean anything. I'm sure being a—"

He suddenly smiled. His grin caught me off-guard. His teeth were blinding white. Long grooves, not quite dimples, carved either side of his mouth, making him look honest-to-God sexy. "I'm kidding, Flor. My dad works in construction."

I laughed in relief. "Nice one." I folded my hands behind my back. "You got me. Still, I didn't mean to imply there's anything wrong with being—"

"Relax. I get it." He turned back to my house, and I didn't sense that he was looking at it anymore. He was looking at what we'd left inside. My father and Dana, preparing chicken mole for two.

He saw more than I wanted him to see, and my smile slipped away. I wanted him gone. Then I could retreat inside and try to make sense of my math on my own and ignore everything else.

"Sunday?" I asked, handing him the thirty dollars I'd been holding.

"Yeah. Does four work for you?"

"Sure. I'll be here."

He lifted an eyebrow, clearly reminding me that I had been late today.

"I'll be here," I promised. "On time."

He nodded once. "See you then."

Crossing my arms over my chest, I watched as he climbed into his car. It was already getting chilly. I was going to have to start wearing leggings under my soccer shorts and my thick headband that shielded my ears.

The holidays would be here soon. Thanksgiving. Christmas. I frowned, suddenly visualizing spending them with Dana. I hardly ever heard from Mom. Just random texts and a few phone calls. In her last text she'd said she was thinking about going to Australia for a few months. Not sure where that left me. I didn't know if that was happening before the holidays or after. I wasn't sure if she was even thinking about seeing me. She'd mentioned flying me out for Thanksgiving months ago, but I knew better than to rely on her.

As Grayson pulled away from the curb, I lingered in the driveway and watched his taillights fade into the night, wishing I didn't have to go back inside the house.

And yet I knew it wouldn't matter to anyone what I did. Whether I stayed out here or went inside, no one would care.

GIRL CODE #3:

Be okay with just being his friend.

Willa

>>———————→

ZACH was sitting in my driveway ten minutes before seven like every Friday.

Tuesdays and Thursdays he went in early to use the weight room or meet with the trainer. On those days Mom or Flor gave me a ride, but the rest of the week I rode with him. Ever since he and Flor had gotten involved, those three days of the week had felt awkward as hell. At least for me. I'd actually considered taking the bus. If that wouldn't have looked weird (and if the bus weren't the seventh circle of hell), I would have.

I hurried out of the house through the soupy air, the sound of a crying child chasing me. I hated that sound. Part of me longed to go back in the house and comfort Mia until she stopped crying. But then I would definitely be late. And Zach would be late too.

I never used to be rushed in the mornings, but ever since Chloe and Mia moved in with us, my mornings were a blur of diapers and flying Cheerios while shouting at my sister to get out of bed and take care of Mia. Oh, yeah, and somewhere in all of that I tried to make myself halfway presentable.

I climbed in next to Zach. "Hey. Thanks for waiting."

He leaned forward to look at something on my shirt. "You got a little something there." He tapped at his shirt for illustration.

Glancing down, I cringed at the stream of applesauce. "Ew." So much for presentable.

I opened his glove compartment, took out some fast-food napkins, and attempted to wipe the yellow glob off my maroon T-shirt. It was game day, so I was wearing my Madison Tigers T-shirt like everyone else would be. I wasn't a big football fan, but Zach was on the team, so I tried to be supportive. Also, *not* wearing spirit wear on game days kind of made you conspicuous, and I was never a girl who liked to stand out from the crowd.

"It's not coming out," I muttered as Zach backed out of the driveway.

"No one will notice."

I shot him a look. "Really? It took *you* all of three seconds."

"Well, it was a big wet blob and smelled funny." He grinned at me before looking back at the road. "It's less wet now."

"But *still* there."

He laughed, his gray eyes glinting. "Cheer up. You don't have to change a diaper for another eight hours."

"That doesn't bother me." It was my sister I resented. Hard to believe that five years ago she was homecoming queen and had a scholarship to Vanderbilt. Now she was this broken woman who could hardly be moved to care for her own child.

I stared straight ahead at the misty morning. "So." I turned to Zach. "Excited about the game?"

He shrugged. "Sure."

He was never big on talking about football . . . or really even himself. That made him pretty much the opposite of every guy I knew. As the varsity team's starting kicker for the last two years he would be justified in a little bragging. I didn't know much about sports, but everyone said he was good enough to play in college. Maybe even beyond that.

"I saw you had company yesterday," he said.

I nodded. It went without saying. He knew Flor's and Jenna's cars. "We were trying to study, but that proved impossible. Thanks to you."

"Me? Why me?"

I gave him a look. "You just broke up with my best friend." The time to point out that they never should have gotten together in the first place had long since passed. If I'd said anything when they started dating, I would have looked jealous. Which I was. If I said something now, I would just look petty.

Actually, when they started dating, I was all encouragement, worried how I would look if I wasn't upbeat and happy about my two best friends potentially falling for each other. Flor actually asked me to talk to Zach on her behalf in the beginning. And I did. I didn't see how I couldn't and not expose my own infatuation with Zach.

I really did want to be a good friend . . . a good person. Only in this, being good meant I couldn't be honest.

I shook my head and felt the bun on the top of my head start to slip. I flipped the visor down. Staring at my reflection, I redid my hair into something only slightly better. "Why did y'all break up, anyway? You still haven't told me." There wasn't much he didn't tell me.

He shrugged and flexed his fingers along the steering wheel. A muscle ticked in his jaw. "Ask Flor about that."

I let out a breath. I had asked. She'd only admitted to me that she'd messed up. No more than that.

"Look," I started. "I never butted in your love life before—"

"Yes." He glanced at me pointedly, a corner of his mouth lifting. "Thank you for that—"

"But it's a hard thing to stay out of it when everyone is talking about it, Zach."

He expelled a breath. "At the moment, I don't have a love life."

"Really?" I arched an eyebrow dubiously.

He frowned at me, clearly catching my meaning. "Didn't take you for someone to listen to rumors."

I continued to stare at him, letting my eyes do the accusing.

Finally, he released a rough laugh. "I've been single for like ten minutes. I'm not diving into anything with anyone."

"But you do have a thing with Ava?" I pressed.

"It's just flirting. Ava knows that. Besides, it's not *wrong* for Flor to see me with other girls. It might help her realize we're really over and she should move on."

"Uh-huh."

We stopped at a red light and he twisted in his seat to look at me. "What's that mean?"

I tried not to squirm under his stare. Those gray eyes always saw too much. It was a constant worry. I lifted my hands and let them drop back down on my lap. "Couldn't you flirt with someone who isn't friends with Flor?"

He stared at me for a long moment, and the skin near the corner of my eye started to twitch. *Don't see me. Don't see the truth.* It was a recurring mantra in my head.

"Flor's popular. She has a lot of friends. I'm going to need a list," he snapped.

A car honked behind us. Zach faced forward again and hit the accelerator, speeding us through the green light with a sigh.

"Sorry," I muttered. He never snapped at me.

I didn't want tension between us. I'd told myself that I wouldn't let Flor and Zach's dating (or breaking up) change anything. Our friendships would stay strong. Nothing would change.

"Why are you sorry?" he asked as he pulled into the school parking lot.

I immediately spotted Flor getting out of her car. We parked in the first vacant spot we came to, a few spots down from her. I stared straight ahead. It was easier than looking at him.

I was sorry about a lot of things. Things I could never confess.

If I didn't want anything to change, I should probably stop interrogating him like this and remember that we were just friends. Friends didn't judge.

"Willa?"

I unbuckled my seat belt. "We're going to be late. Good luck tonight."

"Are you going to Sharla Anderson's party?"

I winced. "Probably not."

He nodded, not bothering to ask why not. He knew me well enough. "Okay. See you later."

I stepped out of the car and walked to where Flor was waiting for me. I knew she would be waiting. Just like I knew the question she would ask.

"Did he say anything about me?"

GIRL CODE #4:

Presence is required if a friend has been dumped.

Flor

"WILLAAA," I whined. "You have to go with me."

I opened her closet and started sliding hangers, searching for something for Willa to wear, because I knew that would be one of the excuses she was going to throw at me. I cringed as I pushed past ancient hoodies that looked like they might have belonged to her mom. I shook my head. She needed a serious wardrobe makeover.

"You know I hate parties like this," she complained. Just like I knew she would. "And I promised Chloe I'd watch a movie with her."

"I need you there, Willa. And it will be good for you."

She motioned in the direction of the street, where Jenna was waiting in the car. Almost on cue, Jenna honked several times. She was clearly anxious to get to the party. "You have Jenna, and a hundred other people you know will be there."

The football game had ended an hour ago, but I'd gone home

to shower and change before heading to the after party. I wanted to look my best. Tonight was important. I felt it. There was something in the air. Things were about to change. I believed in the power of positive thinking. Or maybe it was just because I refused to believe things could get any worse.

Willa had said she wasn't going to the party, which was totally like Willa, but on a whim I'd made Jenna swing by here, determined to persuade her otherwise. I wanted my best friend with me tonight.

I started counting off on my fingers. "Jenna is going to bail on me to make out with someone. I bombed my math test. I know it. And Zach still hasn't talked to me. Overall, it's been a sucky day. You're the girl I want at my back. Just like when we were in Mrs. Grossman's class, remember?"

I was pulling out the big guns mentioning Grossman.

Our third-grade teacher never liked me. She didn't even try to hide it. Mrs. Grossman preferred the smart kids. The quiet ones who never talked, who did their work and got straight As. That wasn't me. I always talked and had trouble remembering to raise my hand.

At recess she'd give me extra assignments to work on as punishment. While everyone was running around the playground and climbing the monkey bars, I sat on a bench by myself and struggled through math worksheets. One day I looked up and Willa was there.

"Hey," she greeted me, her shorter legs swinging off the side of the bench, her feet barely skimming the ground.

"Hey," I returned.

I had never really talked to her before, but she sat with me and helped me with my work. She stuck by me on that faded purple bench, missing her recess for almost an entire year. Just to help me. Just so I wouldn't be alone.

"C'mon," I pleaded. "I need to cut loose!"

I needed this party. It would be the perfect way to get Zach alone. We could talk. I could try to explain that night to him. Maybe this time I would find the right words. I could convince him how sorry I was and that we belonged together.

"I don't have anything to wear," Willa complained.

"Aha!" I yanked a striped V-neck out of the closet. Willa had a nice rack even if she hid it in baggy tops. "This one."

She shook her head. "That hasn't fit me since freshman year."

"Which is why it's perfect. You can show off the girls."

She scowled at me from where she sat on her bed and crossed her arms. "I don't like showing off the girls."

"Believe me, I'm aware. But I don't think you want to go to a party in a stained T-shirt. C'mon, Willa." I motioned wide with my arms. "Is this what you want? To spend your Friday night hanging out with your jaded divorcée sister who bitches about her life to anyone who will listen? You're seventeen! Don't go down that road."

She sighed and I knew I had her. Just in case, I decided to hammer the nail in deeper. "I am the one who just got dumped. I thought that automatically gets me my way for a month . . . six weeks at least." Or until Zach and I got back together. "If that's not a girl-code rule already, then it should be."

"Fine." She swung her feet to the floor. "But we leave the party when I'm ready to go." Willa exhaled as she yanked her T-shirt over her head and reached for the shirt I held.

"Fine," I agreed, loving her right then and feeling a small spurt of happiness. "Your curfew is midnight, so not a moment before eleven thirty." I turned away before she could lodge a protest. "Meet you in the car!"

Willa was going to a party with me. That hardly ever happened. She would be at my side just like all those years ago on the purple bench. Immediately I felt lighter inside.

Maybe it was going to be a good night after all.

GIRL CODE #5:

Never knowingly wear an outfit another girl already owns.

Willa

»——————→

THE party was out of control by the time we got there. Probably a bad omen.

And yet here I was, getting tossed in a sea of bodies because Flor had begged me to come. Why did cutting loose for her have to involve loud music and a mob of kids under the influence of booze and other questionable substances? Cutting loose for me meant fuzzy pajamas, Chinese takeout, and reruns of *The Vampire Diaries*. Apparently that was me.

Sharla Anderson was rushing from room to room with a panicked look on her face as she snatched up discarded cups and other trash.

"That's what she gets for inviting the football team." Jenna tsked and shook her head. "You know how rowdy they can get. Especially after a win."

We were sitting upstairs in the massive game room, squished

like sardines on a couch. Sharla's house was as big as Flor's, and even so it was wall-to-wall bodies.

"Have you seen Flor?" I asked over the music, stretching my neck to peer through the crowd. I'd lost sight of her half an hour ago. Something broke in the distance, and Sharla shrieked from the other side of the room.

"Think I saw her heading to the media room," Jenna said mildly, side-eyeing the couple making out next to her on the couch. "Zach is in there."

That made sense. I sent up a silent prayer that Zach wouldn't dive behind the furniture when he saw her coming, and that Flor wouldn't turn into some crazy stalker ex and dive after him.

I squeezed out from the couch and started toward the media room, hoping to save both my friends from each other. That's what I did. Or tried to do, anyway. When I was in preschool the teachers called me Mama Munchkin because I was constantly trying to resolve the quarrels of the other children. I guess some things never changed. I was still Mama Munchkin trying to keep the peace and make everyone happy.

"Want to come?" I looked back at Jenna.

She was staring across the room. I followed her gaze to where a girl stood, staring back at her. I vaguely recognized the girl from somewhere. Maybe her locker was near mine? That was the thing about attending a 6A school. It was so huge you couldn't possibly know everyone.

Suddenly I remembered where I'd seen the girl before. I moved closer to Jenna. "Isn't that the girl you—"

"Yeah. Abby Morton," she was quick to reply, her tone a touch defensive. "It was a dare. At Parker's pool party over the summer."

I considered Abby for a moment, watching the blush steal its way beneath her makeup as she gazed at Jenna. There wasn't a lot of blushing going on at this party. It was kind of sweet. "You know it's okay," I said.

"What's okay?"

"If you like her."

Jenna looked at me for a long moment, opening and closing her mouth a few times before finally saying, "I'm not gay, Willa."

"Okay." I shrugged, not wanting to push.

"I made out with her because it was a dare. And Hayden told me he thought it would be hot. We don't even need to go over how stupid in love with him I am."

I winced. Hayden Manchester was the star quarterback and worshiped accordingly by the denizens of Madison High School—especially the females. He was also a giant dick, treating girls like they existed for his entertainment and pleasure alone. He cared for no one more than himself. Flor and I were waiting for the day that Jenna woke up to that.

"And it wouldn't be okay," Jenna added. "Not with my parents." She snorted. "My dad makes gay jokes in front of anyone. Can you imagine if I . . ." Her voice faded and she just continued to shake her head, a look of fear crossing her face.

I sighed because she was right about that. Jenna's parents were judgy bigots who controlled every aspect of Jenna's life. Or they tried to, anyway. Honestly, if they didn't approve of me or Flor, they wouldn't let Jenna hang around us.

My parents had never been that controlling, but they used to be strict. Before my dad got laid off and he had to take a job four hours away. Now he was only home on weekends, and then he and Mom were too busy arguing over bills and what to do about my mess of a sister and her daughter to worry much about anything else. Still. It was a good reminder that despite my parents' flaws, it could be worse: they could be closed-minded too. There was comfort in knowing they weren't. I knew they would support me no matter who I dated—regardless of gender.

"But speaking of okay . . ." Jenna stood and made a show of checking out a group of thick-necked football players. "Trevor Webber is looking *very* okay tonight."

I watched as she made a beeline for a football player. I winced at her choice. Webber wasn't the brightest bulb, but at least he didn't treat girls like meat, so that was an improvement over Hayden at least.

She slid her arm around Trevor's massive shoulder and pressed against him. Maybe I was wrong and she was into Webber after all.

Or maybe I was right. And that made me sad. Too many of us pretending.

Including me.

I headed for the media room. I had friends to save.

I finally tracked Flor down. The room had stadium-style seating and she was standing on the upper tier, friends on either side of her. They were laughing and talking, but she was the only one who didn't seem to be having a good time. Her stare was fixed with searing intensity on the room's bottom level. I followed her gaze and spotted a familiar form. *Zach.* He was lounging on a bench with several others. They were staring down at something on the floor. I couldn't see what because several more bodies were standing around the circle, blocking my view.

I reached Flor's side.

"Can you believe it?" She nodded at the group. "They're playing spin-the-bottle like it's fucking middle school." Her dark eyes shot fire. "Oh, and you'll never guess who suggested it."

I glanced back and assessed the dozen faces around the bottle, immediately marking Ava among them. I let out a breath.

Flor heard my sigh. "That's right. Ava. Some friend." She lifted her Solo cup and took a swig from it. "And look what she's wearing."

I looked the girl over. "Is that your sweater?"

"No! But she went out and bought the same one. The nerve, right? I wore that last week. Right before Zach dumped me."

Wearing the same sweater seemed a small infraction, but I didn't voice that. Just like there was no sense pointing out how Ava had scooted close to the bench and was leaning her head on Zach's thigh from her position on the floor. The pose made them look very couple-like.

"I'm sure she didn't mean—" I didn't finish my sentence.

Flor grabbed my hand and pulled me down the steps, closer to the bottle-spinning crowd. More people were gathering to watch, the promise of a spectacle too tempting. Flor stopped once we could actually see the bottle within the middle of the crowd.

Zach's gaze collided with mine. I gave him a *what the hell are you doing?* look. He shrugged imperceptibly, his storm-gray eyes steady as he stared back at me. That was the thing about Zach. He had these eyes that were wise and thoughtful. Almost like they belonged to someone much older. Even when we were six years old they had been like that. So self-assured and confident. Other guys had glazed and vacant eyes from video games or too much beer or hours of ESPN. Not him. Whenever I looked into his eyes I felt . . . I don't know. Understood, I guess. It was easy to feel lost and invisible in life, but I never felt that way around him.

I didn't let those eyes placate me now, however. I very pointedly swerved my gaze to Flor, trying to convey that this was a bad idea, and yet he didn't glance at her.

What was wrong with him? She was unmissable with her Angelina Jolie lips and all that dark hair rolling like black waves over her shoulders. Every guy in the house was checking her out, but Zach was immune. It was crazy. I should have been offended for her, not feeling this secret relief.

I was a horrible friend, and it only made me more determined to get them back together. To prove that I wasn't this awful. That I was a good person.

Cheers went up as a girl leaned forward and spun the bottle. I held my breath. Around and around it went until I grew dizzy from watching it so closely.

Please don't. Please don't.

It stopped.

Right on Ava.

She slapped both hands to her cheeks as though shocked that

such a thing could happen. Imagine that. She was playing spin-the-bottle and the bottle landed on her.

The girl who spun the bottle rubbed her hands together and declared with relish, "I dare Ava to go in the closet for ten minutes with . . ." She let the pause hang, attempting to build suspense. It was unnecessary. And annoying. Everyone knew the name she was going to say before she said it. "Zach!"

Of course.

One of Zach's friends clapped him on the shoulder like he had just scored a winning touchdown.

Shaking his head and laughing, Zach got to his feet and headed to the closet over loud catcalls.

"No," Flor growled. "Oh, she better not."

Almost as though she had heard her, Ava's gaze darted to Flor. A stare-off commenced. For a moment Ava looked uncertain. I willed her not to do it. To stay sitting on that floor. *Don't get up. Don't get up.*

Everyone in the group kept pushing her to join Zach. Finally she broke the stare-off and got to her feet, turning toward the closet.

And there it was: friendship 0, hormones 1.

"I'm out of here." Flor pushed through the crowded media room.

I hovered there for a moment, unsure what to do. Go after Flor, stop Ava, or strangle Zach?

With a sigh of disgust, I stalked after Ava. For some reason, it seemed the easiest choice. Flor and Zach . . . they were harder.

I caught her just before she was about to enter the closet,

grabbing her hand. "Ava. What are you doing? Stop this. You can't do this to Flor."

Guilt flashed across her eyes. I knew about guilt. Recognized it when I saw it. "Come on, Willa." She rolled her eyes. "They're not together anymore. Why is everyone acting like I killed a puppy?"

"She isn't over him and you know it. You saw how crushed she was when they broke up."

"If it's not me, it will be some other girl," she defended.

"Then let it be some other girl," I shot back. "You're supposed to be her friend. Hook up with someone else." I shrugged. "Not Zach."

Ava bit her lip and cast an uncertain look to the dark closet where Zach waited. She had never been that confident of her popularity, and her place in the social hierarchy at Madison mattered to her. Considering Flor was pretty high up the pyramid, she was clearly rethinking her next move.

I latched on to that insecurity. "If you go into that closet, you're dead to Flor. If you don't, no worries. All is well."

That did the trick—and it wasn't *untrue*. Still . . . saying it made me feel like the popular mean girl threatening social annihilation in some lame teen movie. I wasn't remotely like that girl. For God's sake, I played the cello in the orchestra. Most of the time when I was out with Flor or Zach, no one even knew my name. I was just a vaguely familiar girl.

Ava flinched and took a big step back from the closet like it was suddenly contagious.

I nodded toward the closet. "I'll get Zach and let him know

you're not up for ten minutes in the closet with him tonight." I narrowed my gaze on her pointedly. "Or ever."

Ava nodded, hanging her head, clearly cowed, but longing still glimmered in her eyes when she snuck a peek toward the cracked door of the closet. I well understood the lure of Zach Tucker.

Sighing, I wondered if she was still going to find Zach later and plaster herself over him when there were no witnesses. God. Did Zach have to have so many girls crushing on him? He was stressing me out.

I stepped inside the closet, instantly plunging myself into darkness.

Blinded as I was, the space still felt large. No surprise in a house this size. Stepping forward, I held my hands out in front of me so that I didn't run into anything.

"Zach?" I whispered. Why was I whispering?

And why was my heart beating so hard suddenly?

The door snicked shut after me, dulling the sounds of the party. I whirled around, wondering if it had shut on its own or if someone had closed it for laughs.

All at once I felt like I was in a tomb. Far removed from the party and the world in general.

Turning back around, I flexed my fingers in front of me, meeting only air.

"Thought you changed your mind and weren't coming." Zach's disembodied voice was different—deeper and growly—and I realized this was how he talked to girls when he flirted.

Girls he planned to kiss.

Girls like Flor and Ava.

Girls who weren't me.

Maybe I should forgive all those girls for their infatuation with him. Maybe I needed to be more patient with Flor. Because that voice? It was like cashmere on skin.

Something brushed my shoulder, gossamer soft, and I jumped. The touch solidified, and I identified it as a hand. Zach's hand. The familiar ache in my chest returned, and I pressed a hand there, rubbing as though I could get rid of it.

"I—" The word stuck in my throat. I swallowed and tried again. "She—"

I almost said it. Almost got the words out. Almost explained that I wasn't Ava. That she wasn't coming. That it was me. The girl he'd ridden bikes with as a kid. The girl who'd hunted for frogs with him in the ditch behind the park.

Almost. But then his other hand touched me, tangling in my hair and reeling me in like a fish snared on a line.

I guess he didn't notice that my hair was a wild springy tangle and not Ava's sleek, flat-ironed perfection. He tugged me forward by a fistful of curls, rocking me against his chest.

"Zach." His name rushed out of me in a strangled little croak. Unrecognizable. The hand in my hair tightened. It wasn't a gentle grip but it didn't hurt, either. It felt . . . real. Like how a man might handle a woman he desired. Real and totally out of my experience.

Butterflies took off in my stomach.

He laughed softly. "You're shaking."

I couldn't form words, but my mind was spinning with

responses. *Because guys don't usually touch me like this. Because you never have. Only in my dreams.*

His laugh faded, and it was just the slow rasp of his breath in the darkness. My heart felt like a sledgehammer pounding brutally in my chest. Pressed together like we were, I was sure he felt it too. God. The people outside this room probably heard it.

The moment to tell him that it was me he was holding, that I wasn't Ava, was fading fast. It was already going to be weird and awkward when I announced it.

I took a breath, ready to spit out the truth and put an end to this, but he stole the words, the breath, right out from me.

He kissed me.

GIRL CODE #6:

Never leave a party without letting your girls know.

Flor

←————————«

CROWDS never bothered me, because I was a people person. I always had been. I liked parties. The bigger and louder the better. Except tonight it wasn't helping my mood. I guess when you're trying to flee your life, you resent getting stuck in the middle of a bunch of football players chugging on beer bongs. Too bad I hadn't realized this sooner.

Everyone kept stopping to talk to me or thrust alcohol at me like it was the cure for everything. It was like being at one of my father's family reunions with all my great-aunts pushing pozole on me because they thought I needed fattening up.

I forced a smile. Stopped. Chatted. Sipped from a red Solo cup. *Never let them see you upset.* All the while I inched in the direction of the front door, which felt so miserably far away. Escape.

After what felt like forever I finally managed to break free.

"Hey, Flor!"

I gave the obligatory wave in the direction of whoever had called my name, not bothering to look. I needed to get out of here. This party was a bad idea. Willa was right. I wished I had listened to her.

It was too crowded. Too hot. Too . . . everything.

"Flor!" Jenna's hand landed on my arm. "Been looking for you! You leaving so soon?"

Somehow in her search for me she'd managed to pick up Trevor Webber. He was glued to her side. Ick.

His glassy stare could have been alcohol-induced or just his usual glassy stare. It was anyone's guess.

His heavy arm draped over her shoulders looked sweaty and uncomfortable, and not for the first time I wished she would fixate on anyone other than him. He was wearing a blue shirt, fitted closely to reveal his physique, but it also showcased the large sweat stains under his armpits.

"Yeah, tell Willa for me, would you?"

"Why are you leaving?" Her eyes narrowed. "Is it Ava and Zach?"

"No." I cut a swift glance to Trevor. His gaze fixed on me. Who knew how much he was absorbing? I would assume not a lot, but I didn't want to risk talking in front of him. I didn't need the entire school knowing just how hung up I was on my ex.

He released a beer belch. "You should stay, Flor. Hang out."

Ew. Even the suggestion to "hang out" sounded obscene coming from him.

"How are you getting home?" Jenna demanded.

I shrugged. "I'll walk." It was maybe a mile. The fresh air would feel good after being stuck in this house with all these overstimulated jocks. Forget about the fact that one of those overstimulated jocks was my ex-boyfriend and I wanted him back.

Zach wasn't like them. He was never a jerk. Even breaking up with me, he had been nice about it. Sure, he was mostly avoiding me now, but he wasn't trash-talking, at least. And God knew people were salivating for salacious details.

That was a rarity among my peers. I'd dated enough to know that when things ended . . . well. Things never ended *well*. There was no such thing as that. Typically, you couldn't rely on the guy to be decent. No, that was when his true colors came out. That was when you knew. If the guy wasn't trash-talking you to anyone, then maybe he was a keeper after all.

Zach was honorable. He might have broken my heart, but he wasn't adding fuel to the fire.

No. He was just making out in a closet with Ava right now.

Fabulous.

Even as I was leaving, kids were still pouring in through the front door. I sucked in a bracing breath, letting the crisp air fill my lungs.

This party wasn't long for this world. It was only a matter of time before the cops showed up. I dug into my pocket and fished out my phone to fire a text to Willa. I didn't completely trust Jenna to relay my message to her.

> Walking home. You should leave. Party too big. Cops probably on way.

As I glanced back to the house, it occurred to me that I should have warned Jenna, too. She needed taking care of more than Willa. Especially at parties.

I copied the text and sent it to Jenna before starting down the wide sidewalk for home.

My phone vibrated and I glanced down. It was from Jenna. So lame! Come back.

I typed back: Just find Willa and go home. I tucked my phone into my pocket.

Silent houses flowed past on my left and right. A sprinkler went off, chugging determinedly on the night air.

A car passed me. Then braked. The tiny hairs on my arms vibrated as I stared at those brake lights. I was very aware of my situation. Teenage girl walking alone late at night. It was like I was a *48 Hours* episode in the making.

I froze, ready to bolt as the car reversed back toward me. The window rolled down and I let out an easy breath as Grayson stuck his head out. "Flor. What are you doing?"

I ducked my head to better see him. It was weird. Even in the dark, even with the shield of his glasses, his eyes were gleaming black. I had brown eyes too, but mine weren't like this. His eyes would be visible in the dark, like glittering coal in a dark mine.

"Walking home." I motioned behind me. "Were you at Sharla's party?" I asked, even though it didn't seem likely. I'd never seen him at any parties.

"Me? No. Tutoring a freshman."

"On a Friday night?"

"His parents aren't satisfied with a B in geometry."

"Wow. Tough parents." But I was referring to him. *He* was tutoring on a Friday night. Didn't he have a social life? Didn't he do things for fun?

He nodded, looked straight ahead at the quiet residential street and then back at me. "You want a ride?"

I hesitated for a moment and then shrugged. "Yeah. Sure."

I walked around and opened the passenger door. It groaned like it was dying. I waited as he unloaded all his books and his laptop bag from the passenger seat. There were even books on the floor. I bent and handed those to him so he could add them to the pile in the back.

Sinking into the seat, I slammed the creaky door shut after me. "So this is what you do on your weekends, then? Tutor?"

"And you walk home from parties by yourself?"

I settled my hands on my knees and inhaled, not about to explain why I was walking home from a party alone. This guy had already seen enough of my life. He didn't need another peek inside. The idea was for the world to think I had my act together. I was Flor Hidalgo, soccer player, (mostly) good student, always ready for fun . . . and, up until ten days ago, Zach Tucker's girlfriend.

"Where's your nice car?" I didn't know he even paid attention to what I drove. It seemed the kind of thing that wouldn't interest him.

I seemed like the kind of thing that wouldn't interest him.

"My friend drove me tonight, and I was ready to leave the party before she was." A beat of silence fell. "I never see you at any parties."

"Don't have time. I tutor on weekends because I need the money for college."

"Aren't you a National Merit Scholar?" I heard his name in the announcements. And there was some kind of display with his picture in the library. It was a bad picture. He wasn't smiling, and there was a glare on his glasses that hid his eyes. Not that I had examined it today at school or anything. I'd just noticed. "Doesn't that pretty much pave the way for you?"

He turned onto my street. "Even with a full ride, there are things like food, clothes, a car payment . . . toothpaste." I stared at his profile. A faint smile hugged his mouth. "That kind of thing, you know?"

No. I didn't know. Because my dad might not have been the most attentive of fathers lately, but he paid for everything. He never withheld money. I had my own credit card, and he never said anything about my spending habits. I couldn't imagine what that was like. Working because you had to buy your own toothpaste. Not all my friends were rich, but even those of modest means like Willa didn't have to worry about paying for their own food.

I skimmed my hand along the inside of the door, where the old vinyl was warped and cracked. This ancient car couldn't have cost much. "You make payments on this car?"

He shot me a quick glance and caught my half smile. "Funny."

I laughed lightly and then stopped.

Where had *that* come from?

I hadn't heard myself laugh in . . . Well. Ten days. I winced. Longer than that. Definitely a while. I turned that over in my mind, thinking how that couldn't have been fun for Zach. I stared at Grayson, marveling that he was the one to bring me out of my drought.

"You're home," he announced.

I snapped my gaze off him. Of course it had been a quick drive.

My house sat back from the street in complete darkness, silently waiting for me.

A strange hollow feeling spread through my center. Not only did most of my friends come home to lit porch lights, but they had parents waiting up for them. Willa's mom kept tabs on her all the time . . . even though Wills never did anything wrong. She actually had a curfew.

No curfew for me anymore. Not since Dad started dating. Not that Mom had ever been a stickler about that kind of thing anyway. She would cover for me and tell Dad I got in at eleven when he asked the following morning. Funny how my friends had thought I was so lucky . . . that I had the world's best mom. Only she hadn't done that for me. She'd simply liked me going out, being popular. It was like it validated her, too, in some way.

Sometimes when I stayed over with Willa, her mother waited up for us. She'd ask about our night and make us popcorn. It was nice. My mom had never done that even when she had been around. She was always searching for something, moving through projects and hobbies so fast I could never keep track, but none of those had ever involved making popcorn for me and my friends.

"Thanks for the ride." Still I sat there, hesitating, my limbs like lead.

My house looked so dark. There were outside perimeter lights—sconces on the front of the house and lights buried in the landscaping—but they were all set to a timer. They weren't on because someone was inside and had turned them on in anticipation of my return.

Could something *radiate* emptiness? I guess it was possible. People radiated loneliness. I mean . . . I hoped I didn't, but people did.

"No one home?" he asked, his deep voice jarring me out of my thoughts.

"Just Rowdy." I shrugged. "I'm used to it. My dad and his girlfriend go out a lot. Restaurants. The theater. Weekend trips."

He shook his head. "I can't imagine my parents doing anything like that."

"My dad hardly ever went anywhere before Dana. Work, occasional trips to visit family. A Dynamos game downtown." I cupped my hands around my knees, rubbing my palms into the bone. "Since he started dating Dana, he's become quite the sophisticate. Last month they went to the Russian ballet."

"Not something you'd want to do?"

I'd never even thought about that. I guess it was a moot point. They never invited me to their things.

At my silence, he continued. "Enjoy the solitude. My house is always crowded. Noisy." He started counting off on his fingers. "I've got my parents. My sisters. My two uncles are over so much they might as well live with us too. They work with my dad."

"What's your dad do? Construction, right?"

"Yeah. He manages a crew." One of his hands slid down the steering wheel, his grip white-knuckle tight. "One uncle is divorced. The other never married. They're over all the time, eating whatever my mom is cooking. Drinking beer and watching sports. They're there now." He faced forward like he could see them right then in his living room.

Something in his voice, in the way his lips twisted, told me he hated that. The irony wasn't lost on me. I was avoiding my empty house and he was avoiding his full one.

"You don't like your uncles?"

He turned to face me again, his eyes gleaming darker than the night pulsing around us. "My dad and his brothers were high school jocks. They peaked at seventeen. Can you imagine?" He laughed, but the sound lacked all amusement. "They love to relive those memories. Every night they tell the same damn stories."

I winced. "That sucks."

"Yeah. So I get to hear them over and over. It's especially great when they call me a pussy because I don't play sports like they did."

I flinched, imagining him as a young boy, surrounded by three faceless older men belittling him and calling him ugly names. Staring at him, I understood why he hadn't been roped into football or soccer or any of the myriad sports offered at school.

As though to confirm my conclusion, he continued, "Why would I want to? So I could be like them? They started straight out of high school. Before I started making money tutoring, they made me work summers and after school with them. It was backbreaking work. They have to drink and pop pills every night just to numb themselves to the misery of it. Yeah. No thanks. I'm not going to be them."

I opened and closed my mouth, unsure what to say to that. I

had always just seen the smartest guy in school when I looked at him. I never imagined there was anything else to him besides brains and ambition. I never considered what drove that ambition.

I never considered he might have to deal with his own share of crap.

I released a breath and relaxed my grip on my knees. "I guess family is . . . complicated." Well, that was not exactly profound. He must seriously be questioning my intelligence. *Ha.* He was my tutor. He already knew I wasn't the brightest bulb. I gave myself a swift mental kick. I had my insecurities just like anyone, but I'd never thought I was dumb before. Maybe this was because I was newly dumped.

"Yeah."

Silence fell, and I realized he was probably waiting for me to get out of the car. "Thanks again. For the ride."

"No problem."

My gaze was back on those hands with the slightly reddened knuckles. The longer I stared at them, the funnier I felt inside. My stomach quivered and fluttered. The air felt thin inside the car, stretched humming tight.

What was I even doing here? I should have already left. I just had to grab the door handle and step out.

Instead I remained in Grayson's beat-up car — waiting for what, I didn't know.

Why couldn't I get out of this car? It wasn't like this guy was doing or saying anything so compelling I wanted to stay put. So he had sexy hands. Big deal.

I'd never been one of those girls who needed a boyfriend. Like it was some key to fulfillment. I wasn't that insecure. I didn't jump from boyfriend to boyfriend. I wasn't looking for some kind of affirmation because Zach had dumped me. If that were the case, I could have stayed back at the party and messed around with any number of guys happy to oblige a girl on a quest for a hookup.

Maybe it was just nice talking to someone who didn't know anything about me. Nothing about Zach and me. Nothing about my mom bailing. Who didn't expect anything from me — well, other than thirty an hour. I was just a girl he was tutoring. There was sanctuary in anonymity.

And maybe I *could* see myself kissing him. I mean hypothetically. I'd be open to it. As an experiment. I'd never made out with anyone like him before. Someone who didn't play sports or do parties. Someone who scored near perfect on the SAT.

Of course, he probably wasn't an indiscriminate kisser. I was assuming a lot to think he'd even be into kissing me. Our relationship was strictly professional. He probably kissed girls like him. If he made time for things like kissing between tutoring and getting scholarship offers.

I rubbed my hands harder on my thighs.

His voice rolled between us. "Are you nervous?"

I looked at him sharply. "What? No. No, why would you ask that?"

"Just a sense."

He sensed I was nervous? Great. Did he also sense that I was thinking about kissing? Kissing him? God. I hoped not.

I looked at his hands again and my stomach dipped. Suddenly one of those hands lifted off the steering wheel.

I held my breath, watching as that hand drifted across the space separating us and landed just beyond my shoulder to relax on the back of my seat.

Breathe, breathe, breathe. He wasn't making a move. He wasn't like that. *This* wasn't like that. *I* wasn't like that. Maybe this was just some crazy post-breakup meltdown.

Releasing a breath, I leaned my head against the headrest and glanced out the window at the dark, starless sky. "Do you think there's any place left in the world where you can still see stars?"

"Yeah. Just not here. We're too close to the city."

"So where? Like the desert?"

"Australian Outback," he offered.

"Scottish Highlands?" I returned.

"The Atlantic Ocean."

I laughed. "So basically someplace where people don't live?" A smile played about my lips. "That actually doesn't sound too bad. A million stars and little to no people."

"Really? *You* don't want to be around people?" His seat creaked as he shifted his weight. "You're always surrounded by people."

How did he even know anything about me?

"Maybe I just want to see stars," I countered, my voice defensive even to my ears. I definitely didn't feel like confiding *why* the idea of isolation sounded so tempting to me.

Isolation wasn't what I wanted. Not exactly. I just wanted things to be like they used to be. When my life was easier. When my parents were together, for starters. For now I'd gladly accept the normalcy of even a month ago. Meaning Zach. I wanted Zach back.

Shaking off my introspection, I finally opened the noisy door. I couldn't sit in his car all night being maudlin, after all. "See you Sunday?"

"Sure."

He stayed in park as I walked up the drive, the headlights lighting my path. I knew I'd still feel him, though, his stare on my back, even without the glare of light.

I opened the patio gate, one hand digging out my keys. His car rattled down the drive as I opened the back door and shut myself inside my shell of a house. That was what it felt like—an empty shell. A hollowed husk. It wasn't a home. A home is where a family lives.

I prowled through the house with Rowdy at my heels, peeked inside the bare refrigerator and pantry. Nothing. No note on the counter, either. He used to do that. Leave notes even though he could just text me.

I looked inside my father's room. It didn't even appear that he had come home from work today. He must have gone straight out. Obviously he was with Dana.

I made my way to my room, pulling out my phone and punching the number for Gino's Pizza. I had them listed in my favorites. They had my credit card on file, and the guy who answered the phone even guessed my order before I told him.

"Medium chicken Alfredo pizza. Thin crust?"

"Um, yeah." The moment I hung up, I wished I'd told him no —that he was wrong. Just to be contrary. He didn't know me. Just because I'd ordered the same thing three times in the last week didn't mean I was predictable.

It didn't mean my life had become this.

GIRL CODE #7:

If a guy who has a girlfriend asks you for nudes, tell her.
Solidarity and all that.

Willa

ZACH was kissing me.

I'd been kissed before. I'd had a boyfriend part of my freshman year. Until I found out Evan had asked another girl for nudes.

Evan was always asking me for nudes. There wasn't a text conversation where he didn't ease it into the thread. I figured that was the norm since he was my boyfriend. What did I know? He was the first guy I dated.

I told him no. Constantly. Consistently. I told myself to feel flattered and not annoyed. And yet it was annoying that he couldn't carry on a conversation without wanting to know what I was wearing. It wasn't okay, though. I knew that now. Not when he asked me for nudes and not when he asked Olivia Walters, a girl in my health class. It was hard not to notice her. She was endowed in ways I wasn't back then and she had these overly penciled-in eyebrows.

She walked up to my desk before class started and told me very matter-of-factly that my boyfriend had texted asking her for nudes. I thanked her. Then I broke up with him. He moved to Alabama last year, so at least I didn't have to see him around school anymore.

Jerk or not, Evan hadn't been a bad kisser. I knew a good kiss, and he'd complimented my kissing skills often enough. I felt reassured that I was competent, at any rate.

But even so I was not prepared.

There was good and there was this.

It was no-holds-barred. Soft and firm. Zach's lips slanted over mine, and I gasped when his tongue touched my tongue. Both his hands were in my hair, anchoring me to him. I lifted my own hands, ready to push him away. Because really. That was what I should do. This was terrible. So wrong.

He wasn't kissing me. He was kissing Ava.

It was a horrifying thought. But also . . . freeing.

Instead of pushing him away, my hands landed on his chest. Instead of stopping him and ending the kiss, I kept him close, my palms flat on his broad chest, feeling, absorbing . . . committing all this to memory. His heart thudded beneath my fingers, strong and fast. For me.

No, not for me, a voice whispered through my melting brain. *For Ava.*

Angry, I kissed him harder, scraping my teeth against his bottom lip, wanting to punish him for kissing me while thinking I was someone else. For kissing me at all . . . for making me like it so much. It was better than any fantasy I'd ever dreamed up over the years, and that made me angriest of all.

He pulled back at my aggressiveness, and I waited, wondering what he would do next. I felt his stare, searching the dark, and there was only relief that he couldn't see me.

Our breath crashed between us like surf pounding on sand, as hard and rhythmic as the blood roaring in my ears.

His fingers flexed in my hair, fisting the strands tighter. My pulse hiccupped against my throat, sending the skin into mad flutters. Was this even real? Maybe I was dreaming. If I was dreaming, I could do anything I wanted.

My hands curled into his shirt, bunching the fabric. I willed my racing heart to steady, willed my voice to speak and say the words to make this somehow all right.

He let out a breath that seemed to edge into speech, but then nothing.

I opened my mouth, but before I could say anything, he was kissing me again, hands still tight in my hair, hauling my body against him until there wasn't a thread of air between us.

I kissed him back, pitching myself into him, sending us toppling into a wall. A soft grunt escaped him at the force, but he didn't let me go. He clung to me, hands anchoring my head as he slid slightly down the wall. It put us at similar height, and I wrapped my arms around his neck. If this was what others felt, no wonder they were skipping study hall to make out in the upper level of the theater. I would have to be less judgmental about them. Now that I understood. Now that my entire body burned.

I felt him everywhere, and it was just a kiss.

One of his hands released my hair and slid around to hold my face. Something cracked loose inside me at the touch. Even though our mouths were fused in the most delicious kiss I'd ever had in my life, that single hand holding my face—so tender, so intimate —shattered me.

Dimly, the sounds of shouts outside the closet penetrated. He broke the kiss with a curse that made my stomach do wild somersaults. Not that profanity turned me on or anything, but it was proof that he desired me. Zach Tucker wanted me.

Even if he didn't realize it.

I brushed my fingers over my lips. They felt tingly and numb at the same time.

Light flooded the closet and I froze as the bright yellow cut through the dark and slanted over me. That wasn't supposed to happen. I mean . . . I guess it was inevitable. How was I going to leave this closet and still hide my identity from him? But I hadn't thought that far ahead. What everyone said was true. Hormones robbed you of all judgment.

My heart abandoned my chest and climbed up into my throat.

He could see me now. His gaze pinned me to the spot. *OhGod-ohGodohGod.*

I stared back. Didn't move.

And this was it. When everything broke between us. I waited for all the pieces to fall.

He stared with no expression. It was impossible to read him.

Were those flaring nostrils because he was angry? Betrayed? Or something else?

I realized my hands were still locked around his neck, my body pressed to his. I yanked my arms away. Heat climbed my face as I flattened my palms against the outside of my thighs.

I turned for the door, not about to stick around for him to figure out the right words to fling at me. I'd stolen that kiss from him. That pretty much made me a horrible person—a horrible friend to both him and Flor.

At the door, I paused when I realized I was about to step out into the party and a houseful of eyes. Anyone could take one look at me and guess what had happened. I pressed my fingers to my lips. They felt different. *I* felt different. Would I look it too?

I'd been in here too long with him. How would I explain this? After talking Ava out of coming in here to make out with Zach, I went ahead and did that very thing. *Oh. God.* I was the worst hypocrite. Of course, the longer I lingered in the closet, the worst the talk would be.

Best to just get it over with. Rip off the Band-Aid.

Taking a deep breath, I stepped out. Except when I did, no one was looking at me at all. It was chaos. There was no other description for it. People were fleeing the room. Cups were flying, hitting the floor like artillery shells.

Zach followed behind me. We watched as everyone shoved and pushed to escape the room.

I shot him a wary glance.

Shrugging, he flew up the stadium steps and grabbed a guy's arm. "Hey, what's going on?"

"Cops!" the guy cried breathlessly, and shook off Zach so that he could disappear with the tide of bodies.

"Oh God," I breathed, closing my eyes in a pained blink.

My mother was going to kill me. This was the last thing she needed on her plate. I could already hear the lecture.

"C'mon!" Zach grabbed my hand and pulled me out of the room with him. The house was bedlam. It was like a scene out of *Titanic*. Kids were running everywhere, trampling each other as they tossed cups of beer. A girl screamed as she toppled down the stairs. I didn't know if she'd been shoved amid the panic or had merely lost her balance, but I wasn't looking forward to descending the steps.

A loud voice, clearly a cop's, blared through a bullhorn. "Exit the house and step onto the lawn!"

"My mom is going to kill me," I muttered.

Dad was home tonight, and the two of them were actually out on a rare date. If they got a call from the cops about me, she was going to lose it. Life as I knew it would be over.

"C'mon. This way." Zach didn't follow the rest of the pack toward the stairs. Instead he dragged me down the hall and busted into a bedroom—Sharla's bedroom, from the looks of it. Several homecoming mums decorated one wall. Another wall was riddled with cheer pictures. Her giant megaphone sat on her dresser, MADISON TIGERS and her name emblazoned on the side of it.

"Zach! What are you doing?" I looked around wildly. Did he plan on hiding us? That didn't seem like a good idea.

He let go of my hand and rushed to the window, sliding it open. I watched in alarm as he swung one leg over the windowsill.

I pointed in his direction. "Why do I get the feeling you've climbed out of this window before?"

"Freshman year." He held out a hand, motioning for me to come with him.

"Freshman year? You were climbing in and out of girls' bedrooms when you were a freshman?" I shook my head. "Who even are you?" How was this guy one of my best friends? Or he used to be. The verdict still wasn't in on where we stood.

He let out an exasperated breath. "Not now, Willa. C'mon. I'd rather not get an MIP tonight."

Yeah. I didn't have the money to pay the fine for a Minor in Possession charge either.

I hurried forward. "You sure we shouldn't just go downstairs? We aren't drinking. We can take one of those tests to prove it."

"You don't need to be drinking to get an MIP. You can be at a party with beer and still get one. And why don't you know that?"

I shrugged, not bothering to remind him that I wasn't the kind of girl who had to worry about those things. I hardly ever went to parties. "But they can't honestly ticket every—"

My words were cut off with a yelp as he took my hand and tugged me out the window after him onto the roof. I followed him down the slight incline awkwardly, clearly lacking his athleticism. He walked the sloping roof with ease. We reached the edge and he dropped to a sitting position.

I peered over the side and gulped at the sight of green lawn *much* too far below for my comfort.

Zach turned on his stomach and lowered himself down until he hung off the edge by his fingers. Then he let go and dropped soundlessly onto his feet. He looked up at me and held out his arms for me. "Your turn."

I blinked. He had to be kidding.

I glanced behind me. Maybe I should go back inside and take whatever fate waited for me with the cops. Looking down at him, I shook my head. "Hate to break it to you, but I'm not Wonder Woman."

That should have come as no surprise. Zach knew me. I was no athlete. I completed the one year of required PE my freshman year, squeaking by with a B. That pretty much said it all. For everyone else with a pulse, PE was a guaranteed A. You showed up. Did what you were told. Easy A. Not me.

He waved his fingers, the gesture impatient. "Don't be scared. C'mon."

I bristled. "I'm not scared." I was so scared.

"Prove it," he countered.

After lowering to my knees, I copied his move and shimmied myself down until I was dangling off the roof by my fingers, trying not to imagine him staring at my butt. This was Zach. Fifteen minutes ago I wouldn't have cared, because I was confident *he* didn't care. No way would he have even looked at my butt.

But now that we had kissed, I didn't know anything. Not about him. Not about me.

My world had flown from its axis, and I couldn't trust anything anymore.

I didn't know what he was thinking.

Who was I kidding? He was thinking how I had tricked him into kissing me.

"Let go! I'll catch you."

Grunting, I ignored my skepticism. Zach was a jock who never read the books he was assigned. He was a player and someone who spent way too much time on his hair, but I'd never known him to lie.

Holding my breath, I let go.

His arms came around me, catching me and breaking my fall. We toppled together on the ground, my body sprawled over him. Exhaling, I swiped the hair from my eyes and looked down at him under me.

We held still for a moment, frozen, staring into each other's eyes, exerted breath mingling. So close our noses could almost touch. For a moment something was there. That same crackling heat I'd felt in the closet. It must be my melting brain.

"Hey!" A distant voice called out, deep and authoritative. I wasn't even sure if the voice was shouting at us, but it jarred us out of our stare-off. We bolted apart and jumped to our feet.

Zach grabbed my hand again and then we were running across Sharla's back lawn. We vaulted over a white rail fence into the neighbors' yard—probably the very people who'd called the police. We cut through a few more lawns before breaking out onto a street. A stitch in my side stabbed at me and I clutched my ribs.

I couldn't run anymore. I pulled on his hand. "I gotta walk."

He slowed and looked down the street behind us, dragging a hand through his perfect dark hair and sending the strands everywhere. "I think we're okay. Let's keep walking, though."

Nodding, I tugged my hand free from his grip. It was weird to hold hands with him now that we weren't running for our lives. We'd never done that. But then we had never done a lot of things before tonight.

I fixed my gaze straight ahead. Our houses weren't too far away now. We had one major thoroughfare to cross once we exited Sharla's subdivision and then we'd enter our neighborhood. Maybe twenty minutes.

"Where's your car?" I suddenly asked, wondering how he got to the party.

"At home. I rode with Josh."

"We could call someone for a ride," I suggested.

It was understood there would be no calling of parents. And I wouldn't even consider calling my sister. Not that she would answer. If she wasn't in the shower crying, she'd be buried in a pint of Ben & Jerry's and ignoring her phone. Unless her ex called. Then she would answer to scream at him. Obviously he rarely called.

"Do you know anyone who wasn't at that party?" he asked.

I thought for a moment and shook my head. Farah was my only friend who wasn't there, and she was in Austin visiting her dad.

Silence fell between us. I sent him several wary glances as I kept pace with him, my mind drifting back to that closet. Mortification washed over me. Had I actually bit his lip?

My heart was still pounding, and I suspected it had nothing to do with our mad sprint. I wiped sweaty palms on the sides of my jeans.

He finally spoke, and it seemed like even the night stopped. The wind died and crickets fell silent all around us. Or maybe it was just the rush of blood in my ears, overpowering everything else.

"Why did you follow me into the closet?"

And there it was. I felt like I was standing under a spotlight. No hiding or pretending. Nowhere to run.

I moistened my lips. "I stopped Ava and—"

"Why?" he interrupted. "Why did you stop her?"

"She's friends with Flor." It seemed the most obvious thing. But then I guess it wasn't obvious or he wouldn't have been so willing to lock lips with Ava.

He stopped and faced me on the sidewalk. "What does that have to do with anything?"

"Do I really need to explain the nuances of girl code to you? Flor was right there in the room." I waved as though demonstrating something. "She saw you go in the closet and then Ava was about to follow you. Does your first rebound girl have to be a friend of Flor's?"

Zach stared at me for a long moment, and then he did the unbelievable. He laughed.

I propped my hands on my hips. "What's so funny?"

"This." He waved between us. "You getting all self-righteous after *you* kissed me in that closet and Flor is your best friend."

Heat erupted in my face. "*You* kissed *me*."

He stopped laughing and looked at me. "And you kissed me back."

I shook my head, hating that bit of truth. "You . . . surprised me is all."

He lifted a single eyebrow. "I thought you were Ava."

I snorted and shrugged. "That much was clear. It was a mistake. You thought I was Ava. I was surprised."

"Surprised because I was kissing you?" There was a strange light in his eyes, and I felt pretty certain he was mocking me. His eyes seemed wider, watching me with an intensity I had never seen from him before.

"Yes. Of course."

He angled his head like he was trying to figure out a puzzle. "So *surprised* girls kiss guys back? When they get kissed? Just asking for clarification."

I hated where this conversation was going. There was no outcome where I didn't end up exposed and looking stupid. I shook my head and opened my mouth, but I didn't know what was going to come out. I didn't have a plan. Which probably meant I should say nothing at all.

Suddenly there was a chirp of a siren as a police car pulled up alongside us. I let out a relieved breath, and that was all kinds of messed up. I welcomed getting grilled by the police as long as I got to avoid an uncomfortable conversation with Zach?

The officer behind the wheel put the car in park and stepped out. "Evening, kids."

I felt myself wither inside as the man's sharp gaze fell on us.

Please, please, please. Don't have him take us to the police station. Or call our parents. Or both.

Zach dropped back beside me and took my hand again. I let myself have that comfort. It didn't feel weird at all right then. Not when I was massively freaking out inside.

"Evening, sir," Zach returned. He was always great with parents. Adults loved him. It could be his manners or his good-boy looks. Or maybe the fact that he was a local football star. This was Texas, after all. That always mattered to people. No one cared that I got straight As, but every member of the city council knew and cared that Zach Tucker could kick a ball from fifty yards.

"Little late to be roaming the streets, isn't it?"

"We were just on a walk," Zach replied, his voice even and easy. I didn't know that he could sound so normal in a tense situation like this.

The officer glanced at me, then at our clasped hands. I forced a smile.

"You two didn't happen to be at a party a few blocks over from here, did you?"

Zach was quick with his response. "A party? No, sir."

It was impressive. Zach actually sounded bewildered at the question. Apparently tonight was a night of realizations for me. Zach could both kiss and lie with astounding skill. I'd have to remember that.

A second officer emerged from the passenger seat and called out over the roof of the car. "You Zach Tucker?"

He nodded. "Yes, sir."

The second officer was younger. Maybe in his thirties. He looked fit, and I figured he must be the one that chased down suspects while the other one radioed in for backup. He motioned at Zach and addressed his partner. "He's the kicker for Madison." He leveled his stare on Zach again. "Hell of a game tonight. That was some field goal in the third quarter."

"Thank you, sir."

Of course. Football.

The officer gestured toward the back seat. "Why don't we give you and your girlfriend a ride home?" Even hearing myself mistakenly being called his girlfriend was jarring. "It's late," he continued, "and everyone is rounding up kids from that party a few blocks over. Would hate to get you thrown in with that bunch."

Because he was Zach Tucker and no cop would ever dare bust him.

Poor Jenna and Flor. Hopefully they got out in time.

"Thank you, sir." Both officers lowered back inside the car. Zach opened the back door for me, gesturing for me to go ahead of him.

I slid into the back seat, grateful to end the handholding.

Except when he slid in beside me, he picked my hand up again. I glared at him and tried to tug it free. He clung to it and shook his head once at me. What was the deal with holding my hand? Clearly he thought it was important for the sake of these two cops. I didn't see why it mattered, but I gave up and let him keep my hand.

I leaned back and tried to relax as Zach directed them to our street, talking football with them like we weren't sitting in the back of a police car. His thumb brushed a small circle against the inside of my wrist and I fought back a little shiver. I was sure it was unintentional. A knee-jerk reflex for him. He flirted with a lot of girls. Touched them too. This was probably just a result of holding hands with the opposite sex.

My mind strayed ahead . . . to the next couple of minutes, when I would pull up to my parents' house in a cop car. It was going to be awkward. If Mom was home already, she was going to flip. I considered various explanations in preparation, hoping to come up with the one that would get me in the least trouble.

They were just giving us a ride. It wasn't as though I'd gotten arrested. I reminded myself that I had nothing to feel guilty about.

Nothing except a kiss.

The police cruiser pulled up in front of my house, and right away I saw that Mom's car wasn't in the driveway. They'd taken her car to dinner. My shoulders sagged. I might get out of this without getting grounded for life.

"Thanks," Zach said, even as my hand flew to the door handle.

"You both live here?" the driver asked.

Zach pointed to his house. "I live there."

"Next door to your girlfriend?" The officer in the passenger seat chuckled and shared a look with his partner. "That's convenient."

His partner shared his laughter and said something about us being careful not to get into too much trouble.

My face burned. Zach's gaze caught mine but he didn't comment.

I looked away and stepped out into the night, glad to be out of the car. Glad to be home. Glad to be five seconds from escaping Zach.

I hurried to my front door as Zach exchanged a few more words with the cops.

I tried the knob, but it was locked. Damn it. I knew Chloe was home. She never went anywhere, and it was well past Mia's bedtime. I turned and went for the fake rock in the front flower bed that hid a key.

"Willa."

I ignored Zach, searching for the rock and then finding it. I flipped it over and slid open the secret compartment that concealed the key.

He said my name again and I looked up.

"Are you mad?" he asked as he stopped before me.

"No. Why would I be mad?" I'd simply had enough mortification for one night.

"Because you're practically running to get away from me."

"I just want to forget about tonight." I didn't want to continue where we left off before the cops showed up. I didn't want to talk about the closet.

He buried his hands in his front pockets, staring at me mildly. "The kiss." He said it like it was nothing, and I guess that was good. Even if it hurt a little.

"Can we just forget it ever happened?"

He stared at me for a long beat. "Yeah. Sure."

"And Flor . . ." God, it made me feel awful to have to ask him. "Can we not . . ."

"Flor doesn't have to know," he finished with a nod of agreement.

"Good." *Great.* Maybe this night wouldn't convert into disaster.

71

I should have stopped babbling right then, but it was such a relief. I felt like I'd just dodged a bullet. My friendships with Zach and Flor would remain intact. "It will be like it never happened. It didn't mean anything."

I turned around to unlock the door, my promise to text him later on the tip of my tongue, when he said my name again.

"Willa?"

"Yeah." I turned around with a smile on my face, still so relieved, so happy, so *grateful* that things hadn't been ruined. Nothing was broken.

Nothing had to change.

He kissed me without warning. I didn't move, too stunned as his hand cupped the back of my head.

Zach was kissing me on my front porch.

He broke away, his lips a hairsbreadth from mine as he whispered, in a voice that I had never heard out of him before, "I feel like I should confess I knew it was you in that closet the moment I touched you." His voice was growly and deep and sent all kinds of shivers down my spine. His fingers grazed my cheek. "And that was before we kissed."

Before we kissed?

I jerked like I'd been slapped. My stomach plummeted, feeling betrayed and elated at the same time. How two such emotions could coexist I didn't know.

"You said you thought I was Ava," I accused, my breath fanning his lips, and I hoped, irrationally in that moment, that my breath didn't smell bad.

"For about five seconds I did."

His words echoed inside my kiss-addled head, gradually penetrating. *And that was before we kissed.*

How could he have meant to kiss me? Me!

"Okay. But how . . . why did you kiss me if you knew it was me?" That was the sticking point. This was me. Willa Evans. Girl next door. Orchestra geek who didn't even have her own car. Who didn't know the first thing about football. While the two of us had been friends forever, most of his buddies still didn't know who I was or say hello to me in the halls.

"I wanted to."

I stared at him. "You wanted to," I echoed. Well, that explained absolutely nothing. And changed everything.

He had meant to kiss me.

I didn't understand it. Was I just convenient? A warm and willing mouth in a dark closet?

I wanted to think he wouldn't treat me—*us*—so casually. I wanted to believe our friendship mattered too much for him to do that. "I'm not one of your groupies, Zach."

He snorted, and his fingers flexed against the back of my head, sliding against my hair . . . and that was distracting. "You don't need to tell me that. You don't even come to half my games."

"I have things to do," I shot back, feeling sulky.

"Right." He smiled at me, revealing those beautiful straight teeth his parents had spent a fortune to fix. Two rounds of braces. Of course, even when he had braces, girls had been flinging themselves at him. Everything came easy for him.

But not me. I wasn't going to be free or easy. Even if I secretly wanted to be with him, we could *not* do this. Whatever *this* was.

I had Flor to think of. Especially because he wasn't thinking of her at all.

But he was so very good at this. That sledgehammer was back inside my too-tight chest, pounding furiously, urging me to do all sort of forbidden things. His hand slid around from the back of my head, and his thumb brushed my cheek. I felt myself falling, sinking into the Bermuda Triangle otherwise known as Zach Tucker. Hearts entered but never returned.

"Don't play me, Zach Tucker." The words husked out from my lips, my voice unrecognizable as I issued the broken plea.

His eyes darted over my features, his mouth so close that I was certain he was going to kiss me again if I didn't stop him.

The door rattled behind me a split second before it opened. Zach's hand fell from my face. I stepped around to face my sister.

"What are you two doing out here?" Chloe snapped.

She was wearing one of Mom's too-large T-shirts, and her hair was knotted in a wild bun atop her head that bobbed dangerously with her movements. "I can hear your voices upstairs. You're going to wake Mia."

"I forgot my key." I held up the fake rock as though needing proof.

Chloe eyed the two of us distrustfully. It didn't mean she actually suspected anything. That was generally how she looked at the world since her divorce. Everyone was guilty.

I slid the key back into its rock and returned it to the flower bed, dusting my hands together as if the chore had soiled them.

I faced Zach and forced a smile. "See you Monday." It was a silent message. I didn't want to see him any sooner than that.

"You want to watch a movie?" He nodded toward his house.

The offer caught me off-guard. "Um . . ." Apparently he wasn't accepting my "see you Monday."

I had a flash of us on his couch ignoring some movie while we made out. Kissing and petting and groping furiously . . . his hands going places no boy's hands had gone before.

My cheeks caught fire and my breathing hitched.

What was happening?

His eyes fastened on my face, and I was mortified because I knew he knew what I was thinking. And he was probably only suggesting that I come over so that we could talk. So we could set things right. He couldn't want to go there and do those wild things with me.

I couldn't assume that, just because he'd kissed me again. Could I?

I wasn't the kind of girl a boy did wild things with anyway, and he knew that.

"It's kinda late," Chloe interjected, not that she really cared. Lately she was only concerned with her own misery.

I felt torn. I wanted to shut down my sister with the reminder that she wasn't my parent. Naturally. But the last thing I could allow myself to do was go next door with Zach.

"Yeah," I agreed with Chloe. "It's late and I have a lot to do tomorrow."

His gaze held mine, and I knew he wanted to say a lot more on the subject, but my sister's presence stopped him. "Yeah. Okay."

"Night, Zach." I ducked inside the house.

Chloe followed, locking the door. I was halfway up the stairs when she asked, "What was that about?"

I paused. "What do you mean?"

"I could swim in the tension out there."

"I don't know what you mean."

She plopped a hand on her hip and rolled her eyes. "Yeah. You do. You've had a thing for Zach forever. What? Did he finally make a move?"

"No!"

She snorted. "Right."

"Nothing happened. He's Flor's ex-boyfriend!"

She shrugged. "So."

"As in eleven days ago they were together," I reminded her hotly.

"I would say you work fast, but since you've loved him since you were in utero, I guess you're kinda moving at snail speed here."

"Chloe!"

"Stop shouting. You'll wake Mia."

I resisted reminding her that I usually did that anyway. "You don't know what you're talking about, and I'd appreciate it if you kept your theories to yourself about me and Zach."

"Ah. Already in cover-up-mode?" She nodded as she dropped down onto the couch and reached for the remote control. "Let me just give you a bit of advice. He's not worth it. It's going to cost your friendship with Flor, and in the end he'll only break your heart. That's what guys do."

"God, you're being bitter again." I stifled a moan.

"It's true. He has a penis, doesn't he? Then he's basically a prick."

"Not every guy is like Braden." I'd done it. Said his name. It was an unspoken rule: no one talked about her ex.

She leaned forward and blasted me with an arctic stare. "It's in their DNA. You're just too young and dumb to know it, but you'll figure it out soon enough. They say whatever you want to hear. They even believe it in the beginning. They just change their minds. Fall out of love with you. It's easy to fall out of love. Maybe even easier than it is to fall *in* love with someone."

"Dad isn't like that," I shot back. "He and Mom have been together forever."

She stared at me for a long moment before arching an eyebrow and asking, "Are you so sure he's not like that?"

My skin flushed cold. "What are you talking about?"

"He's gone during the week for work." She gave another one of those indifferent shrugs. She was all about shrugging these days. "Who knows what he's up to?"

I shook my head. In fact, all of me was shaking, so angry at her . . . and at myself for letting her affect me. "Do you even hear yourself? This is Dad you're talking about. That's so messed up."

For a moment Chloe looked contrite, her eyes full of doubt and vulnerability. She looked young again. Like the sister I once had before she went away to college and got married. The one who was always laughing and happy and busy with her friends.

Mia started crying. The look vanished from Chloe's face, and she was hard-eyed and biting again. She stormed past me and marched up the steps. "Trust me, baby sister. Stay away from that one next door. I've watched him over the years. He's the ruiner of girls. You're not unique or special. You're not going to be the one to break him. He'll be the one to break you."

GIRL CODE #8:

Don't forget your family and friends just because you're suddenly dating someone. They were there for you before, and you'll want them to be there for you after.

Flor

DAD was home when I came down around ten the next morning. He must have come home sometime in the night. Or maybe early in the morning when I was dead asleep.

I could see him through the glass doors of his office, his dark hair crisp and shining wetly from a recent shower. Before he met Dana, he'd had silver at his temples. Overnight the gray had miraculously disappeared.

He waved at me as I passed, barely glancing up from his computer.

I made some oatmeal, drank a big glass of water, and went for a run. I kept it short. Only a mile. I had soccer practice this afternoon, and I'd get plenty of running in then.

I sent a text to Willa, apologizing for bailing on her the night before; then I decided I'd try to get a head start on homework. I didn't need to let my other grades slip too. I had enough to worry about.

I was an hour in and had just finished reading the assigned chapter for economics when I picked up my phone. There were a few group texts from the girls on my soccer team. Nothing from Willa. I went to my thread with Zach. I still had a little red heart next to his name. I couldn't bring myself to delete it yet. That would be me admitting things were well and truly over. That wasn't happening yet.

My last text to him was still unread, and that stung. I'd sent it on Wednesday, asking him if he wanted to come over and hang out. Yeah. I knew. It smacked of desperation. I'd never been like this over a guy before. Usually I had more pride. Usually I had the upper hand in the relationship, acting indifferent and casual.

It embarrassed me that I was being this way . . . and still. I couldn't stop myself.

My fingers hovered over my phone, poised, considering sending him another text.

"Gah!" I flung my phone down on my bed before I could do something that stupid. I wasn't going to get him back by coming off as desperate and clingy. No. I needed to figure something else out. I needed to remind him why he fell for me in the first place. A large part of that had to do with my confidence. I needed to be the confident girl I once was. I needed to get back to her somehow.

Feeling a little better, I nodded and went back to my reading. I worked until it was time to leave for soccer, then drove to the park where my team practiced.

I played on a select team with girls from all over the city. There was school soccer, of course, but if you were shooting for college recruitment, you needed to play year-round for a competitive soccer club. I tried out for Club Storm when I was eleven years old and had been advancing through the ranks ever since, making my way up the ladder until I was on the club's most advanced team for my age group.

Only one girl on my team went to Madison with me, and she was racing across the parking lot toward me now, her backpack bouncing behind her, her red braids flying wildly.

"Oh my God!" Molly exploded. "Were you at Sharla's party last night?"

I nodded as I got my backpack out of the back seat.

"Did you get an MIP? The party got raided and I heard they lined everyone there up on the front lawn and gave out MIPs like they were candy bars. They even arrested a few kids who were so drunk they couldn't stand."

"No." I frowned. I really should have trolled my social media this morning. Apparently I had missed a lot. "I must have left before that happened."

But what about Willa? Was that why she wasn't answering her texts? Did she get into trouble? That would make sense.

Suddenly I felt like the worst friend in the world. I shouldn't have left her. I was so caught up in myself, in Zach and my dad and his girlfriend and the fact that I was failing math and losing my chance to be varsity captain. I wasn't there for Willa. Not like she was always there for me.

I took out my disappointment and frustration by throwing myself into practice, putting at least three girls on their butts. Two hours later I was drenched in sweat and felt a little better. The endorphins had kicked in . . . but I still felt bad about Willa. I needed to check on her and apologize.

I reached for my phone as soon as I got into my car. No text from Willa. I started my car, then went on social media, quickly seeing evidence of Sharla's party as I waited for my air conditioner to kick to life. There were even some photos taken after the cops got there from the kids waiting in line on the lawn just like Molly had mentioned. I rolled my eyes.

I spotted Jenna in one shot, standing in a line next to Hayden as cops issued tickets. Her face was caught mid-speech, and it wasn't a pretty expression. She'd hate it.

It was ridiculous that people would post such inflammatory material, but unsurprising. Every nuance of life was subject to documentation. Nothing was sacred.

I called Willa on the way home, listening on my car's speaker as it rang and rang. Eventually her voicemail came on. I left a message. She must have gotten into big trouble to not have access to her phone.

When I got home, Dana's car was in the driveway. I blew out a frustrated breath and sat in my car for a moment, composing myself before going inside. Couldn't Dad go a night without seeing her?

Sighing, I grabbed my backpack and went in.

I took my cleats off on the back porch, spying through the blinds on them in the kitchen. They were cooking again, and the delicious smells carried outside and wrapped around me. My stomach grumbled as I opened the back door and entered the house.

"Flor!" My dad said my name like he was surprised I was

home. Like I didn't live here. Like I didn't have practice every Saturday and come home at this exact time.

Dana eyed me over the rim of the wine glass she lifted to her lips.

I smiled overly brightly at her, dropped my backpack on one of the barstools lining the island, and headed for the refrigerator, glancing at the oversize skillet on the stove as I passed. "What are you making?"

"Paella."

It looked as good as it smelled, but I kept that to myself.

I took out the chocolate milk and poured myself a large glass. "Is it ready?" I asked, trying to act casual and like I didn't want to dive face first into it. I was always starving after practices.

"Yes. Just waiting on the bread warming in the oven."

I nodded and took a bowl out of a cabinet and a spoon from a drawer. I moved to the stove and dished a healthy portion for myself.

Dana glared at me. I glared right back. It was my house. I lived here, and I would bet my dad had paid for the groceries to make this meal. I set the bowl on the counter and took the grated Parmesan out of the fridge and sprinkled it over the top.

"My, my, that's a lot of calories," Dana murmured, helping herself to more wine.

Did she really just say that to me?

I forced myself not to ask how many calories were in her wine and said instead, "I ran about a thousand miles today. I think I'll be okay."

She fixed a smile on her face and shared a knowing look with my father. "You'll have to adjust your eating as you get older. You won't have that kind of metabolism after high school."

I rinsed out my milk glass and refilled it with water. "Thanks for the advice."

Balancing spoon, bowl, and drink, I started out of the kitchen, calling over my shoulder, "Thanks for cooking."

Dad's voice stopped me. "Would you mind eating with us?" He motioned to the table.

I turned and stared at them warily. This was the first time he had requested me to eat with them. Well, other than the time we went out for sushi when he first introduced us.

I had been stupidly, naively excited then. Dad had a girlfriend who he really liked. I imagined us forming a unit together. I knew she couldn't take the place of the mother I'd lost to the beaches of Playa del Carmen the majority of the year. But for some reason I had a vision of Gloria from *Modern Family*. He'd mentioned she was younger than he was.

Dana, however, was no Gloria.

I gathered within five minutes that she viewed me as competition for my father's attention. Every comment I made, she one-upped me. Every story, she had a better one. Even when I was talking about something that had happened to me at school, it reminded her of something that had happened to her.

By dessert, I had given up and was saying very little, and that seemed just fine with the two of them. They carried on talking like I wasn't even there. I told myself not to worry about it. She and my father wouldn't last forever.

I still told myself that.

"I need to go work on my math."

"Oh, how is that cutie tutor of yours?" Dana waggled her eyebrows at me.

"It's not like that. He's just my tutor." I muttered, still confused at this invitation to eat with them. They liked it when it was just the two of them. They preferred it that way.

She waved a hand dismissively. "Whatever. When are you seeing him again?"

"Tomorrow," I reluctantly admitted as I pushed up from the table. "If you'll excuse me, I need to shower."

Dana wrinkled her nose as if she could suddenly smell my stink.

Dad motioned to the table and moved to take the bread out of the oven. "Sit down, Flor." It was a command. A command from my father was rare these days. "This won't take long."

I obeyed, moving to the table and setting my bowl down with a thud. I pulled out a chair, sank into it, and waited for them to join me.

They dished paella into their bowls and set them on the table. They sat side by side, always in touching distance. I sat across from them, feeling like a suspect on one of those police dramas with the two detectives across from her.

Dad placed the bread on the table along with some butter. The bread was rich and dark and smelled like heaven. I couldn't remember the last time I'd had dinner with Dad at this table. I eyed them both cautiously, waiting for them to start eating.

Dad tore off a piece of bread and then offered the basket to Dana.

She motioned to her bowl of paella—a quarter of my portion. "This is more than enough carbs for me. I'll have to work out for hours tomorrow as penance."

Dad nodded and handed me the basket. I practically tore off half the loaf, feeling rebellious. Then I reached for the butter, lathered the bread with a generous smear, and took a big bite, moaning in enjoyment.

Her eyes narrowed.

It was petty, but I took my pleasures as they came.

I swallowed my bread, then tasted the paella and rolled my eyes in exaggeration. "Dad, this is so good."

"I'm glad you like it. I found the recipe online."

I ate a second bite and sighed in contentment. "You can make this anytime."

He chuckled and reached for Dana's hand where it rested on top of the table next to him. I watched as she took a dainty bite of her meal.

"What's this sausage?" I asked.

"Andouille," he replied. "Too spicy?"

I shook my head and took another bite. "No. I like it."

A beat passed, and then I heard my father clear his throat.

My wariness returned in full force. I paused mid-bite, certain something was about to happen that I wasn't going to like.

I lowered the spoon back to the bowl and stirred idly, suddenly too uneasy to take another bite.

Dana and Dad exchanged a look. My father's hand flexed around his girlfriend's and she gave him an encouraging nod that made my throat tighten as though a rope were wrapping around my neck and squeezing.

"Dana and I have some news."

News. The word pounded feverishly through me. Oh, hell. I'd been set up. This was no friendly dinner. Of course not.

I stared at the meal spread before me, seeing it for what it was. A carefully orchestrated trap.

I leaned back in my chair, forgetting all about the paella and bread. I stared back and forth between them and then looked down at their joined hands on the table. "What kind of news?"

"Well. Dana's lease is about to end . . ." His voice faded away.

I braced myself and exhaled, understanding dawning.

"We've discussed it." He turned his gaze on Dana, his smile shifting into this besotted, infatuated, disgusting thing. He didn't even look like the father I knew. I'd never once seen him this way with Mom.

There was no saving him. He was lost.

"She's moving in with us." I said the words. Spit them out.

Dad faced me again, his eyes bright with excitement. "It's going to be wonderful, Flor. For all of us. I'll be home more." He squeezed Dana's hand and gave it a small shake. "We both will now."

Because he won't be out with her all the time. They'll be here. Together. I'll get to see Dana every day.

I was going to be sick.

"Flor," he prompted. "Say something. Are you happy?"

Dana watched, her mouth curved in an expectant smile. A knowing smile. She knew I wasn't happy, but my feelings didn't matter in this. Dad had made up his mind, and I would only come across as difficult and immature if I threw a fit. I suspected she wanted that.

"Of course," I lied. "It's wonderful."

Dad turned to Dana. "See. I told you she would be happy."

Really? I sounded convincing?

She stared at me. "Yes. You did."

"So happy," I confirmed.

I reached for my bowl and resumed eating even though my appetite had fled.

She would not win. I would not give her the satisfaction of seeing me throw a tantrum.

She looked pissed. I could see it in her eyes. She'd been ready for a scene. I wouldn't give her what she wanted. I'd wait. I'd wait until they broke up. It couldn't last forever.

Sadly, I knew that.

Nothing ever did.

GIRL CODE #9:

A secret really isn't a secret if more than one person knows it.
It's just gossip waiting to happen.

Willa

$$\gg\!\!\longrightarrow$$

S UNDAY morning we sat down to a huge brunch before Dad had to head back out of town for work. Mom went all out. Eggs, bacon, pancakes, and orange juice.

I couldn't help watching him and Mom closely. It was Chloe's fault. She'd put that stuff in my head about Dad. I wasn't a suspicious or cynical person, and I resented her for putting doubts in my mind.

"How's work?" I asked him, cutting into my syrup-drenched pancake and peering at him closely.

He looked up from where he was feeding Cheerios to Mia. "Great." He smiled mildly, and I tried to read past that smile, but there was nothing there. He was just . . . *Dad*. He liked Monty Python and big plates of barbecue and going to ren fests. This was not a man living a double life. "How's school? Still getting As, I hope."

"Oh, you know Willa, Daddy. She's got her eye on the prize.

She'll get her pick of schools," Chloe said with exaggerated cheer-fulness, stabbing at her eggs.

I stared at her coolly. "Did I mention how great it is to have you living with us again?"

"Willa," Mom chided.

I blinked at her innocently. "What? Isn't it? Just great."

The rest of the meal passed uneventfully. We all hugged Dad goodbye later when he was ready to go. Mom walked him out to his car. I stared at them through the blinds, watching them hug and kiss, and I decided my sister didn't know what she was talking about.

I buried myself in homework, pausing to exchange some casual texts with Flor, which I took as a good sign. Everything was fine between us. Nothing had changed. Nothing was going to change.

Zach, on the other hand, sent me several texts and even Face-Timed, all of which I ignored. I'd told him I'd see him on Monday. That would be soon enough. Friday was still too fresh. I'd stared into the dark half the night, thinking about him, reliving those kisses and convincing myself things could go back to the way they were before.

I had finished my homework and started practicing my cello when my phone rang. I looked over at it where it sat on my dresser. Zach's name appeared over a picture of him in seventh grade when he was smiling really goofy big and showing off his braces. I'd thought it was funny. He'd just rolled his eyes.

I resisted the impulse to answer the call, glancing outside my window to where his house sat, a looming presence in my life as large as the sun. Eventually my phone stopped ringing and I went back to my cello, escaping into my music.

I lifted my head some time later, noticing it was almost dusk. My room had gotten darker, and I stood up to turn on my overhead light. I thought about going downstairs to see if anything was going to happen for dinner when I heard something at my window.

I walked over, wondering if it was a squirrel — they were pretty rampant on our street — and that was when Zach's head popped into view.

I yelped and lurched back, a hand flying over my heart.

He grinned and tapped on the glass. "Hey." His muffled voice carried through the window.

"What are you doing?" I stepped forward and peered out the glass to confirm that he was standing on a ladder and not in fact levitating. "There's a front door." He'd been using it for years.

"Since you were ignoring me, I decided not to risk you turning me away." He tapped on the glass again. "Mind letting me in?"

"No," I snapped, crossing my arms over my chest. "I mean yes. I do."

"Willa . . ." He crooned my name and gave me puppy-dog eyes in a way that I'm sure he thought was adorable. And, unfairly, it was.

"This isn't right, Zach. Go away." I shooed him with my hand. "I'll see you in the morning."

"I think you want me to come inside."

"No. I don't."

He angled his head. "Um, pretty sure you do. Otherwise I'll have to follow you around at school tomorrow until we have our talk and clear the air."

"You wouldn't!"

"I would."

Just the idea of that was panic-inducing. People watched Zach Tucker. Always. There was no way the sight of him stalking me around school would go unnoticed. It would attract attention. People would wonder. They would talk. And if anyone overheard us . . . I shuddered.

I crossed my arms and glared at him. "This is just to talk?"

"What's the matter? You don't trust me? Or *yourself*?" His eyes glinted and he looked smug enough that I wanted to hit him. Instead I unlocked the window and slid it open, letting him in.

He climbed in, his feet landing lightly on the floor. We stood there for a long moment in front of each other in a room that we'd been alone in countless times.

And it felt different.

It felt unbearable.

"God, this is awkward," I mumbled.

"As awkward as avoiding me?"

I winced. "Yeah. That's awkward too." I guess he was right about clearing the air. It was good to do it before school tomorrow. "Not to mention difficult." I motioned in the direction of his house. "We've known each other too long. Things shouldn't be weird between us."

He nodded. "True."

In theory, that sounded right. But I didn't know how things

could *not* be weird now. I'd made out with Zach. That changed everything.

How could things ever go back to the way they were before?

There were a lot of reasons I'd avoided him, but maybe the main reason was because I didn't want to face the possibility that my friendship with Zach Tucker was over. The last two nights I'd stayed up trying to convince myself things could go back to the way they were before. I'd been lying to myself.

My eyes burned and I realized that I was on the verge of crying.

I moved away, putting some distance between us, determined he not see those tears and that I was one breath from breaking down. "I guess maybe *When Harry Met Sally* was right." I choked out a laugh. "Men and women can't be friends, because the sex part always gets in the way."

I froze. Had I just said that?

Had I just introduced the idea of *sex* between us into the conversation?

Excuse me while I *die*.

I babbled, rushing to fill the silence, to fix what I said: "I mean, you're a guy. I'm a girl. We're around each other a lot. It was bound to happen once."

"It?" he echoed, his gray eyes dark and intense, fixing on my face as it exploded into heat.

Ohmigod. "Not *it!* I didn't mean *that*." God, he thought I was talking about us having sex. My body pulsed. A thousand pinpricks attacked my skin like a swarm of bees.

I looked away from him. Away from that face. Away from that body, which was tall and lean and hard and perfect . . . and the

93

obsession of too many girls to count—including my best friend. "I'm talking about the closet thing," I clarified. "And what happened on the front porch."

God, it was like words were my enemy. They fell from my lips like clumsy nonsense.

He lifted an eyebrow. *"When Harry Met Sally*? Is this another one of your movies I should know?"

I nodded and suddenly remembered that Harry and Sally got together at the end.

I stopped nodding and started shaking my head no. The very last thing I wanted was for him to watch it and think that's what I was implying. That I wanted that. That we should be together in the end.

This was real life. We weren't Harry and Sally.

We're never going to be Harry and Sally.

God, that shouldn't hurt like it did.

Of course I was in love with him, but that wasn't public knowledge. It was a *true* secret. As in only *I* knew it and no one else.

"You really don't believe that, do you?" he asked, looking disapproving. As though I had somehow disappointed him. "That we can't be friends?"

"No. Of course not. We've been friends forever. We're around each other so much."

He grinned. "It was kind of crazy." He rubbed the back of his neck, chafing where the hair was cropped close to his skull.

It was a gesture I'd seen him do countless times when he was flirting with a girl in the hallway at school.

When he's flirting with a girl at school.

Oh. My. God.

Flirting. The word reverberated through me. My heart started punching faster and harder, a drum in my chest. No. *Yes*. NO. He couldn't be flirting with me. I couldn't be one of those girls to him. Someone he was attracted to. Someone he wanted to . . .

My mind turned it over feverishly, considering it. It didn't seem possible, but yet there was Friday night.

That night, which had kept me awake and tossing and turning and feeling . . . things. Aching tingly things.

Friday wasn't an aberration. It had been real.

He wasn't kidding when he called this weird. Zach looking at me like he was now, like I was a real-life girl, was the stuff of my secret fantasies. I didn't have to wonder about those lips. I knew them. I knew them, and I needed to forget them.

Reality and fantasy weren't supposed to collide. I was pretty sure that would be like the polar icecaps flipping and the harkening of Armageddon. Who wouldn't do everything to prevent that?

I moved to the far side of my room and sank down on the edge of the bed, stretching my legs out in front of me. "I'm just saying it was inevitable that something like this *might* happen." I waved between us. "We're around each other so much. Things got confusing. So we kissed."

"There were kisses, in fact," he corrected. "Multiple."

I shrugged like it was no big deal. Like I hadn't thought about it every waking moment since it happened. "Kisses. Whatever. What happened between us was a fluke."

He nodded slowly, watching me, and there was still that sense of disappointment that vibrated from him. I did not like it at all.

In the years we'd been friends, he'd always approved of me. He'd never been angry with me. Or disappointed. He'd never looked at me like he did now. Further evidence things were different.

"I've been thinking a lot about what you said."

"What I said?" I asked nervously, perfectly aware that I'd said a lot and not all of it very smart. I was in new territory here with him, and the words that fell from my lips were not to be trusted.

"Yeah. That I surprised you, remember? And that's why you kissed me back. You claimed that's why you were into it."

Oh God. He was going back to my totally craptastic logic. My heart punched hard in my chest. "Uh-huh," I murmured.

"Well, what if I didn't surprise you?" He advanced slowly on me, and I remembered I was on the bed. Not the best place for me to have decided to sit. "What if you knew it was coming? What if I told you I was going to kiss you and then I did it?" His gaze dropped to my lips and my heart lodged itself in my throat. "Would you kiss me back?" He lowered beside me on to the bed. His eyes moved back and forth between my eyes and lips. "Maybe we should experiment with that?"

Experiment. Now that word roused all kinds of images.

I couldn't breathe. My lungs had stopped working.

He lifted a hand and pushed back the hair from my face. Had he moved closer? I glanced down at the space between us. It definitely seemed to be shrinking.

"No, we shouldn't." My voice escaped unnaturally high. I leaned away from his body.

"I think it's a good idea," he countered. "Let's see if you kiss me back when you know it's coming."

96

I didn't need to try this little experiment to know I *would* kiss him back. I needed to avoid this experiment at all costs.

He leaned in, and I pressed a hand to his chest—which was a danger in itself. Touching him was a risk. "Flor."

The single word, her name, spoken out loud, was enough.

He went still.

I continued, "Please don't pretend like she doesn't matter. Even if she wasn't still hung up on you, I can't do this with you. It breaks girl code."

"Girl code," he echoed.

"Don't act like you don't understand."

He sighed. "I get it."

"I won't do anything to hurt Flor."

His broad chest lifted on an inhale. "She doesn't need to know."

I frowned. All of a sudden, I felt dirty sitting there with him on my bed.

"So this experiment will be just between us? Your ugly little secret? Convenient for you."

His gray eyes turned fierce. "Don't twist this. You're the one that doesn't want anyone to know."

"That's right! Because this would be the worst betrayal ever to Flor."

"This is one of those no-win scenarios." His face screwed tightly in anger. "Keep it a secret and you think I'm ashamed of you. Tell the world and I'm wrecking your friendship with Flor. I'm fucked either way."

I flinched at his language, but it went hand in hand with the emotion flashing in his eyes.

I moistened my lips. "I know you don't care about Flor's feelings anymore, but I do. I don't know what happened between you two, but she really misses—"

He shook his head. "No. Don't do that. It's not that I don't care about her feelings and you know that. Don't make me the villain just because I don't want to be with her. I don't want *her*."

The words fell hard between us. He stared furiously at me, his breathing a little heavier. Something hovered in the charged air. The unspoken answer to the question *Who* do *you want?*

I was new to this thing swelling between us, but I understood it. Felt it at an instinctual level.

He wanted me.

For however incredible or wrong it was. For how little sense it made. Right now, maybe only right now and not next month or next week . . . maybe not even tomorrow, he wanted me.

He continued, his voice lower, thrumming like the sad echo of a note fading on my cello. "I'm talking about you and me. You don't think we should at least see if there's something here between us? Something real? You don't think you owe that to yourself? To us?"

I shot up from the bed and pointed to my window. "This is stupid. Why are we even having this conversation? It's impossible. You should go."

He pushed to his feet too. The disappointed look was back on his face, and I hated that it made me feel so sad.

He stared at me for a long moment. "All right, then."

"All right?" I shook my head, marveling that his agreement should surprise me a little.

"What do you expect me to do?" One corner of his mouth curled, but there was no mirth in it. "Stay and force you to kiss me? It's fine. We'll just be friends, Willa. Like before."

Like before.

I sighed in relief. The tension eased out of me. This was good. Great, even.

He turned back for the window and slid a leg over the edge. His gaze found mine. "See you in the driveway tomorrow?"

"Same as always." I nodded . . . hoping, praying, that was true. That it would be the same as always. That things could go back. That the little niggle of guilt inside me would disappear.

GIRL CODE #10:

Make sure you're not unfairly judging your friend's taste in guys. Just because it's not your taste doesn't mean it's wrong.

Flor

I was still stewing the next day.

I'd hardly slept a wink the night before. Staring into the dark, I'd wondered how my father could be so gullible. So taken in by a pretty young face. He was such a cliché. Didn't he want substance in a woman? Someone closer to his age who had seen some of the world? Who had lived and accomplished things? The only thing Dana had accomplished was two semesters of community college and a job in retail. What could she and my father possibly have in common?

My mind took a hard turn into gutterville and I had to stifle my gag reflex—and that definitely made it hard to fall asleep. Eventually I did.

But the following morning, I opened my eyes to the framed picture of Dad and me at a Chivas game when we went to visit his uncle in Guadalajara. His uncle had gotten us great box seats because his wife's cousin played for them. It was awesome. We even got to meet the players after the game. The trip had taken my mind off Mom leaving us. Made the wound a little less raw. The trip had given me hope that Dad and I would be okay. We could be happy just the two of us.

I released a pent-up breath and dragged myself out of bed. Sure. I couldn't expect Dad to live as a monk forever. He was entitled to . . . *companionship*. I wasn't blind to that. I would be gone at college soon, and then Dad would be alone. But this quickly? And Dana? He could do better.

I spent the rest of the day avoiding my father and Dana. Out of sight, out of mind. At least that was what I told myself.

I did homework, then went to the store so I would have stuff to eat this week. I was used to fending for myself and wasn't going to change my ways just because Dana was moving in. On a whim I even decided to give Rowdy a bath. He was starting to stink. Unfortunately, after I finished showering him, *I* smelled like wet dog.

I spotted the time on my alarm clock sitting next to the photo. Damn. Grayson was going to be here in half an hour, and I knew that guy would be punctual. I didn't want to kill him with my BO. Not that I wanted to impress him or anything, but I could spare him that out of courtesy. He had given me a ride the other night and had actually helped take my mind off of stuff.

I grabbed a fresh pair of shorts, panties, bra, and T-shirt and vaulted toward my bathroom, where I planned to take the world's fastest shower.

After turning the shower to hot, I jogged back out to check my phone while the water warmed. Because priorities. There was one from Willa, which I replied to quickly. Nothing, of course, from Zach. It was like he'd just disappeared from my life. With a disappointed grunt, I flung my phone on the bed and rushed back into my bathroom.

Washing my hair, my mind played over the fact that Dana was moving in. She would be sharing a room—a bed—with my father. My gag reflex rose again.

She'd be bringing her stuff with her too. God knew what that would all entail. She'd take over my mother's huge walk-in closet.

I turned off the water, dried off with a towel, and tried to shove thoughts of Dad and Dana far away. Even if Wills called me back right now, I couldn't talk to her. I had Grayson coming over. I needed to focus on that. On math. On passing my next test. On *better* than passing it, because face it: Getting a C on a single test wasn't going to much help my 66. It might only bring me to a D average.

Dressed, I stood in front of my mirror and dragged a brush through my wet hair, working through the snarls. I'd just managed to get the last tangle out when I heard my dad shout from downstairs.

"Flor, your tutor is here!"

At least he wasn't calling Grayson my boyfriend like Dana had.

I yanked open the door and shouted down, "Send him up."

I dashed back into my bathroom and wrung out my hair. The top half of my T-shirt was wet, but at least I was clean. Dana couldn't accuse me of smelling anymore.

When I emerged from the bathroom, Grayson stood hesitantly on the threshold of my bedroom.

He looked incongruous standing there in his dark long-sleeved shirt and jeans and black Jansport backpack. My bedroom was mostly pale colors: white and gray with accents of yellow. I'd picked the colors out two years ago with my mother. She loved to decorate. She was constantly redoing rooms. Almost like with every room she redid, she would finally find something to make her happy. Some change that would be enough to fix whatever was empty inside her, to fill the void.

I tried to shake off thoughts of the way things used to be with my mom. I'd see her over Thanksgiving break. That would be good for us. We'd have a good time together reconnecting.

I'd spent so much time being mad at her when she left, but now I realized things had never been that great when she was here. I'd been angry and mourning something that had never been perfect . . . even if that was the image I had projected to the world.

Maybe I could start over with Mom and rebuild a relationship that was better than what we had before. And let's face it. Thanksgiving break in Playa del Carmen would be amazing. It would beat staying here with Dad and Dana.

Maybe Zach and I would have patched things up by then and he could come with me. We'd talked about it. Before we broke up. We'd talked about lying out on some gorgeous beach during one of our school breaks, fruity drinks in hand, sand between our toes, warm sun on our skin. We could still have that. Once he stopped being mad at me.

"Come in." I waved Grayson inside the room, forcing a smile and trying not to let my sour mood spill over. He was here to do a job, and I needed his help.

He entered, weaving between the pillows scattered around the room. "Sorry about the mess." I bent down and quickly snatched up all the pillows, throwing them back on my bed.

He didn't say anything. Just stood there like he didn't know where to go.

I grinned. "What's the matter? Never been in a girl's room before?"

"Never one this messy."

My smile fell at his quick retort. "Yeah. Well. Mustn't have been in too many, then." I motioned around me. "'Cause this is about what you can expect."

He grunted, and I felt like a jerk rubbing in the fact that he wasn't exactly fighting girls off with a stick.

"Right" was all he said, and in such a curt way that my mortification was only magnified. Whenever he looked at me I felt like he saw a stereotype—the rich, popular mean girl.

I grabbed my backpack and dropped down at the foot of my bed and vowed to be nice. Patting the floor beside me, I invited, "Pull up some rug."

"You don't have a desk?" His voice faded as his gaze found my desk, littered with the clutter of my life.

I smiled brightly. "Of course I do."

He settled down next to me, his long legs stretching out before him. He really was tall.

"You ever thought about playing sports? Football? Basketball?"

He shook his head. "They're just games."

"Yeah. So?" I shrugged.

"I don't have time for games." He unzipped his bag and pulled out a notebook and pencil.

I bristled, offended. Soccer was a game, but I needed it in my life like I needed food and air. Clearly, he didn't get that. Zach understood. He felt the same way about football. I guess there was no sense trying to explain that to some people.

I shot him a disgusted look as he turned and faced me full-on.

I forgot about being offended and gasped. "What happened to your face? That wasn't there Friday night!"

A thick gash cut into his eyebrow and crept down onto his eyelid. It had scabbed over, but I couldn't help thinking it had probably needed stitches. The sensitive flesh surrounding it was bruised a nasty shade of purple.

I brushed his eyebrow with my fingers without thinking, my touch careful against the severe-looking wound.

He flinched and pulled away from my hand. "It's nothing."

"Doesn't look like nothing."

"I ran into a door."

"A door," I echoed in disbelief.

"Yeah. Now, how'd you do on your test?"

Clearly he didn't want to talk about his eye anymore. I wondered if he'd gotten it from some bully from school. Madison had its fair share of pricks. Or maybe even his dad did this to him? My stomach turned and twisted sickly at the idea that he might be stuck in that kind of home life.

"Flor," he prompted. "The test?"

"Um . . . Yeah." I shook my head slightly and looked away from him then . . . from that eye, which hurt my stomach to see. I cleared my throat. "We're gonna have to really prepare for this week's quiz."

"That great, huh?"

I opened up my notebook and took out the worksheet I got for homework on Friday. "I tried starting it. Got through some of them."

He looked over my work and took out his pencil. He started marking up the paper. I watched his hands as he worked. His knuckles were scratched up. These looked like new scratches. Maybe he'd been working outside. He handed the paper back to me after a few minutes.

I glanced down at it and then looked back at him with an eye roll. "So I might as well erase everything and start from scratch?"

He shrugged. "Yeah, that'd be fine. Let me watch you work through it."

I took a sheet of paper and rewrote the first problem, feeling him watching me. The paper, yes, but me, too. For some reason it made me self-conscious. I tucked my damp hair behind my ear and reminded myself that I wasn't usually self-conscious. Guys looked at me. Especially teenage guys. They weren't exactly discreet. And they didn't only *look* at pretty girls. They gawked.

I paused over the problem, tapping the end of the pencil to my lips, not sure of my next move on it. "You must think I'm pretty dumb."

A few moments slid by and he said nothing. I turned to glare at him. He was already looking at me. "This is when you say, 'No, not at all. I don't think you're dumb.'"

His eyes were no less brilliant behind those lenses. Not this close. "You have people complimenting you all day and telling you how great you are. Do you really need me to do it too?"

I sucked in a breath. "That's not true."

"Isn't it?"

"I don't need constant affirmation," I insisted. Was that what he really thought of me? What other people thought of me?

He cocked a dark eyebrow. "Okay." He shrugged. And that shrug totally killed me. So cold and indifferent. What was with this guy? The other night he was decent and gave me a ride home. I thought we had entered a kind of truce. "Look," he said, "I'm just here to tutor you. That's what you're paying me for."

"Right," I snapped, and turned my attention back to the problem. I worked through it angrily, pressing my pencil deep into the paper, breaking the tip more than once and having to push out more lead.

"Shouldn't press so hard," he commented after I finally successfully completed one problem.

I moved on to the next problem without comment. He leaned closer to watch what I was doing and I felt his breath on my cheek. It was distracting. I turned to tell him that he didn't need to be so close, and our noses bumped.

"Ow." I cupped my nose. "How about some space?"

He pulled back. "You write small."

"You're wearing glasses. Maybe you need your prescription checked."

His nostrils flared and I knew he was annoyed. Good. So was I.

"God. Why are you so popular? It's not like you're nice."

The words shouldn't have stung, but they did.

"And you're a jerk," I flung out. "You think you're so smart and superior. Well, if you were smart you would know that popularity and *nice* have nothing to do with each other." Sad but true.

We glared at each other, our insults vibrating between us. The air was charged and tense, and then suddenly I was looking at his mouth. Talk about distracting. But also ridiculous. Not to mention wrong. *So* wrong. I couldn't be thinking about kissing again. Not him. This was becoming chronic.

There was nothing remotely attractive about him. At least not to me. He would be Willa's type. I was surprised she hadn't mentioned him before. She always liked the guys with brains. He had to be on her radar. But then she wasn't boy crazy. She never really got excited over guys.

"Hey." The partially open door creaked, swinging wider, and Dana walked in.

I blinked and scooted a little away from Grayson. She already had a problem remembering he wasn't my boyfriend.

Her smile turned catlike and my defenses rose higher. "Ever heard of knocking?" I demanded. My father wasn't in the room. I didn't have to fake nice.

"Oh, Flor." She cocked her head and said my name in a chiding way that set my teeth on edge. "Should you be in here with the door closed? With a boy?"

I gawked at her. "Are you serious? He's my tutor."

She tsked. "He's a cute boy." She looked Grayson over and I wanted to hurt her right then. She was enjoying making me uncomfortable. And him, too. "I remember the hormones. I was in high school not too long ago."

"Yeah. Like ten minutes ago," I mumbled.

She laughed overly loud.

God. When had my life become this? I was living a teen movie, and it was me versus the wicked stepmother, digging on each other every chance we got.

I shook my head. "Why are you in here?"

"I wanted to see if you kids wanted some popcorn."

Was she serious? "I'm fine."

Dana looked at Grayson. "No, thank you," he answered, then added, "ma'am."

She giggled. "Such manners." She turned back for the door, swaying her hips and not for my benefit. At the door, she made a show of pushing it wide open. "We wouldn't want you two to get carried away and do something other than math." She winked at us.

My face burned hot. *Kill. Me. Now.*

She left then, and I stared at where she once stood, my brain tripping over the fact that she was actually going to be living here with me. That I would see and interact with her every day.

"Hey. You okay?"

I reluctantly looked at him, mortified at Dana's parting remarks. "Yeah. Peaches." I stabbed my pencil in the air after her. "That she-devil is moving in here. They just told me last night."

He looked to the door. "That sucks."

I laughed miserably. "You have no idea." I stared down at my paper. The numbers started to swim and I realized I was about to cry. In front of the smartest guy I knew. Who, I was starting to realize, was kinda hot but thought I was the absolute worst.

How was this my life?

He nudged me with his elbow. "Hey."

I shook my head, an unbearable lump forming in my throat. I dropped my head lower so that my hair fell in a dark curtain around me.

"Flor?" He pushed my shoulder, forcing me to look up.

Reluctantly I lifted my gaze.

He stared at me, his eyes moving over my face, taking it all in . . . including the tears that blurred my vision. "I'm just having a bad day." *A bad month.* I gave a wobbly smile. "I'm okay."

He turned his body to fully face me and leaned in slightly, propping his hand on one thigh. "You can't change any of this. So take *this.*" He pointed to my heart. The stupid organ actually jumped at the brush of his fingertip through my shirt, just above my breast. "And these tears." He tapped lightly at the corner of my eye. "You use them. Turn them to fuel." He nodded his head in the direction of where Dana had been moments ago without taking his gaze off me. "How pissed off you feel, how hurt . . . you use that as incentive to pass math. To do everything better. To become stronger so you can graduate and get the hell out of here. You don't like your life? Then make the life you want for yourself." He gestured to the books and paper between us. "That's why I do this. Why I work multiple jobs and do shit I hate and study my ass off." He took a breath. "So I don't have to live with my old man forever."

It was the most he'd ever said to me at one time, and I was a little stunned. I nodded slowly. I tucked a bit of my long hair behind my ear.

"I'm sorry."

Suddenly he was human again and I couldn't stop staring at

him. He studied me back, and I wondered what he saw. Still the spoiled brat who he thought was mean?

After a moment his stare shifted, caught on something over my shoulder. "Is that your mother?"

I looked over my shoulder and followed his gaze to the photo of me with my mom on my thirteenth birthday. We had gone to Dave & Buster's. It so wasn't Mom's kind of place. She kept calling it a kid place even though there were more grown-ups there than kids. She watched with a pained expression on her face as Dad and I played Skee-Ball.

The picture sat on my nightstand in a white metal frame. I wasn't sure why I hadn't moved it yet. Buried it in a drawer. I probably should have.

It was the last thing I looked at before turning off my lamp at night and plunging my room to darkness.

I loved my mother. Adored her, even. And maybe that was never as it should be. She was like this beautiful moon in the sky, something I was always reaching for, stretching out my fingers to touch, to hold. She had always been just out of my reach. Even when she lived with us. I hadn't realized it then. I realized it now. Now I knew.

I stared at that photo a lot. Mom was smiling in the picture, but I kept searching her face, looking for something. Some sign. Some indication that she was going to leave. Did she know even then?

The curve of her lips looked a little brittle. A shadow of something lurked in her blue eyes. Every time I looked at those eyes I imagined I saw something different in that shadow. I was determined to figure it out. Maybe one day I would.

"Yeah. That's my mom."

"Wow," he said in an even voice. Despite his comment, his expression was mild and not salivating like a lot of boys when they first clapped eyes on my mother. There was some comfort in that. It would have bothered me if he'd looked at Mom with lust in his gaze and made some crack about MILFs. I'd heard plenty of that before. I just really really didn't want to hear it from him.

"She's really beautiful," he added. Just a statement of fact.

I nodded. "Everyone says that." Which was true. Everyone said how beautiful my mother was. She was one of those rare individuals who actually got better with age. Maybe Botox had a hand in that, but for the most part it was just good genes.

"You look like her."

I made a sound and gave him a funny look. "Really? You're the first to say that."

"What? You don't get told you're beautiful like fifteen times a day?"

Heat slapped me in the face. I wasn't starving for compliments. I got my share. I wasn't insecure with my looks. Hearing him say this, though . . . I didn't know why it affected me. I didn't know why it made my stomach churn with butterflies.

I looked back at her with her blond hair and blue eyes. "I look more like my dad."

"Your coloring," he agreed. "Not your features."

And how hadn't I seen that? I studied Mom's face every night, but I never saw me in her. Maybe that was why I couldn't figure out that shadow in her eyes. Because I couldn't see her as she really was.

"Come on," he said. "Let's finish these problems."

Nodding, I returned my attention to math as he walked me through them step by step, patiently, breaking them down so that I could figure them out.

He made things sound easier. Doable. Fixable. Like life was really what you made it and all those clichés. He made me believe I could do this. That I could get things right.

And I wasn't only talking about math. Grayson was one of the good guys.

I really should set him up with Willa.

GIRL CODE #11:

No group pictures shall be posted to social media without consensus . . .
unless you look really really good.

Willa

LITTLE niggles of guilt didn't go away. No, they just grew and grew and became bigger niggles.

I supposed they would go away with absolution, but there could be no absolution coming from Flor, because she would never know what happened.

I would never confess what had gone down between Zach and me.

I was all about justification. Why should I tell her and ruin our friendship? It was a freak collision of lips and hormones, and Zach and I had agreed to move on and put it behind us. It would never happen again. It meant nothing.

The last thing I could admit to was breaking girl code. Especially as today at lunch we'd spent forty-three minutes inventing girl-code tenets to add to our manual. Yeah, that wasn't secretly awkward at all.

"Oooh, I got one!" Jenna exclaimed as she fished a carrot stick out of her plastic bag. "No one shall take a picture of a friend drunk and getting an MIP *and* post it to social media."

She was pissed about that photo from Sharla's party. Her parents had seen it.

"Yeah, but is that a violation of girl code when it comes to you and Hailey Hines?" Farah asked. "I mean, you're not that tight with her. Does she owe you loyalty?"

"She lives a few blocks from me," Jenna protested. "We used to be in the same Girl Scout troop."

"Tenuous thread," I offered.

"I agree," Flor declared. "I mean, I don't see Hailey sitting here with us. Is she even in your contacts?"

"Well, then maybe there should just be a common-decency code," Jenna grumbled. "I'm grounded indefinitely . . . or at least until my brother or sister manages to screw up and take the focus off me."

"Knowing your little brother, that won't be long," Flor reassured her.

"Well, I had to miss it to go visit my stupid dad again." Farah swung her hair over her shoulder. She had the most gorgeous hair. It hung almost to her waist in dark thick waves, and she was always styling it in various braids she learned from YouTube. "I mean, I feel like I'm missing out on our entire senior year!"

"Maybe you should be glad you were out of town this weekend. You could have gotten busted," I pointed out.

"I would have been smarter." She nodded confidently as she tore open a bag of chips. "I would have gotten out of there in time like you and Flor did."

Jenna rolled her eyes. "Right."

"At least your dad wants to see you all the time," Flor interjected.

I studied her, detecting an undercurrent of anger in her voice.

We all knew about Dana moving in and how Flor wasn't thrilled about it. I'd only met Dana twice, but it was enough. I wouldn't be happy either.

The table fell quiet then as Zach walked by with a few of his friends. He didn't look over at us, but we all followed him with our eyes.

All except Ava. She knew better. She kept her gaze down.

She'd been allowed back into the fold, but she'd been quiet since taking her old seat at the table. I brought her into the conversation every chance I got and even offered her one of my cookies, making sure she felt included.

I was self-aware enough to acknowledge that my kindness to her was driven partly out of kinship. I understood the allure of Zach Tucker. Like me, she had resisted it. Rejected it. Unlike me, she had been strong enough to turn away before that first kiss. I couldn't stand by and let the others punish her when I had done far worse.

Flor hadn't spoken to her yet, and we were all waiting for that to happen. I was confident it would. Eventually. Flor wasn't a mean person. And Ava hadn't done anything irreparable.

Would Flor consider *my* actions irreparable? My gut told me yes, but I wouldn't risk finding out.

I bit into my sandwich. Turkey and Swiss. My favorite, but it was tasteless on my tongue as I watched Zach.

Even among his friends, jocks like him, he stood out. He walked with confidence, lean and strong, laughing at something one of the guys said. It didn't seem fair. He'd just turned eighteen. Guys his age were supposed to be struggling with acne and be awkward around girls. Not him. Clearly.

Jenna leaned in. "Did you hear he asked Ashlyn out? They were in the parking lot arm in arm this morning."

An invisible ripple passed over the table. All eyes swung to Flor to await her reaction to this.

"I heard that too," she admitted, her expression stoic.

"What are you going to do?" Jenna asked.

"I haven't decided." Flor looked at me. "Did he say anything about it to you?"

I didn't know whether Zach had actually asked Ashlyn out or not, but they'd been in the parking lot together this morning. I knew that because I'd been there.

All eyes on me, I picked at the corner of my sandwich. "On the way to school this morning he mentioned they were talking."

It was true. The agony was real.

He'd dropped that little bomb on me almost casually as we pulled into the school parking lot and we both spotted Ashlyn waiting next to his usual spot. Her gaze locked on him through the windshield like a lioness zoning in on a gazelle.

"What's she doing?" I'd asked him.

"Waiting for me." He'd volunteered the information simply. No inflection in his voice. As he might have done before we fooled around. And I guessed that was a good thing. I'd wanted things to be the same as before.

But he'd caught me off-guard, and I said the first thing that

117

popped in my head. "Wow. Ashlyn Morgan. You don't waste any time. When did this start? I mean, last night you wanted to *experiment* with me."

He slammed on the brakes and turned to stare at me, leaving Ashlyn waiting there across the parking lot, indifferent to the annoyed teenage drivers swerving around us. "Why do you care?" He angled his head and looked almost amused. "Jealous?"

I pulled a face and shook my head. "Not at all. You and Ashlyn? Okay. Fine. But tell me, how is that a step up from Flor?"

His amusement fled. He looked angry again. He turned around in his seat, his fingers tight on the steering wheel. "Can I tell you how much I hate hearing Flor's name coming out of your mouth? If I never hear you say her name again, it will be too soon."

I flinched, realizing that when it came to getting my two best friends back together again, I might have done more damage than good.

He swung forward and parked. Ashlyn unleashed her wide-lipped, sensual smile on him as she stepped off the curb, waiting for him to emerge from the vehicle.

How had she learned to smile like that? If I tried it, I'd look like an idiot.

She was one of those girls who owned her sexuality. It was like she came out of the womb knowing how to apply liquid eyeliner. She was with different guys all the time.

He waited a moment, releasing a breath. Without looking at me, he said, "She texted me last night." His gaze connected with mine then, his gray eyes dark and meaningful. "*After* I left your room."

After. After I told him to go. After I told him we could only ever be friends.

He exited the car then and joined Ashlyn. She looped her arm through his, leaning all her lush curves into him. He didn't look back at me as they headed into the building, even though I couldn't tear my gaze off him.

Flor sighed. "Maybe that's it, then. It really is over."

"You're just gonna give up and let Ashlyn have him?" Jenna tsked in disappointment. "Everyone knows you're the perfect couple."

Agreement echoed around the table. Even Ava nodded.

No one noticed that I didn't.

"Willa." Jenna looked at me. "What did you tell him? Did you tell him that Ashlyn is a slut?"

I winced. I was never comfortable with slut-shaming. I didn't get why guys could sleep around and get high-fives for it and girls who did the same got called names. How was that okay? It was a definite imbalance made only worse in my mind when girls perpetrated the ugliness. Where was female solidarity? Maybe if our girl code got around, it could help in that endeavor. Sure, I had broken one of the major tenets of girl code myself, but I knew I was wrong. I knew it and I wouldn't let it happen again. I believed in the code.

Farah snorted. "Yeah, 'cause that's going to really repel him. Guys always run the other direction when they hear that a girl is up for sex."

Jenna glared at Farah.

"No. I didn't say that, Jenna," I snapped. "Why aren't guys condemned when they hook up with a lot of girls?" I cocked my head and looked around the table. "What even makes a girl a slut? Is it truth or rumor?"

Jenna looked at me in confusion. "What are you talking about?"

Of course she didn't understand. Jenna had grown up in a family where you were judged and condemned if you didn't wear twin sets and *go steady* with football players. Sure, she hadn't managed the whole exclusivity thing with anyone yet, but she was hopeful. Which was sad, because I still suspected she was into Abby. Too bad her parents preferred her with someone like Hayden or Trevor instead of someone who might actually treat her well. At least she'd be out from under them soon. Maybe at college she would finally feel free to be herself.

"Guys. It's fine. Let's not argue," Flor said, her tone even and reasonable. She exhaled and stared across the cafeteria for a moment. "Maybe he needs to kiss a few frogs to realize I'm his princess." She grinned and winked at all of us, but her voice lacked conviction. After a while, she shrugged and added, "Maybe I should go out on a date."

"Oooh, yeah. Make him jealous," Jenna agreed.

"I think we all need dates," Flor declared, slamming a hand down on the table. "We need to start thinking about the homecoming dance."

"Haven't you been asked by like two guys already?" Farah stole one of Jenna's carrot sticks and waved it at Flor.

"Yeah, but no one I want to go with."

A vague look came over Flor's face, and she glanced across the lunchroom. I followed her gaze, but couldn't tell where she was looking. It wasn't in the direction of Zach's table.

She returned her gaze to me. "Willa." She said my name thoughtfully. "Do you know who Grayson O'Malley is?"

"Isn't he that super-smart guy?" Ava said, finally finding her voice.

"Yeah. He's a National Merit Scholar." I nodded. "We're in NHS together." Not that I had ever talked to him. It was a big school. A lot of kids were in NHS.

"He's tutoring me in math, and I have to tell you . . . he's kinda hot in a nerd kinda way."

"I can see it." Farah nodded.

"I'd totally do him," Jenna volunteered. We all laughed. It was what she said every time she thought a guy was hot.

"Let me set you up with him." Flor hopped in her seat. She loved nothing more than playing matchmaker.

"No," I groaned.

The other girls all made approving sounds.

"Oh, y'all should go to the game together this Friday," Jenna suggested. "It's a big one against Travis."

Farah frowned. "Hello. Willa doesn't go to the games. And I doubt he does either."

"That's not his thing," Flor confirmed. "They'd have to do something else."

"Hello." I waved a hand. "You're talking about this as though it's a done deal. The last time you fixed me up with someone, it was a disaster." It was a guy on the football team. Anthony, one of Zach's friends. We had nothing in common and sat there like two lumps on a log during our double date with Zach and Flor.

"It won't be like that. Grayson has a brain."

Jenna nodded. "Yeah. A big brain."

"I don't know." I glanced across the lunchroom where she had looked before, presumably where Grayson was. I spotted him. He was getting up from a table. He moved toward a garbage can and tossed away his trash. She was right. He was hot in a Loki kind of way. Tall and lean. There was an actual grace to his movements, and that was saying something for a teenage boy.

Maybe you do need to go on a date.

Not necessarily with Grayson, but with someone. Kiss another guy. Get Zach out of my system. Move on.

That seemed to be what he was doing. It was what we had agreed to do.

"Sure," I agreed. "If he's interested, I'll go out with Grayson."

GIRL CODE #12:

Sometimes it's okay to let your friends lie to themselves. They have to figure stuff out on their own.

Flor

I wasn't even sure where to find Grayson, but I figured the library was a good place to start. It was last period of the day, and a lot of kids who didn't have athletics had study hall. Coach gave me a pass when I told her I needed to meet with my tutor. She wanted me passing, obviously. I couldn't play otherwise.

Before reaching the library, I detoured into the bathroom. I checked my appearance, although I didn't know why I bothered. I was in my soccer shorts and an athletics T-shirt, my hair pulled up into a ponytail.

Jenna walked in as I was smoothing out an eyebrow with a fingertip.

"Oh, hey there." She squared off in front of the sink and pulled out her makeup bag. "Hayden is waiting outside. He's skipping athletics for me." She smiled and winked at me like this was cause for celebration.

"Greaaaaat," I said slowly.

She tossed me a look. "Don't go there."

I held up my hands. "I wasn't going to say anything."

She made a sound of disbelief followed by an eye roll.

I lingered, suppressing the urge to let my full distaste show as I watched her reapply lipstick. I was about to turn and leave when Abby Morton walked in. She froze for a moment, her gaze clashing with Jenna's.

Jenna stilled mid-lipstick swipe.

Suddenly, I couldn't move either. I watched the two of them, not about to miss a moment of this.

"Hey," Abby greeted her.

"Hey," Jenna returned, her cheeks pinking up. Abby moved and disappeared inside a stall. I looked at Jenna's reflection in the mirror. She busied herself searching through her makeup bag, pretending like nothing was out of the ordinary.

Moments later, Abby emerged from the stall and washed her hands, her long dark ponytail swishing with her movements. She glanced at both of us, murmured a quick goodbye, and left the bathroom.

Jenna released an audible breath. "Where is that pencil brush?" she muttered.

"Okay, that wasn't tense," I said, watching Jenna carefully as she continued rifling through her bag, her movements agitated. "You okay?" I asked.

"Yeah. Sure. Why wouldn't I be okay?"

I lifted my eyebrows. "You're talking really fast and loud."

Her head popped up, her gaze meeting mine through the mirror as if seized with a sudden thought. "Do you ever wonder if we'll survive this?"

I shook my head, bewildered. "What?"

"High school." She waved a hand. "Adolescence . . . being a kid, whatever." She shrugged awkwardly. "I guess we're technically kids until we have our diplomas in hand, right?"

I didn't feel like a kid anymore. I felt old. Some days I felt damn old. And tired, too. I didn't say any of that, though. Instead I said, "Of course we'll survive." I nodded with sudden determination. "We will."

I had to believe that. Had to say that. Because I didn't want to think things could get any worse. I mean, I knew they could. Things could always be worse. Other people were worse off. I wasn't so naïve not to realize that. Bad things happened all the time. Tragic things that made absolutely no sense. You just had to turn on the news or scroll through social media to see evidence of that. It was always there. Noise. Images. All of it ready to drag you down and pull you under.

I refused to think things could get worse for me, though. I had to stay positive. If I didn't, then there was just despair.

"Jenna, all this . . ." I fluttered a hand. "It won't matter later on."

She nodded. "I guess you're right. Real life begins when we're free to be ourselves."

"That's kind of profound. Is that a bumper sticker or something?"

She looked offended. "No."

I studied her then. Really looked at her. I supposed she would have theories on that. With parents like hers she was hardly in a position to be herself.

She capped her lipstick. "Don't look so shocked. It's insulting. I do have my moments." She zipped up her bag and faced me. "That's what I tell myself, anyway. That's what gets me through. Someday I'll be free to be anyone I want to be."

And maybe she had more to get through than most, I realized. At least my dad didn't try to control my life and make me into someone I wasn't.

Jenna acted like everything was okay and she was happy to chase guys like Hayden. But that was all it was. Acting.

Stuffing her makeup bag in her backpack, she flashed me a bright smile. "See you later."

The door thudded behind her. Shaking off my sudden introspection, I exited the bathroom and headed for the library, continuing on my earlier mission.

Once inside the library, I searched among the tables on the first level. No luck there. I went to the second and then I spotted him.

I dropped my bag on the table across from Grayson. The sound was louder than I intended, and several kids lifted their heads to glare at me. I smiled apologetically and sank down in the chair across from Grayson.

"Hi!" The word bubbled out of me. I couldn't help myself. I was excited.

He watched me almost suspiciously, one dark eyebrow arched. We'd never really talked much at school before.

I unzipped my backpack and dug around for what I wanted to show him.

He leaned across the table, his voice low as he asked, "You do realize you're in the library."

I paused and gave him a look. "Yeah, smart-ass. I know. I've actually been in here before."

I resumed my hunt through the messy contents of my bag.

"You look happy," he murmured.

"Because I am."

"I don't think I've ever seen you happy."

I paused, realizing he was right. He'd come into my life when things were pretty much at an all-time low. I'd lost Zach and virtually Dad, too. Dana was moving in. I shrugged. "Know me long enough and you get to see all sides of me. See how lucky you are?"

He shook his head, but a corner of his mouth lifted like he wanted to smile.

Finding what I was looking for, I yanked my quiz out with a flourish and slapped it down on the table. Beaming, I pointed. "Bam!"

His gaze landed on the circled 81 at the top of the paper.

He fell back in his chair and smiled slowly, his hand coming up to frame his mouth as though he wanted to shield his delight. It was almost as though he couldn't stop himself from grinning. And that smile. It was a lethal thing.

He nodded. "Good job, Hidalgo."

I performed tiny little air claps on both sides of my head. "Thank you. Thank you. But I can't take all the credit. I had this super-smart tutor. He's kinda rude but he teaches really good."

"Well," he corrected.

I rolled my eyes. "You're off the clock, but fine. *Well.*"

"I bet you get an A on the next one."

"I don't know about that. When can we meet again? Tomorrow? I have this really long review packet due next Monday and it counts as a quiz grade too."

"I have plans after school."

"All afternoon?"

"Yeah. I'm booked."

"Oh. Okay. Busy guy. When, then? I hate leaving it until Sunday. I have a soccer game on Saturday that's going to take most of the day. It's all the way on the other side of town."

"Get as much done as you can. I'll check it Sunday night and we'll go over any you miss or don't know."

"Okay."

He nodded and I realized we were done. We didn't have anything else to talk about, and I needed to get back to athletics and let him work on whatever it was he was doing.

Still I sat there, searching for something to say. And I came up with it. "Do you know Willa Evans?"

He stared at me for a second. "Yeah, she's your best friend. You've got pictures of you two plastered all over your bedroom."

"That's right."

"What about her?"

I felt a stab of misgiving as he stared at me. Then I cast my doubt aside and said it: "You want to go out with her?"

Nothing changed in his expression. In fact, as the moments slid past, I wasn't sure he'd heard me.

I waved a hand in front of him. "Hey, you there?"

"You're asking me to go out with your friend?"

"Yeah."

"Why?"

I laughed nervously. "What do you mean, why? Why not? She's fun and smart." I motioned at him. "You're . . . smart. Super smart."

He snorted. "But not fun?"

I waved that off. "No verdict on that yet. I've only been around you in a tutoring capacity."

"So we're both smart? That's why we should go out?"

"She's cute," I added, "and you're . . ."

My voice died. But the thought was there. Immediate and resounding. *Sexy.*

He stared, waiting.

I was taking too long.

"You're cute, too," I supplied, my face erupting into fire.

"Cute." He gave a single, hard nod and then started gathering his things up in abrupt movements.

"So is that a yes?"

"No."

"No?" I frowned at that emphatic refusal, feeling both offended on Willa's behalf and relieved, too. I had no idea where the relief was coming from, though. This had been my idea. It was a *good* idea, and now I had to explain to poor Willa that he wasn't interested in going out with her.

Zipping up his bag, he pushed up from the table. "Look, I don't have time to date. And no offense to your friend, but she's not my type."

I blinked. "You have a type?"

"Yeah," he bit out, and then walked off.

Grabbing my bag, I took off after him. "Hey, we were in the middle of a conversation."

He glanced back at me as he pushed through the library doors, his expression annoyed. "The conversation is over. See you Sunday." His long legs carried him away, and I gaped after him.

"And you accused *me* of not being nice?" I called after him. Jerk.

A couple of girls walking by stared at me. Freshmen from the looks of them. They worked too hard on the hair and makeup. "What?" I glared at them and then looked down the hall. Grayson kept walking like he hadn't heard me.

He was the rudest person alive. I didn't care how smart he was. He could be friendlier. He'd been happy when I showed him my grade. It was the Willa thing that had gotten his panties in a bunch.

Staring at his back, I wondered if I would still see him on Sunday.

And why was I so bothered by the possibility that now I might not?

GIRL CODE #13:

Don't cancel plans with your girlfriends because a boy calls at the last minute, unless he's really special and they're all cheering you on.

Willa

THE week continued in a blur.

I would like to say that sitting in the passenger seat beside Zach, channeling the Willa Evans of a week ago, was easy. I wanted to say it was starting to feel normal again. Like *before*.

Except it wasn't. Our time together was tense. I never mentioned Ashlyn, although I still saw her flitting around him at school. He didn't seem to mind.

I couldn't meet his gaze, so I pretty much avoided looking at his face. Instead I stared at those hands on the steering wheel, but even his hands put flutters in my stomach. They were nice, big hands. Lightly tan and veined. Blunt-tipped, tapering fingers with neatly trimmed nails. And I could only remember how they'd felt on my face when he kissed me. By the time he put the Jeep into park I was always relieved to escape that small space with him.

That afternoon I stayed late after school. I was coming out of the orchestra hall when I spotted Zach walking across the practice field heading for the parking lot. He spotted me, too.

"Need a ride?" he called.

I wished I could say no, that I had a ride, but I didn't. I was planning to call my sister to come and get me. "Sure," I called back. It was only reasonable. Chloe would complain, and even if she grabbed Mia and left right away, I'd probably have to wait at least fifteen minutes.

"How was practice?" I asked once we were in his Jeep, rubbing my palms over my jeans and willing myself not to be nervous. Things were supposed to go back. We were supposed to be friends like before.

"Good. How was yours?"

"Good." I nodded. "We have a recital coming up."

We lapsed into silence, which I guessed was better than inane conversation.

When we pulled up in the drive, I could see Mom's car wasn't parked in the open garage. I knew Chloe wouldn't have started dinner yet. I'd have to come up with something.

I climbed out of Zach's Jeep and started across the lawn to my house.

"Hey, you got any graphing paper?" he asked. "I'm out."

"Sure. It's in my desk."

He followed me up my porch. I tried not to think about the last time I'd stood on this porch with him.

All thoughts about that night fled when I pushed open the door to the sight of my sister asleep on the couch and Mia sitting before the TV, systematically destroying Mom's magazine collection.

"Mia!" I dropped my backpack and sank down on the carpet beside her, plucking a shredded copy of *Cooking Light* from her hands. She squealed at the sight of me and flung her chubby arms around my neck. "You shouldn't do that," I lightly reproved, hugging her cuddly little body. "Phew. Someone needs a diaper change."

"Uh, Willa?"

I looked up at Zach's voice. He was standing over my sister, who was asleep on the couch.

"Chloe?" I called.

No response. Hair obscured half her face. Zach shook her shoulder gently. Then harder. Nothing.

I hurried over and shook her. "Chloe." Alarm tinged my voice.

Zach must have heard it. He reached in and felt the pulse at her neck. "She's breathing."

"Chloe!" I shook her again even as my stomach sank. I knew she was taking antidepressants, and that probably wasn't all. Her bathroom was like a pharmacy. So many pills.

Mia giggled, clapped, and copied me, leaving out the *l* sound. "Coey!"

My sister opened her eyes. "Ugh. You." She moaned and slapped at my hand. "Go way. Leave me alone," she slurred.

I looked up at Zach and held his gaze. Understanding filled his gray eyes. "What's she on?"

I sighed and shook my head. "Who knows?"

Nodding, he bent down and scooped her up in his arms. "Let's get her upstairs."

I picked Mia up and followed. He carried my sister up those

steps and down the hall without breaking a sweat. I watched the play of his back muscles beneath his T-shirt. Yes, even his back mesmerized me. Gah. I was terrible. Salivating over him wasn't helping put things back to the way they were before we kissed.

I followed him into Chloe's room, watching as he lowered her onto the unmade bed. Just as he was about to pull away, Chloe grabbed a fistful of his shirt, tugging his broad chest down toward her. "Hey, what are *you* doing here in my room, sexy thing?" She arched, stretching her too-small MADISON CHEER T-shirt tighter across her chest. She circled a hand around his neck. "Always knew you had a thing for me."

"Chloe!" God, she was a menace.

She turned bloodshot eyes on me. "Oh. You." She let go of his neck. "Little Miss Perfect."

I blinked. It was funny she called me that. I didn't feel perfect now. Far from it. *She* had been the perfect one, once upon a time. Yeah. Hard to imagine that, looking at her now.

She'd been the cheerleader. Homecoming queen. Straight As. Near-perfect score on her ACT. She'd gotten a full ride to Vanderbilt. Even when she'd gotten married to Braden, a grad student, the world had been hers. Beautiful bride. Handsome groom. Lovely church wedding. They moved into married student housing, and if Mia arrived less than forty weeks after the wedding, no one mentioned it. Her life was picture-perfect. At least that was what I thought. Until Chloe showed up on our doorstep with Mia and a car full of her belongings. Apparently Braden was going to complete his doctorate at Cambridge, and he preferred to do it without

Chloe. In fact, he preferred to instead take the student he was currently sleeping with.

Groaning, Chloe collapsed back down on the bed and waved a hand in the air in a little circle. "Why don't you two just do it and get it over with? You've been dancing around it for years."

I gasped. I would kill her. Later. When she was sober and we were alone.

She closed her eyes. She was out again.

I moved into the hall and toward the bathroom. Adjusting Mia on my hip, I poured a glass of water, sneaking a glance at my reflection. My cheeks burned red.

Returning to the bedroom, I thrust Mia at Zach. "Hold her a second."

To his credit, he took her without hesitation and managed not to look afraid.

I slid an arm under my sister's shoulders and lifted her up. "C'mon. Take a drink," I coaxed, hoping it would help dilute whatever was in her system. I wasn't sure if it would work, but it seemed the thing to do. I felt Zach beside me. The warm crawl of his gaze . . . the heat radiating from him.

Chloe opened her eyes. "What the hell!" She swatted at the glass I bumped against her lips, sending water sloshing over her face.

She surged upright, arms flailing. I fought back a laugh. She looked so outraged, coughing and wiping at the water running down her face . . . but she also looked a bit more sober, so that was comforting.

Mia giggled in Zach's arms.

"Take a drink, Chloe," I encouraged.

"Stop being such a buzz kill! Go away. I'm fine." With a huff, she rolled over on her side.

I stood back with the glass. "I guess she's fine."

"She'll be okay."

"God! Both of you just go away!" she shouted over her shoulder at us.

We left the room. Zach closed the door behind me. Standing in the hall, I took Mia from his arms. "Thanks for that." I looked down at my niece. She played with my hair, babbling. Her big eyes locked on my face and she demanded, "*Moana*?"

Smiling, I shook my head. "Not right now, Mia." I looked back at Zach. "I need to change her diaper. Give her a bath. My graph paper is in my desk. Help yourself."

It was a dismissal. I couldn't bear looking at him right now, and not because of the new tension that had come between us, but because he was witness to this.

He glanced at my sister's shut door and then looked down at Mia. I held my breath, hoping he wasn't going to want to talk about what just happened. Looking at it through his eyes, it definitely looked messed up. He probably thought my family was dysfunctional, and I don't know that I didn't agree.

"Okay." He moved down the hall toward my room and I turned for the bathroom.

I spent about thirty minutes bathing Mia. She was squeaky clean and smelled of soap by the time we emerged. Chloe's door was still closed. Who knew when she would surface? I'd have to check on her periodically.

Carrying Mia, I headed downstairs to fix us something to eat, pausing when I reached the bottom. Something smelled delicious.

"Mom?" I called. Maybe she'd brought dinner home.

Except when I entered the kitchen, it wasn't Mom. Zach puttered around my kitchen, looking totally at home. He hadn't left.

"What are you doing?" I bounced Mia into a more secure position on my hip. She grabbed a fistful of my hair in a non-gentle grip. I leaned my head into the pressure but didn't look away from Zach.

He lifted his gaze to mine. "Making dinner."

I glanced around the kitchen. "I can see that." Two pots simmered on the stove, and the oven read 350 degrees. Evidently something was baking inside it. He'd done all this in half an hour? "Maybe I should lock the doors around here. I thought you were going home."

"I thought I'd stay and cook y'all dinner. You don't mind, do you? Seems like you got your hands full." His gaze held mine, the gray of his eyes sucking me in.

Did I mind that he was cooking for me and I wouldn't have to eat cereal for dinner? I shook my head slowly. "No. Thank you."

The front door opened, and Mom called out hello. She entered the kitchen and dropped her bag on one of the barstools. "Something smells amazing."

"Zach cooked dinner," I said.

"Zach!" A smile spread across her face. "How great are you?" She moved forward to press a kiss on Mia's chubby cheek. She brushed a hand over my hair. "I didn't know you knew how to cook. We'd have you over every night."

"I cook exactly three things," he volunteered. "Spaghetti. Tacos. And French toast."

"And what are we so fortunate to get tonight?" Mom asked.

"Spaghetti." He bent and slid a tray from the oven, which held garlic bread.

"Looks delicious," Mom murmured in approval as she leaned over the cooktop to inhale.

I moved and plopped Mia into her high chair. After buckling her in, I locked the tray into place.

"I'll just go change and fetch Chloe down."

"Oh, she's asleep."

Mom paused. "She's already in bed?"

"Yeah." I flicked a quick glance to Zach. He lifted an eyebrow but said nothing, just continued to stir sauce. Even without saying anything, I felt him nudging me on.

"Maybe you should check on her?" I suggested, fiddling with the bib around Mia's neck. It was the most I could say. Especially as tired as Mom looked. She always looked tired. Since Dad took the job out of town and Chloe and Mia moved in, she looked worn to the bone.

"Hmm. Okay." She turned and headed upstairs.

Zach lifted a pot from the stove and poured the pasta into a colander waiting in the sink. I fetched a bowl for Mia from the cabinet and prepared a bowl of noodles for her. Zach approached and poured a little meat sauce over Mia's noodles. I stirred it and blew on it to cool it down.

"You know you should tell her."

I glanced at him. "My mom?"

"Yeah. She needs to know that your sister is a hot mess up there."

"She's got enough to worry about."

Zach shook his head. "You can't avoid it forever. I mean . . . she'll figure it out eventually. Why not go ahead and break it to her?"

I nodded like I agreed.

He continued. "I know you'd rather pretend everything is fine."

I set the bowl in front of Mia along with her toddler fork. I walked around Zach and tore off a piece of warm bread, then handed it to Mia. She snatched up the buttery goodness eagerly, forgetting about her pasta.

He clasped my shoulder and forced me around to face him. "I mean . . . I know you're a pro at avoidance—"

"What's that mean?" I snapped.

He smiled. "C'mon, Willa. You know I mean us."

I bristled. "It's not the same thing."

"Situations are different, but you're handling it in the same way. I know you. You don't do confrontations and you don't do conflict."

I walked to the fridge and poured some milk into a toddler cup, uncomfortable and desperate to look anywhere other than at him. I screwed the lid back on and handed it to Mia. "What are you? A shrink?"

"No. I just get it. It's easier to pretend. To run. I know. I'm guilty of that too. I guess it's just . . . human."

I blinked suddenly burning eyes. I didn't want him to be right.

He continued, "I pretended with Flor." I froze. *Are we going to talk about this?* "Almost immediately I knew it wasn't right. I went out with her because she liked me. Because everyone told me we should get together." He looked at me pointedly. "Including you."

"Yeah." I fidgeted. That was true. Flor had wanted him and I had done my best to get him for her—encouraging him and telling him he should go for her. Because it was easier than admitting I wanted him for myself. "Sorry about that."

"It's not your fault. I should have been honest from the start, but it was easier to pretend. To ignore my feelings. Bury them deep."

Yeah. I definitely knew something about that.

Mia started cheerfully banging her cup on the tray. "Why did you stop pretending?" I whispered over the noise.

He held my stare. "The night she got trashed just confirmed what I already knew. We weren't right for each other." He paused, holding my gaze. "And . . . when the three of us were together . . . I was always thinking more about you than Flor. You remember that double date with Anthony?"

I winced. "Yeah. That wasn't such a good idea."

"You're telling me. Anthony is a decent guy, but I wanted to kill him when he started talking about your butt."

My stomach knotted. "My butt?"

Zach angled his head and gave me a meaningful look. "C'mon. You know you have a great ass."

I blinked. I did? I thought it was too . . . *too*. It was a pain finding the right jeans. "What did he say?"

"You really need a play-by-play? Suffice to say it gave him all sorts of ideas that made me want to throat-punch him." He sighed. "And the fact that I cared so much was kind of messed up considering I was dating someone else at the time."

He couldn't mean that. I couldn't breathe.

"That's not true." It couldn't be true. "You said it had to do with you and Flor. Something happened that night you were at her place."

"Yeah. I said that. I couldn't say that it was *more* than that, could I? That would mean I would have to stop pretending. To myself. To you. We've been one thing for so many years, it was hard to think about breaking out of that."

I fought to swallow the golf ball lodged in my throat.

He continued, "I don't know when it got to be so hard, but being with Flor was hard. We're young. Relationships should be *fun*. There shouldn't be so much struggle. So there was all of that . . . and you." He shook his head. "I won't pretend having feelings for you didn't have something to do with why I broke up with her."

The sweetest, most awful words I'd ever heard. And in no way could they be true.

In no reality did someone prefer me over Flor. That didn't make sense.

I shook my head fiercely. "No. No." Mia started mimicking me, shaking her head and blabbing the word *no*. I swallowed and continued, "No way. You hopped in that closet with Ava—"

"Because I was trying to move on." Like he was evidently trying to move on now. With Ashlyn. "And you were still trying to get me and Flor back together." I winced. That was true. "Clearly I didn't think you felt the same way I did. Not until you entered that closet with me and we kissed. Then I knew."

Was the air thinner in here? I still couldn't get enough oxygen into my lungs. It was like something heavy was pressing on my chest. Not that his words made any difference. We'd agreed. We were just friends.

He expelled a breath. "Look. I figured out what I needed to do and I broke up with Flor." He pointed at me then. "You know what you need to do here. You have to deal with this thing with your sister. You can't pretend forever."

I sank into a chair in front of Mia. A pained smile curved my lips as my niece babbled and ate, dropping more noodles than she actually managed to get in her mouth.

He knew me. I hated confrontation. I would rather ignore something in the hopes it went away. But what if my sister didn't get her act together? What then? I stared at my niece and felt a pang in my chest. I needed to be brave for her.

"I know." But it was easier said than done.

I blew out a frustrated breath. Why couldn't things just go back to before? Go back to being easy?

Mom's footsteps sounded on the stairs. Zach moved back to the stove and dished spaghetti into three bowls. "Let's eat."

Mom entered the room. "Chloe is out like a light. Just checked on her and she's snoring louder than Grandpa."

Zach's gaze cut meaningfully to mine as he placed our bowls on the table. I nodded at him. I needed to talk to my mother. As much as I dreaded giving her more to worry about, it had to be done.

Mom oohed and aahed as she picked up her fork. "Zach, you really should move in with us."

He smiled, and I couldn't help wondering if Mom would say that knowing that a few nights ago we had been making out in a closet . . . and on the front porch. I gave my head a small shake. Didn't matter. Not anymore. We weren't anything but friends.

He'd said himself he was trying to move on. And I was going to let him do just that.

Dinner was actually nice. We talked about school. Mom asked Zach about football. She followed the sport more closely than I did. He regaled her, filling her in on all the player drama on and off the field. And there was Mia. She always put on an entertaining show.

"This was wonderful," Mom said, gathering her dishes and smiling in a way she always used to do. When things were more carefree. "I insist you head home now, Zach. I'll do the dishes." She leveled her gaze on me. "And you, too, Willa. Upstairs. Get on that homework."

Zach and I took our dishes to the sink and left the kitchen. I walked him to the front door. "Thanks for tonight," I said.

He shrugged, burying one hand deep in his front jeans pocket. "Think about what I said. You should talk to your mom."

I nodded. He was right, of course. "Okay. I will."

He looked at me pointedly, cocking an eyebrow.

"I mean it. I will." I shoved him in the shoulder good-naturedly, realizing the moment my hand connected with his very solid body that it was a bad idea. It only made me want to keep touching him in a way that was more than friendly.

"Good." He fist-bumped my shoulder in a buddy move that I totally hated. Even though we had agreed this was the way it would be between us.

"You didn't have to do any of this, Zach."

Carry my loaded sister upstairs. Cook dinner for my family. Make small talk with my mother.

"That's what friends are for, right?" He held my gaze for a long moment.

"Yeah." I nodded, fighting down the lump in my throat. Friends. That was right. We were friends. I wasn't going to lose that.

I watched him walk down the drive and cross the yard into his house. Closing the door, I turned back to the kitchen. Mom had already put Mia to bed, and now she was cleaning up. I inhaled a fortifying breath. We were alone now. There would be no better time to talk to her about Chloe.

She was humming lightly as she wiped down the counters and that made me pause. She was cheerful. In a good mood. I hated to rain on that, but Zach was right. We needed to talk.

Her phone rang from where it sat on the counter and she answered. "Hey, babe. How are you?"

Dad. I took a step back, giving her time to talk with him. They both worked long hours and didn't even live in the same city most of the week.

She sank down on one of the barstools, smiling. "I actually had a pretty nice night. Chloe went to bed early, but Willa and Mia and Zach and I all ate together. Zach cooked. It was really good. Delicious." She crossed her legs. "I miss you, too. Tell me about your day. Hope you didn't hit up another fast-food drive-thru."

Whatever Dad said made her laugh. Brought joy and light to her eyes. She looked happy. And lately she just looked stressed. Overworked. Worried. Not happy.

"Oh, I'm thinking about taking a long bath and watching reruns of *Golden Girls* until I fall asleep . . . Yeah. Wish you were here too . . ."

I backed out of the kitchen. Our conversation could wait.

I'd let her have a relaxing evening. There was time enough for reality tomorrow.

GIRL CODE #14:

Friends say what needs to be said, even when it can be hard.

Flor

←——————»

WE sat in a back booth at Farah's family's restaurant, our books spread out in front of us. I loved study groups here, and not only because Farah's mom and aunts supplied us with endless amounts of pita, hummus, tabouli, and grape leaves.

Cedars Mediterranean Grill was peaceful with mellow lighting and music that reminded me of something that played softly while you were getting a massage. Not that I'd had a spa day since Mom left. Mom used to take me with her. I missed that.

"What did you get for number seven?" Farah asked, scooping hummus onto a triangle of pita and then topping it with a heap of tabouli. She took a messy bite, somehow managing not to spill it on her notebook.

Jenna flipped a few pages in her notebook, scratching her head with the back of her pen. "Um. 'When words are used in quick succession and begin with letters in the same sound group, creating a repetition of similar sounds in the sentence.'"

Nodding, Farah scribbled down the definition for *alliteration*. "Thanks."

Just then her mom came over with a plate that smelled heavenly. "Here, girls."

"Mom, we have plenty," Farah protested.

"Nuh-uh." I reached for the plate. "Leave that right here."

Farah's mother beamed as she handed it over to me. "There you go." She patted my shoulder. "Flor is a good eater."

"My favorite thing," I exclaimed as I plucked a tiny spinach pie off the plate, unashamed that I loved food. No salads for me. I bit into the triangle-shaped pastry and groaned. It was still warm.

Willa reached for one too. "I don't even like spinach, but these are amazing, Mrs. Barry."

"The key is to make a good dough. I still can't make them as good as my grandmother, but I try." She shrugged helplessly.

"I can't imagine them better," Willa said.

"She tries every week," Farah said.

"You make them every week?" I moaned as I reached for another one. "That's it. I'm moving in with you and becoming your sister, Farah." I looked at her mom. "What do you say, Mrs. Barry? Need another daughter?"

Farah snorted. "I already have two sisters. Thanks, but I don't want another one."

"Farah," her mother chided. "You love your sisters. They're your family. No matter what. The bonds of family can't be broken."

I nibbled on the corner of my spinach pie, watching their interaction and feeling a little hollow inside. I could only think of my mother and how different she was from Farah's mother.

Farah's mother would never have left her. She and her husband might have divorced, but they were there for their children. They were unified in that sense. None of their children had been cast aside after they split up.

Farah grudgingly nodded as her mother pressed a kiss to the top of her head and wandered off, stopping where Farah's cousin, the hostess, neglected her duties in favor of draping herself across the old-fashioned wood bar and flirting boldly with the bartender.

Moments later Mrs. Barry was chasing Farah's cousin back to her post at the front of the restaurant.

Farah giggled. "Serves Angela right. He's too old for her."

"I don't know." I took a sip from my straw. "What is he?" I assessed the bartender. "Maybe thirty? Your cousin's twenty-one. Older guys are sexy."

Farah shook her head. "Ew. I'll take a hard pass."

"Maybe that's what you need," Jenna suggested. "A hot older guy to take your mind off Zach and Ashlyn."

I felt my smile slip. Willa cut a hard look to Jenna. One of them must have kicked or pinched her under the table, too, for bringing up the subject of Zach. We were doing fine, I had to admit. It was nice not talking or thinking about him and just hanging out with friends.

"What? What'd I say?" Jenna exclaimed.

"We're trying not to talk about him," Farah said in a tone that made it seem that they had discussed this plan already.

Great. My life had become a topic among my friends. And not in a positive way. It's like I was the senile aunt and they had to talk ahead of time about how they wanted to handle me. I could hear it now . . . the three of them discussing what subjects to avoid. *For God's sake, don't say Zach's name.*

Jenna shot me an apologetic look. "Sorry."

I shook my head. "It's fine, guys. You don't need to tiptoe around me."

"I think we need to add a new tenet to our girl code." Jenna reached for her laptop. "Something about friends never being afraid to say what needs to be said."

"That's right," I agreed. "Even things that are hard to say should be said."

"Everything?" Farah questioned. "I don't know about that. Sometimes people don't need to spill *everything* that's on their minds."

I glanced at Willa. She didn't offer up an opinion.

"You're good at wording these, Wills." I nodded at Jenna's laptop. "You should do it."

"Maybe we should focus on what Jenna said . . . friends should always say what *needs* to be said."

"Needs?" Farah cocked her head. "That's very broad."

My phone buzzed and I glanced down at the screen. I practically dropped my drink back on the table in my haste to reach for it. I gripped it in both hands and stared at it.

"It's my mom." I couldn't help the slight trip in my voice.

Mom barely answered my texts. I only got one-word replies, and they were always delayed if and when she responded. Actual phone calls? Hardly ever. I told myself to be patient. She was going through a thing. I knew the world always talked about men having midlife crises, but I'd learned they weren't exclusive to the male gender. No, indeed. Women could go through them. Women like my mother.

Willa, Farah, and Jenna all exchanged looks and then fell silent, understanding the rarity and significance of my mother's calling me. Farah's eyes widened as she reached for some more pita.

Willa smiled and nodded encouragingly as I answered. "Hey, Mom!"

"Hey, Flor. How are you, baby?"

I smiled at the sound of her voice. There was a lot of noise in the background wherever she was. "Good. What about you? Are you still in Playa del Carmen?"

"Oh no. I'm in Costa Rica now. I've been here for two weeks with my friend Lito."

Lito? I'd never even heard of this friend before. And Mom had never mentioned going to Costa Rica. What happened to Australia? "Oh. So I'm going to Costa Rica for Thanksgiving instead?"

I stared down at my plate with its forgotten food. I could feel my friends staring at me, but I couldn't bring myself to look at them as I waded through this conversation. Suddenly I wished I had taken the call in the restroom, where I could have had some semblance of privacy instead of sitting here trapped in the corner of a booth.

"Oh, baby, Lito lives on a boat and there's not a lot of room."

A pause fell and I couldn't think of anything to fill the silence. My friends had just heard me ask about Thanksgiving, and now they were waiting to hear my response.

"Ah, sure."

They were still looking at me. Jenna and Farah stared expectantly, their gazes bright and optimistic. Only Willa looked a little wary. She, better than any of them, knew the situation with my mother. As much as I would discuss, anyway.

Mom droned on in my ear. "Hope you understand. Maybe Christmas break—"

"Sure," I quickly cut in. "Maybe."

"It's so good to hear your voice, baby."

"Yeah, same here," I murmured.

"The beaches here are amazing. Like nothing else in the world. You really need to come someday . . ." Her voice kept going.

I pretended to listen, murmuring at appropriate intervals, trying to act like I wasn't breaking a little inside. Trying to put up a good front. I should have been over this by now. She'd walked out on us over a year ago, and this was my life now. I should have been accustomed to it.

I guess there's just no getting used to heartache. It finds its way in even when you think you've closed all the doors and windows.

GIRL CODE #15:

True friends listen . . . and eat burritos with you.

Willa

>>———————→

O N the way home from school on Thursday, I finally got up my nerve and asked Zach the question that had been burning on my mind. "Are you going out with Ashlyn now?"

I figured we were back on solid footing as friends, and friends could ask each other anything. The guy had cooked my family dinner, after all. The old Willa would have asked him without hesitation, and I was trying so very hard to find my way back to the old Willa . . . to get back to her. To the way we were before.

Hopefully, I didn't sound jealous. I only wanted to project friendly interest. No more than that.

He shrugged a non-answer as he stared ahead at the road. "We're going to the party after the game."

The party. He meant Kennedy Watson's party. It was outside town at her family's lake house. Flor and the others planned to go. There was going to be a long caravan of kids heading out after the game. No one cared that it was a forty-minute drive. The party would be big and probably wouldn't get busted because there were no neighbors for miles around. No one to complain about the noise.

"What about you? Any plans for the weekend?"

"Yeah. I might go to the party too." I hadn't planned on that until I said it, and then it was too late. It was out there.

"Really?" He shot me a skeptical glance. "Well, look at you. Going to parties now."

I smoothed my hands over my knees. "It is my senior year. I should live a little."

He sent me another glance—this one looked a little puzzled. As though he didn't know me at all, and I guess that was about right. I didn't quite feel like I knew myself anymore, so maybe he didn't either.

"That's right," he finally agreed. "You only get one senior year. Might as well do it right."

Was he trying to say something? Like he didn't think I was doing my senior year *right*? Or was I just mind-fornicating the situation? I expelled a breath and looked out the window, staring unseeingly at a blur of shopping centers.

So now I was committed to going to a party I didn't really want to go to just because I didn't want Zach to think I was at home moping for him. Even if I was the one who'd demanded we keep our relationship limited to friendship. Still.

Flor was probably right. I needed to go out on a date. It would be like one of those juice cleanses that flush out all the toxins. Instead of a juice cleanse, it was a boy cleanse.

Only that date wasn't going to be with Grayson. He hadn't asked me out. Which was kind of awkward because I knew that Flor had talked to him. She'd told me she was going to. Evidently he wasn't interested in me. That could have been a blow if I had wanted to go out with him.

Zach and I parted in the driveway, and I escaped into my house. He didn't follow this time. No surprise dinner, I guess. I tried not to feel deflated.

The TV blared loudly. Chloe looked up for a split second before her gaze shot back to the TV. "*Project Runway* marathon," she volunteered as though I'd asked. "I missed this whole season. I should be all caught up for the finale now."

"Is that what you've been doing all day?" From the smell of it, Mia needed a diaper change.

Her eyes shot to mine, full of fire. "I've been taking care of my daughter. It's hard staying home with a kid all day. It's not the life of a carefree teenager, to be sure."

My phone started going off in my pocket. I grabbed for it eagerly. Anything to end this conversation before it turned into full-fledged ugliness.

"Hey," I answered a little breathlessly, glad to escape Chloe— and I hadn't even been home for two minutes yet.

"I'm on my way," Flor announced in my ear. "I'll be there in five."

"Where we going?"

"I'm craving burritos." Burritos only meant one place.

"Yesss."

I dropped my backpack and scooped up Mia from where she played on the floor. I couldn't leave her in a dirty diaper, and I wasn't going to waste another breath on Chloe. In less than five minutes, I managed to change her diaper and return her to the living room.

"Where you going?" Chloe asked as she fished chips out of the bag on her lap.

"José's."

"Ooh, bring me back a burrito. Chicken with black beans, sour cream, and guac."

Annoyance trickled through me. She had her own car. Not that she went much anywhere in it. "I might not be coming straight back here. It will get cold."

"Fine," she pouted.

Flor honked from the street and I hurried outside.

"It's like you must have some sixth sense," I said as I shut the door after me and buckled into my seat.

"Let me guess. Chloe?"

I nodded with a sigh.

"Is she *ever* moving out?"

I laughed briefly. "I think I'll be moving out before she does."

We got our burritos to go. Neither of us, however, felt like eating at either of our houses. I'd seen Chloe watch *Project Runway* before. It usually involved a lot of screaming. Especially if her top picks didn't make it through. José's was loud and crowded as usual, so we drove to the Fielding Elementary playground. It was our spot —where we first met.

It was empty in the evenings after school. We parked along the street and walked across the lawn until we settled onto the bench the teachers always sat on while kids played. At least that's how it had been when we were students here.

We took out our burritos. Unwrapping the tin foil around mine, I watched as Flor took a bite out of hers. The cheese immediately dribbled down the sides of the tortilla. She always asked for extra cheese in addition to steak, sour cream, and guacamole. I loaded my burrito with veggies. No cheese.

I bit into mine and caught a strip of red bell pepper from falling onto my lap.

"I can't get over how you can ruin a perfectly good burrito by putting vegetables in it." She shook her head like this was a travesty.

"I like roasted veggies," I defended. "Plus, I can't eat like you. I don't run up and down a soccer field every day."

Flor sniffed and shrugged. "You could run with me. Or Jenna."

I laughed. "Yeah. Or not." We ate for a few moments in silence before I asked, "So how's your dad's girlfriend?" It seemed a safer topic than bringing up the phone call from her mom. I knew it had hurt her.

Flor made a face. "Yeah. Let's not talk about that."

Apparently the subject of Dana was little better.

"That bad?"

"Well, it's not like I get to ever see my dad without her there too."

I nodded. "Maybe . . . she's all right? Once you get to know her?"

156

She cut me a swift look at the suggestion. Lifting her straw to her mouth, she took a swallow as she leveled me an *Are you kidding me?* look. "You're such an optimist. It's like you think we're going to have one of those movie moments that makes everything all right."

"Sometimes that can happen in real life."

"Really?"

I peeled back more foil off my burrito. "Well, if not, at least you'll have her wardrobe to raid."

She chuckled. "And that's why I love you. You always see the silver lining." She unraveled more of her burrito and continued to chomp away.

"What about your sister? She looking for a job yet?"

I snorted. "Um. No."

"She's got a degree, right? Can't she work?"

"Oh, she *could*." I yanked a section of tin foil off my burrito.

"Well, your mom needs to boot her from the nest."

"Mom said she's been through a trauma and we need to be patient and supportive."

Flor shook her head. "She's been with y'all for almost . . . how long now? Eight? Ten months? Is she ever going to move out?"

I shrugged. "Dunno." Another subject I didn't push with Mom. As much as I wanted Chloe gone, what would happen to Mia if I wasn't around? Or Mom? Chloe needed us right now. Mom was right about that.

Our phones dinged almost simultaneously. I glanced down at mine on the bench between us and read the text. "Jenna wants us to come over."

Flor finished the last bite of her burrito. "Are her parents home?"

"You know it. That's probably why she wants us to come over. To act as a buffer for her."

"I guess we should go." She sighed.

It wasn't Jenna's fault her parents were generally miserable to be around. You couldn't hang out at her house without having to deliver a state-of-the-union address on your life. They wanted to know about your family, your grades, your college plans, and if you'd been to church the previous Sunday.

We wadded up our tin foil into balls and stuffed them in the brown paper bag.

"C'mon." Flor got to her feet and extended a hand, pulling me to my feet. "Let's go save Jenna. Just think. Next year we'll all be at college, and then we can be who we want to be."

I thought about that as we walked toward the parking lot, and how being who we wanted to be . . . who we were . . . shouldn't be so hard.

GIRL CODE #16:

If you see a girl acting awkward with a guy, don't make fun.
We've all been there.

Flor

I got to school early on Friday to meet with the trainer. My hamstring was tight and bothering me lately, so she worked on it for me until it felt better. Looser. Hopefully I wouldn't injure myself. That was the last thing I needed.

Excitement buzzed in the air as I exited the athletic wing and crossed the courtyard. It was game day. Bright signs hung everywhere, and everyone was decked out in school colors. Not that there were too many people milling the halls yet. I walked past a hall clock: still fifteen minutes until first period. Another five minutes and the place would be hopping.

A door slammed. I glanced down the hall and spotted Grayson stepping out of a classroom. He was in a dark gray shirt. Of course he wasn't in school colors. Idly, I wondered if he even knew it was a game day. Although with banners everywhere, it would be hard not to know.

"Hey," I called. "You're here early."

He turned as I approached. At first the overhead lighting reflected off his glasses and I couldn't see his eyes. As I drew closer, they became more visible . . . the dark depths fastened on me.

"I'm always here before school starts. Physics tutorials."

"Oh." I glanced at the door from which he'd emerged. I didn't know the teacher, but if this was a physics classroom, that would explain why. I wasn't in physics. That was for honors students. "She helps you in the mornings?"

He hesitated and then replied, "No, I help her with tutorials."

"Oh. Of course you do." For a moment I'd forgotten I was talking to *him*. "It must be nice."

"What is?"

"To be so smart." It would certainly help with some of my problems.

He angled his head slightly. "You think it's easy?"

A pair of cheerleaders walked past us, carrying a rolled-up banner I guessed was for the pep rally later. "Hey, Flor." They eyed Grayson speculatively. I wanted to think it was because I was talking to him, but I wasn't so sure anymore. I didn't view him the same way I once had. He had his own appeal.

As they moved on, I answered him, "Not everyone can do what you do."

"Sounds like an excuse."

I fumed. Why did this always happen? I wasn't trying to offend him. I was actually trying to be nice. Shaking my head, I walked around him. "See you Sunday."

A moment passed and then I heard, "Flor, wait." He caught up with me. I didn't slow down. "I wasn't talking about you."

"Weren't you? I was calling you smart. You could just say thank you."

"Yeah, well, you keep doing that."

"What?"

"Talking about how smart I am."

I shook my head. "So?" Why would that be offensive? He'd pretty much implied I was lazy. That seemed much more insulting.

"Because I'm more than that," he snapped.

I stopped and faced him. Obviously he was more than that. He'd told me about his home life. I knew everything he had to overcome. "I know that." I shifted the strap of my backpack over my shoulder. "Why do you care so much what I think about you anyway?" Our relationship was professional.

"I don't." He blinked. "Why do *you*?"

"I don't," I echoed, even as I saw myself storming away from him because he'd implied I was too lazy to be smart. We were lying to each other and we both knew it.

Looking at him, all at once I didn't know what I was doing or what this was about anymore. With him everything was always confusing and awkward.

Suddenly the bell rang, signaling we had five minutes to get to class. I hadn't even noticed that the halls had started to fill up.

"I've got to go," I said. Without waiting for his response, I turned and headed to class.

GIRL CODE #17:

Slut-shaming and tearing another girl down hurts all of us.

Willa

>>>———————→

FRIDAY arrived. AKA game day. It was like a carnival. The school was decked out in banners and posters heavy on the alliteration. *Tromp Travis. Take Down Travis. Mop the Mustangs.* The mascot ran up and down the halls at various points during the day. It was like one nonstop pep rally. That was Madison for you . . . and Texas football.

After school, I found Chloe in her room, the shades pulled, lost in a dead sleep that was likely drug or alcohol induced. Again. I lifted her wrist off the bed and checked her pulse just to make sure she was breathing.

Mia called for me in happy shrieks from her crib against the wall. If earsplitting screeching didn't wake up Chloe, nothing would. I shook my head in disgust. Mia might as well have been alone. I picked her up, balancing her sweet, solid weight on my hip. I took her to my room and played with her for a while. Then I took her downstairs and fed her. After a dinner of SpaghettiOs and peaches, I plopped her in the bathtub and washed her, getting all the food out of her strawberry-blond curls.

I rubbed her dry with a towel, carrying on a conversation with her like she wasn't only eighteen months old and could understand everything I was saying.

"The thing is, I'm not even looking forward to this party. Why am I doing this to myself? I mean, what am I trying to prove? So maybe I should stay here with you. We can stay up late and watch *Moana*." I pulled her nightgown over her head. "For like the five hundredth time?"

She perked up as her head popped through the neck hole. "Moana!" she exclaimed, clapping her hands. A yawn quickly followed. I knew it was probably bad parenting—or aunting—but I pulled out the foldout couch in the upstairs game room and settled her in the middle of the bed. I just couldn't bring myself to stick her back in the crib in my sister's room. I turned on the television and started *Moana* for her. She settled in happily, fixing heavy-lidded eyes on the TV screen.

The door downstairs slammed. "Hello! I'm home," Mom called.

"Up here. Just putting on a movie for Mia," I shouted back, tucking a blanket around her and then hurrying into my room. I didn't have a lot of time to get ready for the party. The evenings had gotten a little cooler, and I could have worn my typical sweatshirt and jeans, but something made me choose differently. I went with a skirt and a loose, off-the-shoulder blouse. Knee-high boots that used to belong to Chloe. I got all her size seven shoes. After her pregnancy her feet grew and she wore a size eight now.

I didn't examine what it was I was doing. I just felt compelled to look my best. Believing that I did would make me feel better as I watched Zach and Ashlyn flirt, and that mattered. It mattered a lot.

I only had time to touch up my makeup and run a brush through my hair. I'd made an effort with it that morning, actually drying it and flat-ironing it, so it still looked decent.

Flor texted me when they were outside. I shoved my phone in my pocket, checked on Mia, now fast asleep with the light from the TV casting dancing shadows on her sweet face, and launched myself downstairs.

"Whoa there, hold up. Where are you going looking so fancy tonight?" Mom eyed me up and down.

I stopped at the base of the stairs and stifled the impulse to roll my eyes. Lately, Mom had been too busy to even check on my comings and goings. But Dad wasn't home this weekend, plus Chloe and Mia were passed out upstairs—I guess she had a little extra time to grill me.

"I'm going out to a party. Tonight was the big game against Travis. We won." I knew that because Farah had texted that information when she'd texted to say they would be here in thirty minutes.

Almost on cue, a car honked from the driveway.

"That's it? No asking me if you can even go to this party? No telling me who you're going with?"

I just stared at her. Was she kidding me? Lately she'd been so caught up in the Chloe drama and not having Dad around and having to put in so many hours at work. I didn't even think she cared.

Swallowing down the impulse to tell her what I was thinking (which would only lead to a fight), I asked, "Can I go to the party,

Mom? I'll be with Flor, Farah, and Ava." My usual friends. Why was she suddenly going all parental on me?

She took her time staring at me, making me wait for her answer.

Farah honked the horn from outside again.

"I guess so," she finally said, but it was grudging, and that made me grind my teeth. What did she have to be so grudging about? Honestly. She worked and worked while I went to school and then came home to take care of my sister's neglected daughter.

Did she really mind me going to one measly party?

I held it in, though.

"Be home by midnight." She gave me a sharp look like I chronically broke curfew or something.

I nodded and muttered thanks, then reminded her that Mia was asleep on the foldout before I plunged out of the house.

"Wow! You look hot, girl!" Flor shouted as she hung out the window. As far as cheering me up and making me forget about Mom, it worked.

I giggled as I slid into the back seat of Farah's mom's SUV.

"Yeah!" Jenna chirped from the front seat. Apparently, her brother had gotten into trouble as predicted and taken the heat off her—she clearly wasn't grounded anymore. "I'd totally do you." We all erupted into gales of laughter.

It took almost forty minutes to get out to Kennedy's lake house, and the party was in full swing by the time we got there.

Part of the reason tonight's game had been such a big one was that Travis happened to be the high school closest in proximity to ours. We were rivals, but also friendly enough to go to a lot of the same parties. I immediately knew that it was going to be one of those parties by the number of vehicles in the yard with Travis slogans written on the windows in shoe polish.

"Oh goody." Jenna rubbed her hands together with glee. "Beau Sanders will probably be here."

Beau Sanders. A name that was known all over town. He was the Travis High School quarterback and undeniably beautiful. I'd never met him, but I'd seen his photo blasted all over Instagram and in the local news.

Even though Madison had beaten Travis 21 to 18 tonight, spirits were high when we entered the house. Students from both schools mingled.

Jenna stood on her tiptoes and attempted to peer through the main room. "I'm going to go find me some Beau Sanders."

Flor rolled her eyes. "You'll have to wade through his fan club to even get to him. Especially after tonight's game. He scored two touchdowns, and scouts were there."

Jenna pointed at her. "If *you* were with me, I bet he'd take notice. Hell, we should all go. We're hotter than all these girls." Jenna grabbed Flor's hand and led her through the house, craning her neck so that she could assess as they walked.

Farah shrugged and followed.

"I'm going to find the keg," Ava said.

"Want me to come with you?" I said, lifting my voice over the din.

She gestured for me to continue without her. "Go on. I'll find you."

Nodding, I plunged back into the crowd, trying to catch up with Flor, Farah, and Jenna. I couldn't catch sight of them. The house was packed, and they were somewhere far ahead of me. It took me forever just to make it halfway through the main room.

The house was open concept, with a large upper balcony that wrapped around the living room. Looking up, I could see people standing on the second floor. A few were familiar. And then I spotted Zach. I almost wished I hadn't seen him. My goal tonight was to come here and try to have fun. Not stalk Zach. But there he was and there *she* was. Ashlyn was plastered to his side.

I quickly looked away before he could see me looking at them, and I resumed my hunt for my friends. I barely managed five feet.

This was exactly what I hated. Wading through a party packed with bodies, alone, my friends lost somewhere in the house and I couldn't find them.

Maybe it was my imagination, but I thought I felt Zach's gaze on me from above.

I snuck another glance up at the second floor. The scene was the same. Zach surrounded by Ashlyn and several other people, all laughing and talking. Except Zach's attention was on me. He lifted a red Solo cup to his mouth, smiling as all the others were laughing, but his gaze didn't stray from me.

I tossed my hair back off my shoulders, feeling at least better knowing I looked my best. I didn't have to be self-conscious because I wasn't dressed well. I was wearing makeup and having a decent hair day too.

Tendrils of loose hair danced over my shoulder as I squeezed past overly warm bodies, searching for a friend—any familiar face, really.

Another quick glance revealed Ashlyn standing on her tiptoes to say something into Zach's ear. She spread one red-nailed hand over his stomach and then slid it down until she curled her fingers around the waistband of his jeans, tugging him closer to her.

I smacked into a body. I wasn't moving fast, so it wasn't too jarring, but the body was hard. A veritable mountain. I practically bounced off him.

"Hey! Watch where you're going!" The guy turned to glare down at me. His forehead was broad, jutting over a thick unibrow.

"Yeah, sorry about that," I muttered. "I mean, what was I thinking bumping into you in a house crowded with three hundred people?"

Someone chuckled low and deep near my ear. I whipped around and gasped a little. Another guy was standing there. Right next to me, which was really the only way anyone could stand in this party—pressed right up on each other. Except this guy was not sporting a unibrow. He was hot. And smelled good. And was vaguely familiar.

"Hi, there." He smiled down at me as he lifted a cup to his lips, his eyes sweeping over me as he took a slow drink. Lowering the drink, he announced, "You're funny."

I smiled weakly, feeling a little dazzled by that smile. "At times."

He chuckled again.

"Oh, hey, Beau," Unibrow greeted him, holding out a hand for a fist bump.

And now I knew why he was familiar.

He was Beau Sanders, the very guy Jenna was on a quest to find at this party.

Beau gave him his fist bump without taking his eyes off me. It was disconcerting to have myself under the scrutiny of a strange guy this good-looking. The only hot guy who looked at me with any level of interest was Zach. And right now a girl was upstairs happily pawing him. Not that I was angry about that. He was free to do what he wanted and with whomever.

At the thought of Zach I looked up to the second floor again.

He was still watching, but now his gaze skipped between Beau and me. His body was fully turned, one hand braced on the railing as he looked down at the first floor.

"Did she hurt you, Mac?" Beau asked, his lips twitching as he surveyed me up and down again. "I mean what is she? A buck twenty?"

I weighed 135, but I wasn't going to correct him.

"Huh?" Mac said, looking bewildered. "No. I'm okay, Beau."

Shaking his head with a chuckle at his dimwitted friend, Beau held out his hand for me to shake. "I'm Beau Sanders. I've never seen you around. You go to Madison?"

I accepted his hand and shook it, thinking how few times a guy my age ever introduced himself to me with a handshake. "Yes."

The tide of the crowd shifted in the room, and I was pushed forward, directly against him. He still held my hand, his fingers stroking lightly where we touched. I huffed to find myself pressed against him.

He bent his head to ask into my ear, "What's your name, pretty girl?"

Pretty girl? Did that really work?

"Willa," I replied, feeling a warm flush spread through me. And

I guess that was my answer. I was rarely on the receiving end of flirtation, but now I knew.

Yes. Yes, it worked.

"Want to go someplace less crowded, Willa?"

My heart hammered. I glanced up at Zach. He was still watching, both hands clutched on the railing now, his gaze intent on me.

"You know Tucker?"

I looked back at Beau to see he had followed my gaze. "Uh, yeah. We're friends."

"He's not looking at you like a friend right now."

And for some reason that gave my stupid heart a stupid thrill. "We're just friends," I insisted.

"Good. Then c'mon, Willa." He was still holding my hand. His warm grip on it tightened and he led me from the room, passing through the crowd with much more success than I'd experienced on my own.

GIRL CODE #18:

Let your friends be who they are.

Flor

←———————≪

I was on the second floor laughing as Jenna persuaded one of the football players to take off his shirt so she could write on his chest with whipped cream. Don't ask me where she got the whipped cream.

"I'll get sticky," he whined.

"Baby boy." She clucked her tongue and batted her lashes. "It'll be okay, and if I like what I see, I might lick it off for you." She waved her can of whipped cream in the air with a flourish. We all laughed again.

He looked at Jenna hopefully, obviously giving clear consideration to her offer. "For real?"

"Hey, Flor."

I looked up and blinked at the unexpected sight of Zach. Zach, who was ignoring me like a pro these days. He pushed into our circle, his expression tight and agitated. "You seen Willa?" He shifted impatiently on his feet.

My girls around me went still. I stared at him for a long moment before answering. I couldn't help it. I was processing that he was really here, in front of me, *speaking* to me.

He hadn't talked to me in days. Hadn't responded to my texts. We'd been together for months, but he'd been treating me like I was invisible. Now he stood here, dragging a hand through his hair and asking me if I'd seen Willa. Like it was no big deal. Like it was nothing.

I held out a hand. "Let me see your phone."

"What?"

I held out a hand. "Your phone, please."

He hesitated a second and then reached inside his pocket, pulling out his phone. He handed it to me. I typed in his code. He hadn't bothered to change it since we dated.

"What are you doing?" he asked, impatience tingeing his voice.

"Just checking to see if it still works. You know, since you haven't replied to any of my texts."

People around us tittered and laughed.

"Oooh," someone said. "Burnnn."

Zach snatched his phone back. "Not now, Flor. I'm looking for Willa. Have you seen her? It's important."

"We haven't seen her in a while," Farah answered. "But you know Willa. She'll be fine. She probably found one of her orchestra friends and is in a corner somewhere talking about their upcoming recital."

"Yeah. Sure," he grumbled, and left.

I wasn't done with him, though.

I pushed through the bodies, following him down the stairs. He was moving at a fast clip. I didn't catch up with him until I emerged outside onto the attached deck. The covered deck was aglow in an eerie yellow light.

There were fewer people around, and I could finally stretch my legs to catch up with him. I grabbed his arm and pulled him around to face me. "Hey," I bit out. "What the hell?"

"Not now, Flor. Please." He still wore that agitated expression.

"Not now? When, then? When are you going to talk to me again and treat me like I exist?" I took a deep breath. "Tell me why we broke up. The real reason."

I hated asking. It humbled me to do it. He'd given me the standard breakup speech. *I just want to be friends. It's not working out. Blah blah blah.*

None of it meant anything.

"I told you—"

"You told me *nothing*." I swiped a hand through the air. "I want the truth, as hard as that might be."

He looked out off the deck toward the lake. I followed his gaze. A lone speedboat zipped across the surface, its lights cutting through the liquid dark. "I never wanted to hurt you, Flor. I still don't."

I moistened my lips. "It's that night, isn't it?"

His gaze swung back to me, sharp and cutting, and I knew I was right.

I continued, "I mean . . . you broke up with me the very next day. What else could it be?"

"It's not *only* that night, but yeah . . ." He shrugged and released a gust of heavy breath. "It wasn't fun anymore, Flor. You're always angry or sad, and it's not like you ever talked about any of it to me. Whenever I asked, you put me off. Either changing the subject or flinging yourself at me."

His words stung, but he wasn't wrong. I listened, suffering through it. I'd asked, after all. No, I'd demanded.

He continued, finally giving me the answers I wanted. "That night, you got shitfaced. Even when I tried to get you to stop drinking, you wouldn't. You wouldn't talk or tell me what was wrong, and then in your room . . ." He released a choking laugh, but I knew he wasn't amused.

I shook my head, heat slapping my cheeks. I wasn't amused either.

That night was fuzzy, but I distinctly remembered wrestling out of my clothes even when he told me — no, begged me — to keep them on. It wasn't an exaggeration to say that I attacked him, kissing him even when his lips weren't kissing me back, and I may have tried to wrestle *him* out of *his* clothes too. He actually had to peel me off him.

Yeah. It had been a bad night even before Zach came over. I'd been angry and hurt and acted badly. Rashly. Stupidly. I thought I could find something with Zach to make it all better. Never mind that I was drunk and had never had sex before and I came at him with all the finesse of a water buffalo. I was aggressive and clumsy and, yes. Drunk.

But none of that was a valid excuse. It didn't matter the circumstances. It didn't matter that I was a girl. It was wrong. *I* was wrong. No one should ever do that to another person.

And the next day he broke up with me.

It was mortifying.

"I apologized," I said in a shaky little voice. If I could go back and undo that day, I would. I'd just been so stupidly hurt.

Dad had taken off for a long weekend to Vegas with Dana, forgetting that I had a big tournament that Saturday. Dad used to make all my games. Soccer was our thing. Something we had always loved together.

I'd found out he was going to Vegas via a text he sent me from the airport. Not that I explained any of that to Zach. No, I just raided Dad's bar and made myself a pitcher of margaritas. I was halfway through when Zach showed up. I even kept drinking after he got there. Even though he asked me to stop.

"It's not about me forgiving you, Flor. I do."

I stared at him. "You just don't want to be with me."

He nodded once.

"Okay." I nodded back, and in that moment I knew it didn't matter. Being with him, keeping him, didn't matter anymore.

He stared at me for one lingering moment and then he turned. His footsteps thudded across the wood deck until he stepped off and headed down the stretch of lawn toward the lake, passing shadowy figures making out in the darkness.

I watched him go. I watched him until he was lost to the night. Lost to me.

I hadn't really lost him, though. I would have had to have had him in the first place to do that, and I realized now that I had never had any real hold on Zach Tucker. Because I'd never let him in. I'd never been comfortable enough, for whatever reason, to do that.

I released a breath and suddenly felt a little lighter.

Ever since Zach broke up with me, I'd looked at winning him back as a solution to my screwed-up life.

Now I was starting to suspect . . . there was no solution. Or at least it didn't rest with Zach.

Maybe it was in me.

GIRL CODE #19:

If you've never actually spoken to a guy before,
you can't call dibs on him.

Willa

>>———————→

I'D never had a guy single me out at a party before. I wasn't that girl. I'd never aspired to be.

Although my self-esteem wasn't so low that I imagined myself unattractive. I had good hair. Nice eyes. I liked my nose.

But I wasn't flashy enough to stand out at a party. Especially not big parties with the all-popular beautiful people from half the high schools in the district.

That was the reality of it. Even with my improved wardrobe, there were a lot of girls here tonight showing more skin than I was. In a sea of bare midriffs, mine was hidden under clothes. These other girls were throwing inviting looks at Beau Sanders regardless of his attention on me. Looks that promised him access to said skin if he would just give them the time of day.

Strange as it was, he was giving me the time of day.

Where was Jenna when I needed her? I knew she would be equal parts envious and proud of me.

As we exited the house and walked outside into the dark, I continually snuck looks at him just to see if he was there and real and truly beside me.

"Whew," he exclaimed, stepping off the porch and inhaling. "Nice to get some fresh air. Kind of tight in there."

We started down the lawn toward the lake. He was an easy conversationalist, asking about me. I felt myself relax. He seemed like a genuinely nice guy. He wasn't just a hot jock. Apparently Zach wasn't the only one in existence. That was good. I needed to expand my experience.

My foot caught on a sprinkler head and I went flying. His strong hand was there, catching me and hauling me back against him with an easy chuckle. "You okay?"

I laughed nervously, feeling like a clumsy fool. "Yeah. Thanks."

"No problem."

I stepped back from him, but he snared my hand and kept hold of it.

My gaze lifted to his face. He glanced at me with a disarming smile.

My skin flushed warm as we walked toward the dock. There were random kids outside. Some making out in the dark, their shadowy figures tucked away under the cover of trees. I noted a trio near the fence, passing what I doubted was a cigarette among them.

"Those are some reflexes. I guess you'd be a handy guy to have around during the zombie apocalypse."

"The zombie apocalypse? Is that an eventuality?"

I nodded. "More like a probability."

"Huh." He nodded contemplatively. "Do you often evaluate

people based on their potential survivability in the zombie apocalypse?"

"Absolutely. You rank high."

"And what about you?"

I winced. "Yeah. Not so much, which is why I hope to surround myself with those with higher survivability."

"Thereby upping your own survivability. Maybe that's your skill. Pretty clever, actually."

"Huh." I angled my head, mulling that over. "Never thought of it that way."

We stepped out onto the stretch of dock. Our footsteps rang hollowly over the wood planks. I was out of my element. Stick Flor or Jenna or any of my friends in this scenario and they would know how to handle themselves.

I told myself not to freak out. He was just holding my hand. Probably so I wouldn't stumble again in the dark. It wasn't like he was trying to jam his tongue down my throat.

Relax, Willa. Don't act like such an amateur. Act like a girl who knows what to do when a boy pays attention to you.

Right now Zach was inside letting Ashlyn rub all over him. I was free to hold hands with a hot guy.

At the far end of the dock a few tiki lights glowed. "You're a senior?" I asked.

"Yeah. You?"

I nodded, gazing out at the water.

"So a year from now where will you be?"

"I'll be at whatever school gives me the most scholarship money."

"Ah. A smart girl."

I shrugged. "What about you?"

"The same."

"Academic?"

He laughed. "Okay, not the same. I'm not that smart. Football."

A turtle's head bobbed above the surface of the lake. I leaned a hip against the railing, peering out at it.

He followed my gaze. "I came fishing out on this lake as a kid. We always hooked turtles and would have to throw them back."

He brushed the hair off my shoulder. The backs of his fingers skimmed my skin and sent a jolt of surprise through me. I took a steadying breath. *Don't be weird. He just touched you, and it wasn't in a creepy or aggressive way. It was called flirting.*

"Were you at the game tonight?" he asked.

I laughed nervously. "No. I don't go to the games."

"No?"

"Yeah. I have a friend that plays. I hate to watch . . . I'm always worried he'll get hurt."

"You don't go to school football games? What kind of Texas girl are you?" He tsked his tongue and shook his head at me.

"Not a very good one, I guess."

"You didn't see me play tonight. Or ever, apparently. How am I supposed to impress you?"

"Is football the only thing you have going for you?" My tone was halfway flirty. I also somehow managed not to choke on the question as I looked at him—because he clearly had other things going for him. That face, for starters. Followed by that deep Hemsworth

180

voice. Good looks and a fair amount of charm. Half the universe would make a deal with the devil for those two things alone.

"I've been told I have a winning personality."

I bet. I waved toward the house. "I'm sure there are dozens of girls back in the house ready to be impressed by you. You can recount your most glorious moments on the field for them."

He flipped around so that his back was to the water and his elbows were propped on the railing. He dug a hand deeper in his front jeans pocket, and that motion stretched his shirt tighter across his broad chest.

Good God. When had all the boys my age suddenly sprouted bodies like this? It seemed like only yesterday I could arm-wrestle most guys my age and win. I didn't feel like I'd changed. I was still the same as I was freshman year, minus the braces.

"But I'm kind of trying to impress *you* right now," he countered. "Is it working?"

I smiled and opened my mouth to respond, but his head suddenly ducked.

He kissed me.

I knew we were flirting, but it was still unexpected. A week ago I had been kissing Zach. I would never have believed another boy would kiss me the following weekend. Or that I would let him.

I just couldn't seem to move.

It wasn't a long or deep kiss. Just a quick press of his mouth to mine. He pulled back, his dark eyes searching my face.

This would be the moment when I pulled away. Or I asked him not to do that again. I still loved Zach. That hadn't changed. The concept was really simple: when you loved someone, you didn't go around kissing guys that weren't him.

Except I'd told him to forget about me, and I was trying to forget about him. Kissing Beau Sanders would definitely be me moving on, and that would be a good thing.

His head lowered again, coming at me, taking his time. I could stop him if I wanted. I felt sure of that. I could.

His lips brushed mine in a series of soft, seductive kisses. He was good at this. There was skill and practice behind his method, but it felt oddly passionless.

Zach had had lots of practice too, but it hadn't *felt* practiced with him. With Zach it had felt raw. There'd been no deliberation. Only longing and desire. Need.

Damn. Why was I thinking about Zach right now?

Because there was nothing aching or desperate about this kiss with Beau. About *me*. Maybe that was the key component—me.

I couldn't feel the passion. I couldn't revel in it . . . because this wasn't Zach. *Damn it.* Why couldn't it be easy? I'd decided to move on. Why couldn't my heart do that? Be a tame, obedient little puppy inside my chest?

"Willa."

Great. And now I was hearing *his* voice as I kissed another boy.

"Willa."

Okay, that time sounded real.

I pushed against Beau's chest and looked around. Zach stood five feet away, his expression hard. Lips unsmiling.

"Come on, Willa."

Guilt flashed through me, which was a totally inappropriate reaction. I had no reason to feel guilty.

"Zach?" What was he doing here? Why wasn't he still with Ashlyn getting pawed? "What are you—"

"It's almost eleven and it's gonna take over half an hour to get home. You're gonna break curfew."

"Oh." He was right. I looked at Beau. "I need to go."

Beau dragged his gaze off Zach. "I can give you a ride home," he offered.

I opened my mouth to decline, but Zach butted in. "No thanks, man. I got this."

I glared at him. He was speaking for me now? Like he was my father? Excuse me, no. The last time I checked this was the twenty-first century and I could speak for myself. "Farah drove me. She'll take me home."

Beau still stood close. "I don't mind, Willa."

"Are you deaf, Sanders? She said no."

Beau swung away from me then. The two guys squared off so quickly I would have missed it if I blinked. One moment they weren't even facing each other. Then suddenly they were like two barnyard roosters puffed up and bumping chests.

"I don't think she wants your interference, Tucker."

Of course. They'd played a game against each other tonight. They were rivals on the field and, I suspected, off.

Did this even have anything to do with me, or was it just an extension of some stupid competition these guys had had since Little League?

"She wants me to give her a ride," Zach said with such certainty I wanted to slap his face. I'd said I'd get a ride with Farah. What was wrong with him? I glared at his profile. I'd never seen him like this. I didn't even know him right now.

They were nose to nose, as close as I had been to Beau a moment ago, and neither one seemed to mind that they were standing close enough to kiss.

"What's going on here, Tucker? You're not her boyfriend," Beau said in a voice like dark silk. "So why you cock-blocking me, man?"

I gasped. Did he really just say that?

Zach shoved him hard in the chest.

Beau collided with the dock railing, and for a moment I thought he might flip over and go into the lake. He caught himself, flinging back from the railing and launching himself at Zach in a move that was right out of the Olympics.

I snapped into action and wedged myself between the two of them. "Stop! Stop it!"

For the first time in my life I felt small and delicate sandwiched between two testosterone-riddled jocks. Their chests heaved on each side of me like living, breathing mountains. "Both of you, knock it off!"

"Willa." Zach dropped my name with heavy emphasis, putting everything that there ever was between us into those two syllables —all the years we'd known each other, all the times he'd given me rides to school, all the times I'd helped him with his homework. "Let's go."

"Okay, okay." At this point I only wanted to defuse the situation.

End the crazy. When we were alone he'd feel my wrath. I'd let him know exactly how this was not okay.

I faced Beau. "Sorry, I—"

"I thought he wasn't your boyfriend," he cut in, his eyes accusing.

"He's not," I insisted.

"Then this is messed up." He waved a finger between me and Zach, and I felt kind of small inside. Like I was the height of dysfunction. And maybe I was, because Beau was right. This whole scenario was messed up.

Shaking his head, Beau's expression turned to disgust as he looked me up and down. "Cock-tease," he muttered.

The word hit me like a slap.

No one had ever said anything that ugly to me. I'd always played it safe, hung back, and blended with the wallpaper (well, discounting the time I made out with my best friend's ex-boyfriend).

Ugly things did not get hurled at invisible girls.

So maybe I wasn't as invisible as I thought. But I wanted to be. Right then, especially.

I wanted to go back to being invisible, where life wasn't nearly so scary and definitely not this complicated.

I felt Zach stiffen behind me and knew he was one second from reacting to the fact that this guy had just insulted me.

I beat him to it. My palm lashed out and connected with Beau's cheek—the *nice* guy from ten minutes ago. Guess I was a bad judge of character after all.

The sound of my slap cracked on the air. Everything fell silent.

The air went still. Even the insects dancing around the tiki lights seemed to quiet and stop buzzing.

The water seemed to barely move, stretching like glass into the night. The party sounded even more distant. Like it was happening several docks down and not just seventy yards away.

"Just because I walked out here with you . . . and *kissed* you . . . doesn't make me a *cock-tease*. That's not the way it works, asshole. The sooner you figure that out, the better your odds that you won't end up in prison."

I stormed off the dock then, stumbling through the dark toward the house, pretty much ready to quit the male species for good right then — and these boots. They had to come off.

To my left a girl was puking in the bushes, two girls on either side of her patting her back. A few feet away, buried in a ivy-riddled fence, another couple made out, indifferent to the less-than-romantic vomiting in the background.

Zach called my name, but I ignored him and fast-tracked it for the house.

The house loomed in front of me, blazing with light and music and voices. Staring at it, I stopped, dreading going back in there suddenly. My earlier optimism fled. Just like that, this had gone from a night of fun to a night of how-soon-could-I-get-home.

The deck was more crowded too. Probably because the house had reached max capacity. I crossed my arms and hugged myself, chafing my skin against the chilly night.

"Willa." Zach jogged up beside me. "You okay?"

"Yes," I snapped.

No, I wasn't okay. I wanted to rip into him for daring to

interrupt me with Beau. But if he hadn't, I'd probably still be kissing that jerk. So he did kind of save me—even if it was only from myself. And I hated that. I didn't want him or anyone to save me. I was supposed to be capable of doing that myself.

"Nice slap." He scanned my face closely, assessing. What was he looking for? Did he think I'd run off to cry?

I shrugged. "Thanks."

"Remind me never to piss you off."

"What makes you think you haven't?"

"Well, you haven't slapped me."

"The night isn't over."

His smile slipped, and he looked uncertain as he gazed at me.

I peered ahead at the house. From the sounds of it the party was just getting started. I really didn't want to have to wade back in there to beg Farah to take me home.

"Fine." Sighing, I looked at Zach. "Drive me home."

Without waiting for him, I turned and started around the house to the front, where too many vehicles to count filled the front lawn and spilled out onto the street. I hoped Kennedy's parents weren't fond of their grass, because there wasn't going to be left much of it.

Once on the road, I spotted his Jeep several yards down. I tried to walk fast, but my boots weren't a fan of the loose gravel. I probably looked like a staggering drunk.

He caught up with me easily. "Now you want me to take you home?"

"You offered." I threw him a look. "Actually, more like demanded." I slipped my phone from my pocket and sent a text to the girls that I was getting a ride home with Zach.

Sliding my phone back in my pocket, I looked up at him. "Shouldn't you text your girlfriend?"

"She's not my girlfriend."

I made a sound in my throat. "Does Ashlyn know that?"

"Yeah. Of course."

We reached his Jeep and climbed in. He'd barely started it before he was asking me, "What were you thinking, going off with Beau Sanders? Do you know that guy's rep?"

I turned on him quicker than a springing snake. "Is it anything like yours?"

His fingers opened and flexed on the steering wheel. "Actually, no. It's worse."

"And don't do that." I stabbed a finger at him as if he hadn't said anything at all. "Don't jump all over me because I went off with a guy and kissed him. What are you? Jealous or something?"

"Course not," he denied, his voice thick and defensive, a tinge on the outrage.

Of course he wasn't jealous. I'd declined to see where things could go between us, and he'd jumped on the Ashlyn train quicker than a jackrabbit. He wasn't pining away for me. He didn't care.

Zach Tucker was a player. I guess he couldn't be blamed. But I was still mad at him. For what had happened on the dock with Beau. Maybe for Ashlyn, too, even though I wasn't supposed to be.

"Good. Because I've watched you do that for years. You fool around whenever the whim strikes you with whatever girl is convenient, so don't you dare get judgy on me."

"Willa," he cut in, his voice placating, "I never said—"

"Oh, and for the record, I should be able to kiss who I want. And that doesn't obligate me to sleep with him! The phrase *cock-tease* should be obliterated from the English language. It puts blame on the girl because she doesn't go all the way with a guy."

"*I* didn't call you that."

"No, but you're looking at me like I did something wrong, which kind of implies that you agree with him."

"I don't agree with him. And I'm sorry that I jumped on your case." He blew out a heavy breath. "I can't help that I was worried about you. I'm sorry that I acted like . . ." His voice faded as he stared straight ahead through the windshield.

"Like a jackass?" I quickly offered.

"Yeah." He nodded. "Sure." He started the engine and pulled out onto the road.

I fell silent beside him, regretting thinking I had to come to this party and flirt and kiss someone else to feel better.

Better right now would be my bed. Wearing my pajamas. With a book or a *Walking Dead* marathon. Even better than better would be if Flor were with me and we had a pint of cookie dough ice cream between us. It felt like we hadn't done that in ages.

His deep voice rose in the confined space. "You going to give me the silent treatment the whole way home?"

I looked at him coolly. "I'm not trying to."

"What are you thinking about?"

"Ice cream," I replied.

"Ice cream?"

"Mm-hmm." I nodded and turned to look out at the dark night again. The hills were vague purple shapes against the blackness.

"A minute ago you were ready to see me lynched. Now you're dreaming of ice cream?"

I shrugged. "Ice cream is always a priority."

"Maybe we could stop through a drive-thru. Probably won't miss curfew if we're really quick."

The offer made me soften slightly. Until I remembered that I was mad at him and not ready to forget about that. "No thanks. I just want to get home."

We drove in silence the rest of the way, and when he pulled up in the driveway, there were still ten minutes to spare until curfew. I unbuckled my seat belt and let it slide home with a clatter.

"Well. Thanks for the ride," I said, just to have something to say. "I know you probably wanted to stay." His parents had relaxed on his curfew this year. He'd told me it was because he was eighteen now. I'd told him it was because he was an only child and they let him get away with murder. Or it could just be because he was Zach Tucker. Even if he was their son, that made him special. The shining prince of the Tucker household.

"I didn't even want to be there."

With one hand on the door handle, I turned back to look at him. "After your big game? How could you miss it? Isn't that punishable by death or something among your team?"

He chuckled. "That's why I went. To make them happy. It wasn't what *I* wanted."

I stared at him, struggling to accept what he was saying. The entire time I'd known him, everything always seemed to go his way. "What do you know about not getting what you want?"

"Not everything goes my way. There are things I don't get."

His gaze seemed to sharpen on me right then. I adjusted my fingers around the door handle. It wasn't real. The way he was looking at me, his words strongly hinting at something more.

Something impossible.

"It looked like you going tonight made Ashlyn happy, too." This bitter, caustic bite of poison welled up inside me and I had to spit it out.

He shut off the engine, slid the keys out of the ignition, and turned to face me, resting one arm along the top of the steering wheel.

I couldn't stop. The poison kept coming out of me. "Bet she wasn't too happy when you left early," I added.

"I'm not responsible for how Ashlyn feels."

I made a sound in the back of my throat that was part laughter, part choking.

Those gray eyes deepened to black in the dimness of the Jeep. "What's that supposed to mean?" he asked, his voice whisper soft.

"Are you responsible for how *any* girl feels? Ever?"

His jaw clenched, and he knew that Flor was part of this conversation now. I'd brought her into it. As always. She was never far.

"*Should* I be responsible for the feelings of every girl that flirts with me?"

I thought about that and knew it was wrong. It wasn't fair of me to put that burden on him. Sometimes it felt like the whole world had a crush on him.

His eyes gleamed in the dark. "What do you want from me, Willa?"

"Me?" I flattened a hand against my chest. My heart was racing under my palm, beating like a drum in my too-tight chest. "I don't want anything from you." I thought I'd made that abundantly clear. I couldn't want anything from him.

I *wouldn't*.

I opened the Jeep door and stepped out into the night. "Thanks for the ride." I slammed the door shut and looked at him for a moment through the glass.

He stared back at me. It felt like a vast sea swelled between us. Endless and impossible to cross. I turned, walked into the house, and didn't look back.

GIRL CODE #2O:

When you say something, you better be sure you mean it.

Flor

←————————≪

THE steady beeping of the garbage truck woke me at the crack of dawn—well before my alarm went off. I'd set it for ten because I had a soccer game at noon. My room was still dark, and I didn't move for a moment, just held still in my bed listening to the truck beeping outside. Finally I lifted my head off my pillow and twisted, fumbling for my lamp with a groan.

I felt hung over and I hadn't even drunk last night. I needed one good day when I could sleep in. Clearly I should have left the party when Willa left instead of an hour later. I didn't fall into bed until a little after one.

Of course, that would have meant getting a ride home with Zach. I winced at that idea. That would have been awkward.

With another groan, I pushed up from the comfort of my bed and staggered bleary-eyed across the room to pull back my window curtains. Outside in the muted light of dawn a moving truck was parked alongside the curb. So it wasn't a garbage truck. I smirked. At least not technically.

Three men hopped out of the vehicle. Dana's Mini Cooper zipped around the truck and parked in front of it as the movers slid open the back door of the truck and started carrying items into my house.

This was really happening.

I sighed. "And so it begins."

Knowing it was pointless to try to go back to sleep for another hour, I shut off my alarm and jumped into the shower. I stood under the warm spray, letting it wake me. I deliberately tried not to think about Dana moving her things into the house right now. It would only drive me crazy.

Instead my mind drifted to last night and the conversation I'd forced on Zach. I felt a fresh sense of detachment. Numbness. I guess that was okay. Maybe I really was moving on. There was no hurt or pain. Maybe there really never had been. I felt around inside myself, probing carefully. Maybe it had only been disappointment I'd felt. Another loss. Another rejection. More of the same I'd been getting lately. I hadn't let myself examine if it was really *him*, really Zach, that I wanted.

Stepping out of the shower, I grabbed a towel and dried off, then put on my soccer shorts and jersey for the game today. I squeeze-dried my hair, getting out as much moisture as I could before pulling it into a tight ponytail and braiding.

Since I had time to kill, I could stop off for breakfast. I really didn't want to linger at home anyway with Dana and her movers tromping through the house.

I gathered up my gear—all except my cleats, which I kept outside—and headed downstairs.

Dana was in the living room, wearing a striped wraparound blouse that exposed her midriff. The movers gawked at her as she directed them, snapping her fingers and motioning where they should put one floral-print monstrosity of a love seat.

Dad watched from several feet away, a stupid grin on his face . . . like he'd just woken up to Christmas morning.

And I guessed that was why they called love blind. It besotted you and rendered you stupid so that you ignored all the other things in your life once deemed important.

I could feel my mood souring, and it was way too early for that. I needed my spirits high and my head in the game. Staring at my father beside Dana, one of his arms wrapped around her tiny waist as she directed a sofa chair into the suddenly crowded living room, I felt the almost violent impulse to say something. I didn't know what, but it would be something regrettable. Something mean. Something like how her furniture was butt ugly and clashed with our brown leather couches.

Hot emotion swept through me, coating my mouth in a bitter wash.

I bit the inside of my cheek and gave myself an internal shake. I couldn't give Dana so much power over me. She would *not* spoil my day before it even got started. I took out my water jug from a cabinet and added ice to it, taking a deep breath and attempting to control my emotions. Endorphins. That's what I needed. I'd get on that soccer field and feel better.

Flipping the faucet lever, I looked up. My eyes collided with

Dana's. Her stare fixed on me from across the living room as I filled my jug with water at the sink.

"Good morning, Flor," she greeted me.

"Morning," I returned.

Dad looked back and forth between us, his expression hopeful and oblivious to the tension. "Flor," he said cheerfully. "Game today?" he asked.

I glanced down at myself in my jersey. I was decked out in full game-day regalia. "Yeah." I nodded, thinking how he used to know my schedule better than I did. Now he rarely showed for a game.

"Good luck," he said, his gaze swerving and seeking out Dana even before he finished uttering the words to me.

"Thanks." Screwing the lid on my water, I hurried out of the house, veering past movers carrying a futon in a pink-and-brown animal print. I grabbed my cleats and sat on the bench outside to put them on, trying to push Dana and all her ugly furniture out of my mind.

I stopped at Whataburger for a honey butter chicken biscuit. Not the healthiest, but it was hearty. Sure, it was five thousand calories, but I would burn it off in the first half of the game.

Despite my vow not to let crap at home get into my head, I couldn't stop thinking about the fact that when I next walked through my door, Dana would be permanently moved into my house . . . into my life.

I could hardly get a foot on the ball in the second half. Their defenders were like linebackers. I was going to sport bruises tomorrow. There was no getting past their defense. We lost 3 to 1 and I felt like crying, which wasn't like me at all. I didn't get emotional on the field. It wasn't how I played.

I held it together through our coach's parting remarks and then grabbed my bag as the rest of the players headed to the sidelines to talk to their parents. It was still early enough that the day had a nice chill to it. The fall air cooled off the sweat on my skin as I walked into the parking lot, blinking burning eyes.

It was just a game. One game. I knew all the mantras. Had the T-shirts.

You can't win them all.

Defeat makes you stronger.

You can't appreciate the triumphs without the losses.

Blah blah blah. Stupid mantras. But I knew the truth. Losing a game wouldn't eat at me so much if other things were going right in my life. Family. Grades. Relationships. I was zero for three. Hopefully I'd at least be turning math around soon, thanks to Grayson.

At that thought, I dug out my phone from my bag and shot a text to him. Still on for tomorrow? I'm free tonight if you get an opening.

I snorted. God. That sounded beggy. An opening. What was he? My shrink? I winced at that.

"Hey, Flor! Wait up."

I looked up. Brianna, the goalkeeper, jogged after me. She was tall with an incredible wingspan. She covered a lot of space inside the net. Balls had a hard time finding their way past her. Except for today.

"Well, that sucked." She panted as she came to a stop beside me. "Want to hang tonight? I know a party."

I shook my head. "No thanks." Right now I just wanted to take a shower, maybe order Chinese, and power through some reruns of *Big Bang Theory.*

"What's the matter? You can't slum it in my neck of the woods? Come to this thing with me." Brianna lived north of the city. It was hardly a slum, just another suburb.

Then it occurred to me that tonight would be the first night with Dana in the house. Who knew what she had planned? I just knew she had something up her sleeve. She was probably busy making her mark in my house right now. Wait. Not *my* house. *Our* house.

Maybe I should go out tonight. I could see what Willa was doing. Maybe spend the night with her. Even if the last time I'd slept over, her sister's child had puked all over me.

"C'mon, Hidalgo. I promise you a good time."

I stared at Brianna's perpetually sunburned face. Freckles scattered across her nose. "Yeah?"

A good time. I hadn't had one of those in a while. Maybe it would be fun to go to a party where no one knew me. Where no one knew that Zach Tucker had dumped me.

"Sure, Bri. I'll go with you."

GIRL CODE #21:

True friends never start a statement with:

"Don't take this the wrong way, but . . ."

Willa

A s the day faded to evening, Jenna, Farah, and Ava texted they were going to see a movie that night.

Of course they invited me, but I told them I had to babysit Mia. Which was partially true. I could take Mom's car and meet them at the theater if I wanted. It'd be okay. But I didn't want to.

After last night, which had been loaded with its share of mistakes, I was staying home. That seemed the best way to ensure no more mistakes happened.

No more parties. No more humiliating moments where I did and said things that weren't me. No more regrets.

Flor chimed into the group text, passing on the movies. She was going to a party with one of her soccer friends. She did that occasionally, hung out with her teammates.

So it was just me, Mom, and Mia at home. Chloe was going out with some old friends from high school, surely to man-bash over margaritas.

Mom heated up leftovers and hid in her room with a bottle of wine and a Hallmark movie marathon that would probably only depress her because Dad wasn't home for the weekend and she was living the life of a single parent without technically being one.

I knocked on her door and pushed it open at her muffled command. As I suspected, she held a glass of wine in one hand. A plate of half-eaten mystery casserole was sitting on her nightstand.

"Hey."

"Hey," she greeted me, looking away from the TV. "Everything okay? Mia asleep?"

"Like a log."

She patted the bed beside her. I moved into the room and climbed up beside her. "Talk to Dad?"

She nodded. "He's eating Whataburger in his room. He had a long day at the plant. There was some kind of malfunction. He thinks the launch will be delayed now." She sighed and lifted her glass in a mock salute and took a long sip.

"Delayed?" He was already stuck working the new plant until it opened in February.

She nodded grimly, the line of her mouth tight. "He's thinking it won't be until March now."

I grimaced, watching as Mom reached for the bottle of wine on her nightstand and poured more into her glass.

"Has Dad thought of telling them no? That he has a family four hours away and—"

"Doesn't work like that, baby girl." Mom shook her head and dug out a package of Oreos I hadn't noticed buried in the bed with her. "There are half a dozen guys under him more than willing to take his job, and they don't mind being away from home for a few months. Now is not a good time to be out of work."

She meant now because they had Chloe and Mia and me to worry about. Chloe wasn't working, and even if I got a scholarship, it wouldn't cover all my expenses.

I decided to go for encouraging. "March will be here before you know it."

She sighed and offered me a cookie. I took one from the package. "No plans tonight?" she asked.

"No. Just staying in. Probably watch Netflix."

She nodded. The bag crinkled as she dug out another cookie. "Don't stay up too late."

"I won't," I promised, and kissed her cheek. "See you in the morning."

I peeked in on Mia in her crib. She slept with her knees tucked under her, her bottom sticking up in the air. I stroked her back softly, careful not to wake her.

Satisfied that she was still sound asleep, I headed to my room. I tapped a key on my laptop and *The Walking Dead* resumed playing. I settled back on my bed to watch it. Not five minutes passed before a text buzzed on my phone.

I stretched across my bed to grab it. My stomach tightened at Zach's name on the screen.

Want to get some ice cream?

My fingers flew over my screen. What? No big plans for the night? He quickly replied. No. Staying in like you.

I resisted the impulse to tell him that he was nothing like me—or ask how he knew I was staying home. I also resisted the impulse to ask him why he didn't have any plans with Ashlyn tonight. I would just sound petty and jealous. Which I was, but I didn't want him to think that.

Want to go get some ice cream?

I frowned. What? Now?

Sure. It's not that late.

I glanced at the time. He was right. It was a perfectly reasonable thing to do at eight thirty p.m. If he'd asked me a few weeks ago, I would already be out the door and crossing to his driveway. And wasn't that what I wanted? What I had told him? For things to go back the way they were before?

As though he could sense me internally debating the question, he typed again: What's wrong? Afraid to go get some ice cream?

I bristled at the challenge. I wasn't afraid of him.

The girl I was before our first kiss (and second kiss) would already be sitting in his car.

Before I could have second thoughts, my fingers flew over my phone. Meet you in the driveway.

GIRL CODE #22:

Fistfights are a spectator sport. Don't get involved.

Flor

←————————≪

"So explain what this thing is again?" Tromping through a field in the middle of nowhere, it didn't feel like any party I'd ever gone to before.

Suddenly I wanted more of an explanation than Brianna's pithy *Come to this thing with me.*

"You'll see." She giggled and ran ahead, with her friend Maddie close to her side. They'd picked me up, music blaring loud enough to make your ears bleed.

I followed them at a slower pace, wishing I'd known it was going to be outdoors. I would have worn different shoes.

Brianna stopped running, letting me catch up with her. Maddie continued without us. The sound of the crowd grew as we approached a circle of cars and trucks. All their headlights were on, pointing inward to the center of the circle.

Music blasted from one truck, easily identifiable from the large speakers positioned in the truck bed. All the other truck beds were full of bodies. Onlookers watched and cheered at something I couldn't see inside the circle. People even sat on the roofs of their cars.

"What are they looking at?"

"C'mon." Brianna waved me after her. We squeezed between two vehicles, pushing past bodies.

"Hey," one guy snapped at us, until his gaze landed on Brianna. He blinked and raked her with his eyes, making no effort to disguise his thorough inspection. His voice softened to silk. "Oh, hey there." His gaze flitted to me and he did another slow survey. "Hello, girls."

Brianna pouted, actually looking demure and nothing like the kick-ass-and-take-names girl I knew from soccer. "My friend and I can't see."

"Well, c'mon, ladies." He took our elbows and pulled us through. "You don't want to miss the show." He splayed a hand on his chest. "I'm Jed."

With Jed's help, we managed to get to the front of the mob, and I finally got to see what all the fuss was about.

It wasn't what I'd expected . . . but then I'm not sure I knew what to expect. I'd already sensed this wasn't an ordinary party.

Two guys circled each other. Both were shirtless. One had so much blood running down his face and torso I didn't know how he could stand, much less prance on the balls of his feet. I think he probably needed a transfusion.

Even in his condition, he managed to pull back his arm and land a blow in the other guy's face. A bare-knuckled punch. The crack of bone on bone carried over the night. I jerked and winced.

The mob went wild. The noise around me was deafening. I ducked my head as though I could escape some of the din.

Brianna elbowed me and grinned. "Pretty wild, right?"

"What is this?" I called out.

Jed looked at me like I was slow. "It's a fight."

"I can see that." I gestured around us. "Why are they fighting?"

Another crack rang out, and the crowd erupted into a roar. A body dropped into the dirt. Someone grabbed the bloody guy's arm and held it high in the air, evidently proclaiming him victor. He didn't look like a victor as he swayed on his feet, ready to drop. He looked like hell.

"It's a fight club." Brianna did me the favor of explaining.

I stared at her and then looked back into the circle as a few men stepped up to scrape the loser off the grass and carry him somewhere out of sight, past the vehicles. "A fight club? That's a real thing?" I'd thought it was only something on TV.

"Sure. Locations change every week. You get text alerts."

I shook my head and looked around me again. That's when I realized not everyone here was a high school student. There were all ages represented. From acne-faced teenagers to middle-aged men with bottles of beer. Everyone had cash in their hands. A skinny guy wearing a tank top that showed off his tatted arms walked around with a ledger, taking money from people.

"How did you find out about this?" I spoke loudly into Brianna's ear.

"Maddie's brother told us." She shrugged. "His college roommate fought in the club. Just once, though." She shivered. "It didn't go well for him. His parents weren't thrilled. The dental work was very expensive."

"So *anyone* can just step up and fight?"

"No, you have to be invited." She shook her head. "It might be underground, but it's organized. These fighters are legit."

An organized underground fight club. I didn't know what to think. I didn't know if I even wanted to stay. I looked around at the crowd. It felt like something out of *Lord of the Flies*, where the mob mentality could take over at any moment.

"Girls fight too, you know," she added with a laugh. "Those are fun to watch."

I shook my head.

"Have you ever tried—"

She looked at me in horror. "Oh, hell no! Maddie keeps talking like she might do it, but she's crazy." She waved at her face. "I'm not messing this up for any amount of money. And can you imagine me showing up for soccer after one of these fights? Coach would freak."

Nodding, I turned my attention back to the space cleared for the fighters.

This didn't seem the same as watching a fight on TV. It felt raw and wild. Unsavory. Like anything could go wrong and probably did. There was something in the air, a bloodlust that filled my nose and mouth like sour copper.

Two more fighters were already stepping into the clearing, talking with a guy in an Astros ball cap who seemed to be in charge of this thing, from his terse manner.

One of the fighters was thick and built like a tank. He wore a pair of overalls with no shirt underneath. Bulging, gleaming muscles swelled around the faded denim. He was just one big fat pile of man meat, and he looked capable of crushing anyone that stood in his path.

The other guy had his back to me. He was tall, lean, and cut. His bare back rippled with muscle and sinew as someone taped his knuckles for him.

"Oh, yesss! Duracell is here tonight." Brianna clapped gleefully.

The guys around us noticed him at the same time, and they started high-fiving each other. "This should be good. Duracell versus Mountain. I don't think they've ever faced off."

Of course the big one's nickname was Mountain.

"Duracell?" I echoed. That one was actually slightly original.

"Yeah. You know. Like the batteries," Jed chimed in. "Because he goes on for motherfuckin' forever," he hooted, and high-fived one of his buddies. They all laughed and started chanting "Duracell" like they were spectators at a football game.

Rolling my eyes, I returned my attention to the two fighters.

"The popular fighters all have nicknames." Brianna pointed at Duracell, who still stood with his back to me. "But yeah . . . he's just got this stamina. Whew." She fanned herself. "Makes you wonder what other things he can do forever."

I laughed lightly. "You're bad, girl."

"I'd like to be. With that guy, for sure. Oh, look." She pointed. "There's Maddie."

Brianna's friend was on the opposite side of the mob, sitting atop the shoulders of some guy so she could see into the center of the circle. She cheered and waved her arms wildly.

Jed held up his hand, waving a hundred-dollar bill madly. "Right here! On Duracell!"

"You're betting on him over that huge guy?" I asked. It wasn't that Duracell didn't look fit. It was just that the other guy was so very large. His hands were as big as my face.

"Hell, yeah!"

"If I had any money. I'd put it on him too," Brianna said, prancing in place anxiously just like she did when she was in the keeper's box. "He's tough to put down. Plus, he's just hot as hell. My girl parts demand he gets my vote. It would be like sacrilege not to root for him."

I snorted and looked back at the fighters. Duracell turned around then, and my heart stopped. I knew him, and his name wasn't Duracell.

It was Grayson.

GIRL CODE #23:

A friend always gives you the shirt off her back . . . and doesn't judge you when you take off yours.

Willa

»—————→

WE drove a little out of the way to go to Ritter's Frozen Custard. Technically not ice cream, but it was even better. They had a few tables scattered outside the front of the building. Half were occupied with families enjoying an after-dinner treat. It wasn't so chilly yet that we couldn't sit outside in October. Plus, it was Houston. It was never really too chilly for that.

We sat down at a round table to eat our frozen custard.

"This isn't like you," I commented as I used my spoon to scoop out some salted caramel custard from my waffle cone. "Even when you're home, you usually have friends over."

"You make it sound like I can never be alone."

I shrugged and let that be my answer.

"I can be alone," he insisted, licking at his waffle cone. No spoon for him. He looked beautiful even doing that. His brown hair was product-free and flopped low on his forehead. His gray eyes were brilliant as usual. His features relaxed.

"You're not really a loner type. You thrive on others around you." I waved my spoon in the air. "I like my solitude. I mean . . . I actually stay up late even when I'm exhausted if it means I can have a quiet house with no one to bother me. Solitude is bliss." I savored another spoonful of custard.

"Yeah. I know you. I've lived next door to you forever."

I stared at him for a moment. He did know me.

I didn't think Flor had ever understood that part of my personality. She was a people person like Zach. That's why they'd been drawn to each other. Well, that and they were both beautiful. Beautiful people flocked together.

"Hey, Zach! What's up, man?" I looked up as a group of kids passed us. I didn't recognize them. They probably didn't even go to Madison. Zach knew people everywhere.

He nodded and waved at them.

I finished off the rest of my frozen custard, then walked to the trash and tossed my half-eaten cone inside it. Dusting imaginary crumbs off my fingers, I returned to the table. "Ready?"

He popped the last bit of his cone into his mouth and stood. "Sure."

We climbed into his Jeep and pulled out of the parking lot for home.

"Want to come over and watch a movie?" he asked.

I hesitated. Tension crept over me, tightening my shoulders. The guilt was there . . . an uncomfortable niggle worming through me. I wondered what Flor would think of this scene. Me eating ice cream with Zach and then heading back to his place to watch a movie. It felt . . . *intimate*. Like a date. Like something a couple would do.

"I don't think so."

"Why not?" he was quick to reply.

"I don't think that would be a good idea."

He shook his head. "Really, Willa? You said you wanted things to go back to the way they were, but the way they were would have been you and me watching a movie. Probably one of your cheesy eighties flicks that I would have made fun of the entire time."

I winced. He was right, of course. We'd done that before. Countless times. I'd recently added *Pretty in Pink* to my watch list. Under normal circumstances—*previous* circumstances—I would have gladly forced him to watch that with me. But watching Molly Ringwald crush on some guy with Zach beside me probably wasn't smart.

I moistened my dry lips. "Maybe I was wrong. Maybe we can't go back to the way we were."

Suddenly he was turning the Jeep, veering off the four-lane road onto a side street in a move that bordered on reckless.

"What are you doing?" I pressed a hand to the window to stop myself from slamming into the door.

He pulled into a vacant parking lot, braked hard, and slammed the Jeep into park. I glanced around, recognizing the building in front of us as the public library. It sat dark and silent. This time of night, no one was around.

He turned in the seat to glare at me, his eyes glittering. "So what's it going to be? Are we friends or not, Willa?"

"Friends, of c-course," I stammered, my hand still pressing into the glass of the window as though I needed to brace myself. "Of course." There. That sounded more emphatic. "But just different friends than before."

"Different than before?" His voice turned mocking . . . almost cruel. He'd never spoken to me like that before. His eyes flashed in the dark confines of the Jeep, and all at once I felt like I was walking a tightrope. Any moment and I might go over.

"Yeah." I nodded, my stomach twisting. Suddenly that custard didn't sit so well. I felt sick.

"*I* wanted things to be different than before," he reminded. "I suggested that very thing. I hoped we—"

"Not *that* kind of different," I quickly cut in. His offer to experiment still rang in my ears and made my face burn. I glanced around the empty lot, uneasy. "Take me home, please."

"That's right. Time to run away. You're good at that. Run inside your house. Hide in your room. Blame *this* not happening"—he waved between us—"on Flor."

I shook my head miserably. Going out for ice cream had been a bad idea. His eyes weren't happy anymore. His features weren't relaxed.

My friend was gone, and I wanted him back.

Only I didn't know how to get him back. I didn't know if I ever could. A vast gulf separated us.

"Look at us. We're supposed to be friends." I released a brittle laugh. We weren't acting like it. He was acting like he couldn't stand the sight of me.

I fought to swallow past a painful lump in my throat. This was what happened when you kissed your best friend. Things got confusing.

Things got ruined.

Something passed over his face, and then he nodded slowly, as though coming to a realization. "Maybe I don't want to be your friend anymore, Willa."

That stopped me hard. Stung in the worst way. It hurt more than I'd imagined anything hurting.

I removed my hand from the glass and pressed it over my heart. It was like I could feel it bleeding inside my chest cavity, ripped open and throbbing.

"I have plenty of friends," he added.

"Okay," I mumbled, looking down to where I now twisted my fingers until I could no longer feel them. "Good to know."

"I don't do this to girls I'm friends with."

This?

Alarmed, I looked up just as he reached for me. I caught a flash of those blazing eyes a second before he pulled me to him.

I'd like to say I shoved him away. Slapped him. Called him a jerk. Anything.

But I wasn't as strong as that. Or as smart.

Or, apparently, as good a friend to Flor as I should have been.

Our mouths came together like two bullet trains crashing head-on. He hauled me over the console and onto his lap, guiding me into straddling his bigger body. I moaned and melted into him, so relieved. A moment ago I'd been afraid I'd lost him.

Mouth devoured mouth, lips and tongues going at it. It wasn't like the other kisses. As good as those were, this was all wild fury. Like two long-lost souls finding each other at last.

The steering wheel was right against my back, so I had to lean forward, mashing my chest into his. One of my knees was wedged uncomfortably against the armrest of his door, but I didn't care. It was a small discomfort when I had *this*.

His delicious lips. His hands sliding under the back of my shirt, skimming my spine.

He groaned into my mouth, his hands stroking and playing against my skin, fingers tracing down the vertebrae of my spine like they were playing the keys of a piano.

"Your skin is like a dream."

I didn't know what that meant. He couldn't be talking about me.

Still, I sighed into his mouth, aching in places I'd never known could *feel* such things. I wrapped my arms around his neck and pressed closer. My body might not have been experienced at this kind of thing, but it *knew*. It recognized what it wanted. My heart had always wanted Zach and now my body did too.

He sucked on my tongue and I pulled back with a gasp, my eyes finding his in the dark as my hand flew to my mouth.

"I dream about you, Willa," he whispered. "I can't close my eyes without seeing you."

I flattened a hand on his chest, feeling the steady thud of his heart. I didn't think I'd felt anything so solid, so strong. "I'm not one of the legions you've kissed, Zach."

It was important that I remember that . . . and that he realize it too.

I didn't want to become as ordinary as all of them. As expendable. Our friendship was special. I'd always taken solace in that. Even Flor had never had that with him. It was something precious just between us.

His eyes flitted over my face. "You don't think I know that?" His mouth was close now.

"We can't do this." My voice wasn't high-pitched anymore. No, just a barely-there whisper.

He eased back a little. Only a little. I was still pinned under his gaze. "You think I haven't thought about this? That I'm just here to play you? I wouldn't do that to you, Willa. I've thought about this. About kissing you." He stopped and let out a gust of air, looking physically pained. "God, it's all I've thought about. I've played it over and over in my mind."

A whimper escaped me at his confession and I leaned in, burying my hands in his hair, scraping my nails against his scalp as I brought my mouth back down to his.

My hair fell around us in a curtain as we kissed. I reveled in sitting high over him. I felt powerful. Like I held this strong guy in the palm of my hand. His desire was mine. *I* controlled it. *Me*, who was never in control of much of anything in my life. Me, who never felt particularly wanted or desired, who watched as Flor and my other friends got asked on dates and went to dances.

He grasped my hips, and suddenly we were rocking against each other. Movement was limited in the cramped space, but we managed it.

I rubbed my breasts against his chest as we continued to kiss. The wild little sounds that broke from me should have embarrassed me. But this wasn't me anymore.

I was some other creature, wild and lacking all judgment.

This must have been what it felt like to be drunk. Why kids did stupid things when they were intoxicated.

I didn't have alcohol as an excuse, though. I was simply drunk on Zach Tucker.

Still under my shirt, his hands slid around my rib cage, tracing the edge of my bra. His palms came up over my demi cups and he was holding me then, cupping me with hands that I had stared at for years. In moments of weakness I'd imagined either one of his hands holding mine. *Handholding.*

And now we were here. Doing *this.*

Now those hands were touching me where no boy had touched me before.

I pulled back from his mouth to look down at him. My breasts heaved where he held them in his hands. The intimacy should have scared me. It should have felt wrong, but I could only draw ragged breaths and want more of his touch.

The air in the Jeep was thick and charged, crackling with tension. If we lit a match, we'd both go up in flames.

His eyes gleamed with emotion I'd never seen from him.

His palms flexed against me, thumbs brushing over the lace of my bra. My mouth dried.

He stared at me, not speaking.

His hands let go of me, dropping to seize the hem of my shirt.

He pulled it over my head in one smooth move while I lifted my arms, helping him.

How was this happening?

How was I on his lap, shirtless, wearing only a bra?

I wished it were a better bra. One of those sexy scraps of fabric my friends traipsed around in when we were changing clothes. *A bra Flor would wear.*

I didn't need to worry about the bra for long, though. His hands found the front clasp and flicked it free. It popped open and I didn't move. Just watched him watch me.

"Willa," he whispered, his voice hoarse and awe-tinged.

My insides quivered.

His hands cupped me then, and I nearly flew off his lap at the first rasp of his palms on my bare breasts. Oh. God. Was it supposed to feel like this? Wonderful and shocking and vomit-inducing at the same time? No one had told me. None of my friends had warned me.

My stomach couldn't stop churning. It was like a thousand butterflies rioted inside me, looking for a way out.

"Willa." He pressed his mouth to my neck, my collarbone, looking up at me, watching my face with intense eyes as he played with my breasts, his thumbs brushing over my nipples, back and forth, back and forth, each swipe making me shake. "Do you like that?"

Ohh. That voice. His hands.

I whimpered as he tasted me with warm, open-mouthed kisses, his tongue hot on my skin, burning, singeing.

I should have been horrified and stopping this. Instead I was galloping straight into it, arching into his touch and sliding my fingers into his hair, sighing and moaning and holding him closer to me.

His mouth trailed down, closing over me, sucking me deep. Pleasure knifed through me.

Oh. My. God.

I gasped as a twisting tightness started in my belly. His hands were at my hips again, gripping me hard, urging me as I rocked over him, grinding down on that hard bulge in his jeans, trying to relieve the ache as much as I could with our clothes between us.

It was clumsy and desperate and wild, but that didn't stop us from trying.

"Willa." He said my name brokenly against my flushed skin.

With his lips on me, I couldn't think. There was only feeling . . . sensation. Fleeting flashes of thoughts that wanted to make sense.

"Zach," I choked, gazing down hungrily at his beautiful face. I heard the plea in my voice . . . a voice I didn't even recognize. Didn't even know.

With a curse, he brought my face down to kiss again, his lips fierce and frantic.

I melted against him, my mouth opening wide. Giving. Taking.

What was happening? I'd give myself over completely right now and not regret it.

Suddenly lights flashed and a siren chirped. My gaze darted over his shoulder to the rear window. "Oh my God! It's the police." My hands flew to cover my breasts.

"Shit!" His gaze clashed with mine as we jumped into action. "Don't worry," he reassured me as I snatched my bra off the console.

"I'll take care of it." I fumbled to get my arms through the straps. "I'm good with cops, remember?"

I nodded jerkily, my heart beating painfully in my chest. It felt like it might burst free from my rib cage. "I remember," I panted, letting myself feel hopeful.

He lifted me off him and deposited me in my seat as I fumbled to bring the bra cups up over me.

I jerked, stifling a scream as a police officer stepped beside the driver's-side window, shining a flashlight into the cab, nearly blinding me. Clutching my bra together, I held up a hand over my eyes.

He knocked on the glass.

"Let me do the talking," Zach whispered as he rolled down the window. "Evening, sir."

"That would be ma'am." The light of the flashlight came back over me then. "I guess I don't need to ask why you're parked here. Licenses, please."

The police officer was a woman. Considering my boobs were hanging out, that made me feel a little better. I finally managed to snap my bra closed. I grabbed my shirt and tugged it over my head. I smoothed my hands over my hair and reached for my wallet.

Zach had already given her his license. She'd studied it with no expression. Apparently his name as a local sports hero didn't ring a bell. Or she didn't care.

With shaking hands, I handed Zach mine and he passed it through the open window to her.

The woman studied it for a moment before shining the flashlight back on me. "Miss Evans?"

I nodded. "Yes?"

"You're seventeen."

"Y-yes." I shared an uncertain look with Zach. She'd said nothing about his age. He was already eighteen.

"That means I'll have to call your parents to come and get you."

GIRL CODE #24:

Don't believe everything you see on social media. Can you say Photoshop? Trust your own eyes.

Flor

I stared in shock as the fight started. Part of me wanted to dive into that circle and stop Grayson before he got himself killed —crushed by some giant who went by the name of Mountain. As if that weren't omen enough.

What was he thinking?

But the other part of me held back, reminding myself that he wasn't Grayson here. Here, in this field in the middle of nowhere, he was Duracell. How strangely messed up was that?

My genius National Merit Scholar tutor was some underground fight-club rock star. How was that possible? And where were his glasses? The random thought almost made me want to laugh.

The other fighter charged Grayson, who stayed light on his feet, dancing out of the way. My shoulders sagged in relief as he dodged Mountain's swinging arm.

"If Mountain gets his arms around him, it's all over," Jed pronounced grimly, sharing a knowing look with his buddies. "No one has ever broken his hold."

I shot Jed a worried look. "Really?" *No one?* My pulse thrummed wildly at my throat.

"C'mon, Grayson," I whispered under my breath, following his movements as he danced out of the Goliath's way.

The shouts of the crowd around me only added to my growing panic. I covered my mouth with both hands to stop myself from crying out like some kind of maniac.

Grayson darted in and delivered a double-punch combo to Mountain. I couldn't help myself then. I slapped the air in triumph. "*Yes!* Get him!"

Brianna looked wide-eyed at me. "Wow. You're really into this."

Mountain roared and got close enough to grab a fistful of Grayson's hair. He swung him around, then flung him flat on his back on the ground. I felt the bone-jarring impact under my feet.

I lunged forward. "Foul! Foul!"

"Flor, this isn't soccer!" Brianna shouted as she and Jed pulled me back.

I struggled against them, watching in alarm as Mountain stepped over a stunned Grayson, placing a foot on either side of his shoulders.

"Get up!" I screamed, my heart squeezing inside my chest. *He's going to be hurt. He's going to be hurt.* It was all I could think: a desperate mantra running through my head.

Brianna tightened her hold on my arm. "Remind me never to bring you to a fight again. You're way too invested."

Still clenching Grayson's hair, Mountain forced his head up. I winced, watching as he pulled back his tree-trunk arm to deliver a blow.

"No!" I screamed, the shrill sound of my own voice ringing in my head.

I must have been really loud, because Mountain glanced at me with a satisfied look on his face.

Grayson came alive then. He took advantage of the distraction and cracked his fist under Mountain's chin.

"Ohh! Here we go!" Jed proclaimed, slapping the shoulders of one of his friends gleefully.

Mountain's head snapped back from the blow and he let go of Grayson's hair. Cheers and boos simultaneously erupted. Grayson didn't stop there. He sent his fist straight up between his opponent's legs, directly into his crotch.

The crowd groaned in empathy. Even I cringed.

Mountain went down with a shriek, holding himself between the legs and landing like King Kong with an earth-shaking crash.

The ringleader of this sideshow jumped into the circle and grabbed Grayson by the wrist, holding his arm up in the air to declare him the victor.

I exhaled, suddenly aware that I had only been partially breathing this whole time.

"Well, that was exciting," Brianna announced. "Ended a little too quickly, but oh well."

I craned my neck, keeping an eye on Grayson as he disappeared into the crowd. I followed, moving through the press of bodies.

"Flor, where you going?" Brianna stayed close behind me as I circled the vehicles and threaded through the crowd, going around to where I'd last seen Grayson disappear.

"Do they fight more than once a night?" I asked, wondering if he could have slipped away and left.

"Sometimes. If they're popular enough and can still stand after their first fight. Are you trying to meet Duracell? I mean, I know you're pretty, but he's got a horde of groupies. He doesn't give anyone the time of day. Don't bother."

Ignoring her, I kept moving, determined to confront him and find out what the hell he was thinking. He could seriously get hurt.

A crack appeared in the crowd, and I spotted Grayson collecting money from the tatted guy with the ledger.

I pushed through the gap. "Grayson!"

His head snapped up, his dark eyes flaring wide at the sight of me. His skin shimmered with a fine sheen of sweat, and I couldn't help marveling that I'd thought he'd make a good athlete. How dumb was I? This guy was in killer shape. He was the real thing. So he didn't wear pads and fight for a ball on a field with a bunch of other guys. No, instead he stripped to the waist and used brute strength against grown men who looked like they ate high school boys for breakfast.

"You know him?" Brianna whispered at my back. "Why didn't you say anything? Oh my God, you have to introduce me."

The tatted guy looked at me and then back at Grayson, holding the last bit of cash in the air, hesitating before giving it up. "What'd she call you?"

"Nothing," Grayson snapped. "You gonna finish paying me my cut or not, Jase?"

Jase looked at me appraisingly. "You know Duracell here?" he called over to me. Suddenly everyone was looking at me.

I started to nod and then stopped uncertainly as Grayson leveled a glare at me.

"Yeah?" Jase pressed. "From where? The marines?"

"The marines?" I echoed. Why would he think I knew Duracell from the marines? Did he think Duracell was a marine? Ridiculous. Even I was starting to think of him by that name.

I shook my head.

Suddenly Grayson was there beside me. He seemed bigger, looming. Shirtless and sweaty. His body was lean and hard, cut with definition. I guess fighting and getting your ass kicked on the weekends did that to a physique. It was like I could smell the pheromones coming off him in waves.

I met his dark gaze, struggling to reconcile Grayson with Duracell. It was like they were two different people.

Yes, I had started to think Grayson was attractive. I mean . . . I'd tried to set him up with Willa, and I had thought of kissing him that time. Okay. Yeah. Grayson kind of did it for me, even before this moment.

But Duracell? He confused the hell out of me. He was sexy hot. One of those dangerous bad boys mothers warned their daughters

225

about. I didn't need this confusion in my life. I already had enough confusion.

I stared at him accusingly. "What do you think you're doing? Trying to get yourself killed? Do your par—"

He crossed the distance separating us, grabbed my face, and kissed me. Hard. I couldn't move. Shock rippled through me, even more intense than when I'd first clapped eyes on him here tonight.

The sounds and voices around me drowned down to nothing. There was only the pressure of his mouth on mine. The feel of him, the taste, the smell. Heat swelled between us. It was like a force field, only drawing me closer instead of repelling me.

I didn't know who he thought he was to kiss me like this, or what point he was making. I should shove him away.

But that's not what I did.

My hands crept up his chest and circled his neck. I didn't even care that his skin was damp with sweat. I only wanted more of his drugging mouth. More of his skin and strong body. I'd kissed my share of boys before. Nothing, not even Zach, had affected me like this.

I broke.

Lifting up on my tiptoes, I kissed him back hungrily. It was impossible not to respond. I opened my mouth to him. His tongue swept inside and touched mine. At that first stroke something busted loose inside me. A shudder racked me. I tasted him back.

He tore away with a ragged breath. Staring down at me, his dark eyes mirrored my astonishment.

"Sooo you two know each other," Brianna asked, dragging me

back to reality. Maddie had arrived and stood behind her with her mouth hanging open.

"Yeah," Grayson replied, his gaze fixed on me, the astonishment fading, replaced by something inscrutable.

I couldn't move. I felt frozen under his stare, exposed. I'd kissed him back in front of all these people.

He turned and faced Jase, who watched us with keen interest. Snatching the rest of his money from him, Grayson said, "She's my girlfriend. Just hates to see me fight. That's all." He lifted an eyebrow at me, waiting to see if I would contradict his lie.

I held silent.

Jase looked me over. "Little young, isn't she?"

How old did he think Grayson was?

Stuffing his money into his back pocket, Grayson said, "She's older than she looks."

Taking my hand, he led me away. The crowd parted for us. It wasn't anything like when Brianna and I had fought our way through bodies.

"What the hell are you doing here?" he tossed over his shoulder.

"My friend brought me." At the thought of Brianna, I tugged on his hand and turned back around, searching for her.

I spotted her hopping amid people, waving an arm as she tried to catch a glimpse of me. "I'll see you at practice, Bri!" I faced him again. "I assume you're giving me a ride?"

He grunted and kept walking, pulling me after him, his hand warm and strong around mine.

Quiet fell around us as we left the throng of people behind and walked out into the field toward the parked cars.

"You almost blew it for me back there," he finally said.

"What does that even mean?"

"They think I'm Duracell. Not some high school kid."

"So? What are you even doing here?"

He stopped and faced me. "I've worked hard to build a rep. They think I'm some hardened ex-marine. That's how they even let me start fighting. I can't ruin the illusion now."

I shook my head. "This is why you can't tutor me half the time? So you can get your rocks off fighting?"

A car started in the distance and headlights flashed across his angry face. His nostrils flared. "I fight because I need the money! Because I don't have a rich daddy to support me through school."

"You're going to get a scholarship."

"God." He made a sound of disgust. "You're such a special snowflake if you think that will solve everything."

"Don't talk to me like that." Like I was so privileged I didn't know anything. Like I was stupid. "There has to be a better way to earn money than this."

"Nothing that pays so well. And I have two younger sisters. They get a roof over their head and that's it." He pounded his chest once. "If they need anything else to make their lives even remotely bearable with our old man, then it falls on me to get it for them."

I stared at him. Seeing him fully for the first time. "They're lucky to have you . . . but I doubt they'd want you hurting yourself for them."

He inhaled sharply. "Don't worry. It's fine. I'm good at it. I know how to fight and I know how to get my ass kicked and get up again."

I could only stare at him in all his righteous glory as he crossed his arms over his chest. Stare at him and remember that kiss from a few moments ago. My lips still burned. My tongue still tasted him.

His gaze dropped to my mouth, and something told me that he was thinking about it too. I held my breath, waiting. Waiting for what, I didn't know. Not another kiss. That would be weird. Wrong.

Once was a mistake. Twice was . . . something else.

The air crackled all around us.

"Why did you kiss me?" I blurted, even though I pretty much knew why.

"I needed to stop you from talking. It seemed the thing to do."

The thing to do. There had been nothing else to it for him, then? "You did a good job making it look real."

"It needed to look real." Matter-of-fact. No emotion. His dark eyes were as unfathomable as ever.

I wanted to point out that he hadn't needed to kiss me so thoroughly. Or stick his tongue in my mouth . . . but then he might counter that I had been fully into it, kissing him back. I could do without that embarrassing reminder.

"C'mon, princess. I'll take you home. Back to your world."

He walked ahead, letting go of my hand, no longer pretending we were something for the benefit of Jase or Duracell's adoring fans.

I stared at the back of him, my fingers brushing the inside of my palm, still feeling the warmth and pressure of him there. His figure faded into a hazy shape ahead of me, swallowed up in the night.

Shaking my head, I hurried ahead before I lost track of him.

GIRL CODE #25:

Lots of friends like the same things, but best friends hate the same things.

Willa

>»——————→

THEY called Mom.

I didn't think anything could be more mortifying than being discovered topless by a police officer, but having that same officer tell my mother that she had found me topless with a boy was definitely more mortifying.

The amusing thing was that the female officer didn't give a flying fig about whether or not Zach was the star kicker of Madison High School. There was a second officer who had remained in the car. She emerged and issued Zach and me citations for public lewdness while the first officer called and spoke to my mother.

Apparently neither one was a fan of local football. I could tell by Zach's expression that this came as some shock to him. For the first time, the town golden boy didn't get a pass. It would almost have been laughable if it weren't so embarrassing. If Mom weren't looking at me like she was so ashamed of me.

The officer handed my mother my citation. Mom glanced down at it and scowled, doubtlessly seeing the fine amount. God. This would have to happen when money was tight.

"Thank you, Officer," my mother said grimly but still ever polite. "This will never happen again."

Just then a car honked as it drove past the library parking lot. It moved at a snail's pace, the brake lights bright red in the night. Several faces peered out from open windows.

"Hey, Zach!" the driver called, his gaze sweeping over us. *All* of us. Zach, me, Mom, and the cops. I tensed. Great. Further public humiliation. Witnesses to my fall from grace.

"Hey, Willa!" a girl called from the back seat.

I squinted at her, recognizing Sydney from orchestra. I stared after them for a moment as the car drove away, the pit of my stomach knotting.

Great. Who knew what the rumors were going to be now that they'd seen us with these cops?

I stood with Zach and Mom as the two officers settled back into their cruiser and drove away, leaving us alone.

I inhaled a shaky breath. "Mom—"

"In the car, Willa."

"Mrs. Evans," Zach began.

"Not a word, Zach. I don't quite know what to think of you right now. I always thought you were a nice boy and someone I could trust with my daughter. I see now I will have to reevaluate my opinion."

"Mom," I whispered. "That's not fair."

Her gaze swerved back to me. *Fair?* The word flayed me like a whip. "I don't think you want to discuss what's fair with me right now, Willa. Now just get in the car."

Not long ago I was making out with Zach and now I was being lectured by my mother. How did I get here?

Hanging my head, I moved around to the passenger side of the car, not glancing at Zach again. I'd never seen Mom look at me the way she was now. It crushed me, and I couldn't bring myself to meet Zach's eyes while my own mother was glaring at me like I was such a disappointment. Something substandard. An unwanted daughter.

I felt his intense scrutiny as I buckled my seat belt, but I stared resolutely ahead. I didn't want to see what I was sure would be pity in his eyes.

When we got home, Chloe was there in the living room, waiting.

"Well?" she demanded.

"She was with Zach." Mom dropped her purse on the table by the door with a sigh. I hated that sigh. Hated that it was because of me. That I was just one more stress in her life.

Chloe snorted. "Course. Should have figured it was that guy she would be making out with." She looked at me. "You two have been eye-fucking for years."

"Chloe!" Mom reprimanded.

"That's not true," I snapped, certain Chloe didn't know what she was talking about. I was the one infatuated with Zach for all these years. It had very much been one-sided. Until now.

I wasn't sure what *now* was. Other than wrong. Now *was* wrong. I knew that.

Chloe kept going, all the bitterness and ugliness festering inside her spilling out and landing onto me. "I don't know why, though. It's not as though you're his type. Cheerleaders and girls like Flor are his type. You? You he'll just use and forget." She looked me up and down and her lips curled back in a sneer. "You don't think he's in love with you, do you? God, you're not in love with him, are you?"

"No!" I denied. "I'm not."

She snorted and shook her head. "You *so* are. Pathetic."

It was like she knew just what to say, the precise words to wound me.

I blinked eyes that suddenly burned.

"Chloe," Mom said in a warning voice. The kind of tone she used when we might have filched one too many cookies. It was like she didn't really care. Didn't care how mean and nasty Chloe was being to me, because she thought I deserved it.

And maybe I did.

My sister propped her hands on her hips and stalked closer to me. "And what about Flor? Your best friend? Does *she* know you're banging his ex?"

"Chloe!" There was Mom again, all outrage. I still couldn't help feeling it was more instinctive, more habit and not genuine.

"What?" Chloe glanced at Mom and shrugged. "It's true, Mom. She just got caught in the act. I hope you have her on the pill. You better take her to Dr. Halloway. If you don't, you're gonna have two grandbabies to take care of."

I balled my hands into fists at my sides. "Shut up!" I shouted.

Mom and Chloe both stared at me in shock.

"Considering *I* probably spend the *most* time out of the three of us taking care of Mia, you can just shut your mouth, Chloe."

Chloe sputtered, angry splotches of red breaking out over her face. "I stay home all day with her."

"And keep her in the playpen while you sleep, out cold from whatever pills you're popping!" I turned on Mom next. Since I was being honest, I might as well go all the way. "And you just go to work. I haven't quite figured out if you're just blind or indifferent to it. Either way, you're enabling her!" I stabbed a finger at Chloe.

Now Mom gaped at me.

"I'm almost eighteen," I said, my voice coming out calmer. "You could both cut me a break. I made a mistake. One mistake. I've never given you any trouble before. I make good grades and I'm busting my butt to get myself to college as cheaply as possible. I've never given you a reason to treat me like an irresponsible kid."

"Before tonight, you mean," Mom said evenly, holding up the citation between two fingers. "Any idea how much this costs?"

"It won't happen again. It was a mistake," I repeated, nodding. "I'll pay for it with my summer money."

"That money is supposed to be for your college savings."

I stared at the slip of paper in her hand, my sense of doom deepening. The citation would be a matter of public record, at least initially. And with all the gossips out there listening to police scanners? People probably already knew about it. I'd be lucky if it didn't get out at school.

God. Flor could find out. I could lose her. She'd hate me.

I rubbed my forehead where it was starting to throb.

It wasn't worth it. Not for something that didn't mean anything. My sister was right. As much as it hurt to hear her say the words. I wasn't Zach's type. He deserved girls who looked like Flor. Cheerleaders. Not a cellist. I didn't think he would set out to hurt me, but that would be the end result. He'd dump me like he did Flor.

Tonight was just some freak anomaly. A reaction to our longtime exposure to each other. It was physical attraction. Nothing more.

An experiment. That was what Zach had called it.

It wouldn't last. If I did this, if I let it happen, this thing between us would run its course and die. Zach would then find a girl more suited to him. Someone pretty and popular. Someone not me.

And then I'd be left with no one. Not Zach. And not Flor.

I couldn't risk it. Couldn't be so stupid to risk that.

"It's late," Mom announced, looking as tired as I felt. "We'll talk about this after I talk to your father."

The disappointment in her voice stung. Nodding, I turned and hurried upstairs, escaping into my room, shutting the door behind me—wishing I could shut out the world just as effectively.

But it wasn't to be.

My door flung open, and my sister strode inside, closing it with a hard crack after her.

"Ever heard of knocking?" I snapped.

She squared off in the middle of my room, hands on her hips. "You think I like being this way? Living this life?"

I sat up on my bed, staring at my sister for a moment, unsure how to respond.

Chloe continued, "I mean, you think I get off living at home

236

with my parents? I can't even take care of my own daughter without help. Oh, and it's awesome knowing both my mother and sister are better parents to her than I am." Her face screwed up tight with bitterness.

"Well," I snapped, "then do something about it. If you don't like it, change." I waved a hand at her. "Help yourself!"

"'Help yourself,'" she mimicked. "That's hilarious coming from you. You've been pining for a boy you're never going to get, but I don't see you helping yourself. No, you're letting him use you."

"At least I'm not the world's worst mother!"

She closed her eyes in a long blink, inhaling through her nose. "I know it doesn't look like I am . . . but I am trying."

I stared at her in disbelief. "You're right. It doesn't look like it."

"I'm working on it. Today was actually better than most," she admitted. "When I woke up, I didn't cry. Usually the first thing I do in the morning is cry. I look to the left of me and I realize Braden isn't there. I realize I'm all alone in bed. Then I remember everything. I remember everything that happened. I see his face when he said he didn't love me anymore . . .when he said he probably never really had."

I flinched. For the first time I thought about how awful that must have felt. How crushing. She'd never talked to me about what happened. I *knew* what happened, of course—my mother had told me the night Chloe and Mia showed up on our doorstep. I knew . . . but I had never really heard the words come out of Chloe before. This was different. It was different *hearing* the words from her. It was hard seeing the pain gleaming in her eyes. Looking at her, I imagined I could feel that pain too. I guess that was love. Because when the people you loved were hurting, you hurt too. I sighed. Damn it. She was my sister. Of course I loved her.

I shook my head in anger.

And for a change this anger wasn't directed at Chloe. It was the kind of anger I should have felt before, if I was any kind of a sister.

"That asshole," I growled. "I hope he gets a taste of his own medicine. I hope one day he wakes up and whatever her name is—"

"Dolores," she supplied, a faint smile playing on her mouth.

"I hope Dolores," I readily echoed, nodding savagely, "dumps his ass and leaves him. Then he'll know how it feels." Breathing heavily, I stared at her in a rare moment of camaraderie.

Then something she said clicked.

I angled my head. "Dolores? Really? That's her name?"

She busted out in sudden laughter. "Right? It's like she's fifty-five years old or something."

I joined her, laughing until my sides hurt. "Sixty-five, at least."

When we both finally stopped laughing, we stared at each other for a long moment.

In the quiet aftermath Chloe whispered, so softly I had to lean in to hear her, "I *am* trying. It may not seem like it, but I'm finding my way. I want to be a good mom. I want to be happy."

"Maybe you need help," I suggested. "Maybe you can't find your way alone." Gazing at her, I conveyed the full weight of my meaning. I wasn't talking about babysitting help for her daughter. She needed the kind of help Mom and I couldn't get her.

"Yeah." She nodded. "I should probably see someone."

We both understood we were talking about therapy. My chest loosened. Suddenly, I felt like I could breathe easier. "That's a great plan."

She nodded. After several moments she smiled at me. "I can't believe you got busted making out by a cop!" She nudged me in the shoulder with a giggle. "And you were supposed to be the good one."

Rolling my eyes, I shrugged. "Yeah. I was supposed to be."

GIRL CODE #26:

Real friends won't listen to rumors.

Flor

←———————»

I woke up late and then lay in my bed for several moments.

The memory of last night flooded me. In addition to being the smartest guy I knew, Grayson was a fighter in an underground fight club. In addition to that, he had a body that wouldn't quit and a mouth that could kiss you until you saw stars. Oh, and he was beyond *beyond* crazy devoted to his two sisters.

I let all that spin around in my mind for a while and percolate. The guy fascinated me and launched butterflies in my stomach. And he was coming over today. He was going to be alone with me in this very room.

I bounced up from my bed and reached for my phone to call Willa, excitement thrumming in my blood. I had to tell her about Grayson. I knew I could trust her to keep his secret. The phone rang for several moments before going to voicemail. With a grunt I flung it down on the bed and collapsed onto my back in the covers with a groan.

I spent the rest of the day working on homework and trying not to stare at the time, anxious for when Grayson would get here.

Later in the afternoon, I got a text from Jenna. Did you hear about Willa?

Frowning, I replied back. No. What's wrong?

Heard she got in trouble. Someone saw her w/Zach last night. They were w/cops.

What did that even mean? And why was Willa out with Zach? She'd said she was staying in last night. My fingers flew over my phone. They were with cops??? Where?

Don't know. In a parking lot somewhere.

In a parking lot? I shook my head. Well, if she'd gotten into trouble, that maybe explained why she wasn't answering her phone. I tapped on her name and sent her a quick text just in case. Hey. Everything ok??? Worried about you.

I went back to texting Jenna then. I was in the middle of asking her where she'd gotten her info from when my phone suddenly started ringing. Willa's face popped up on my screen. The photo was from a sleepover we had a year ago. She was making a crazy face and there was chocolate syrup on her nose from the sundaes we'd made.

I accepted the call and hit speaker. I wasn't a fan of burning-hot phones against my ear. "Hey, what's going on?"

Willa's voice floated on the air in a tinny whisper. She sounded like she was buried under a mound of bedcovers. "Hey, I can't talk. I'm grounded. Mom doesn't know I have my phone."

"What happened?"

"Zach and I ran out for some ice cream and we, er . . . got a ticket."

"Ohhh." I nodded. That made sense. Except . . . "You mean *he* got a ticket? He was the one driving, right? And why are *you* grounded? What did you do that was so wrong?" I felt suddenly angry on her behalf. Her mom expected so much from her, but put up with everything from Chloe.

"Um, I'll explain it all later. I just wanted to let you know," she said in a rush of whispered words.

"Okay," I murmured, not really understanding. There was definitely something weird in Willa's voice. "You sure you're all right?"

"Just . . . I . . . I'll explain everything at school tomorrow. Okay?"

"Okay," I repeated, a little unnerved by her cryptic answer. I hoped things were okay at home.

"Love you, Flor." There was just her breathing between us, but she was still there. She hadn't hung up yet. "See you before first period, okay?"

"Yes. Love you too, Wills."

Hanging up, I stared down at the phone in my hand for a while, wondering at the strangeness of that call. Something was definitely wrong. I hoped it wasn't anything with her parents. Or her sister. Chloe could be a real bitch.

I missed my Wills. We were overdue for a good girls night. And I couldn't wait to tell her about Grayson. A smile spread over my face and it felt good. I hadn't been smiling much these days. I knew it. I wanted that to change. I remembered what Grayson had told me. *You don't like your life? Then make the life you want for yourself.*

He was right.

I touched my mouth, fingers playing over my lips as I remembered that kiss. The rest of the afternoon dragged. I tidied my room, remembering how he'd said it was messy last time.

My father sent him upstairs when he arrived.

"Hey," I said, feeling kind of shy as he stepped inside. Which was weird in itself. I wasn't shy.

The last time he'd been in my room there hadn't been that kiss between us. Now it was there. This great big shadow that stretched over everything in the room.

"Hey," he returned.

I motioned to the desk. "I cleared everything off it."

"I didn't mind sitting on the floor with you."

My heart leapt a little like that meant something. I needed to relax. I was one step from hyperventilating.

"Well, I thought now we could be civilized and sit in chairs." I grinned like I'd made a joke.

Was it my imagination or did he look nervous too? He stood in the center of my room, fingers wrapped around the strap of his backpack.

I motioned to a chair, and his tall body crossed over to it in two long strides. We sat at the desk and started on my homework.

We didn't talk about last night. Not the fight. Not the kiss. Somehow we worked steadily for an hour. We were well-behaved children. *I* was a good girl pretending like my heart wasn't hammering away and my hormones weren't on fire for this boy.

At five minutes past, I cleared my throat and spoke up. "Hour's up."

He glanced at the time on his phone. "Oh. Okay." He leaned back in his chair. "You think you got this?"

I nodded and studied him, my gaze tracing over his profile. It was hard . . . not looking at him and feeling something now. Not *loving* the look of him. "You always make it seem easy." I shut my laptop and tucked my review packet back in my binder.

An awkward silence fell. My gaze drifted to where his hand rested on my desk. I reached out and touched his reddened knuckles, my fingers brushing over the raw flesh. "I guess I know now why your knuckles always look like this."

"Yeah," he murmured, the word thick and rough on the air.

I frowned. "I hate that you get hurt." I let my smaller hand cover his, keeping it there for a moment, not thinking, just enjoying the skin-to-skin contact, however minor it was. He didn't move, but I felt his gaze on me. I couldn't bring myself to look up.

I withdrew my hand on an exhale. *Don't look so desperate, Flor.*

I led him downstairs. Dad and Dana were somewhere else, so that was good. At least I didn't have to run into them.

I walked with him out the back door onto the patio. I fished his money out of my pocket and stuck it out for him to take.

He stared down at it, not lifting a hand to accept.

"Go on." I nodded, encouraging him. He clearly needed the money. He sacrificed his body every weekend just so he could save up money. "You earned it. Take it."

Still he hesitated, and something cracked loose inside me then. He didn't want my money.

He didn't want my money.

My mind raced. Why? Why wouldn't he take it?

"It's okay. Keep it." He turned then and headed for the gate.

Without thinking, I went after him. I grabbed his arm and forced him around. I was breathing fast, my heart lodged in the vicinity of my throat.

Dark eyes gleamed down at me and I had to know. "Why won't you take the money?" Was that strangled voice my own?

A beat passed. He said nothing.

Then his hand shot out. Warm fingers circled the back of my neck and tugged me forward. I caught a flash of Grayson's luminescent eyes. He examined me for the briefest moment before dipping his head. Then those lips were on mine again.

Blood rushed to my ears as we kissed. One hand held my face, his broad palm rasping my cheek, thumb sliding back and forth.

My lips quivered against him. Almost as though this were the first kiss I'd ever had. And in so many ways, it was. It was nothing like anything before. He made me burn and throb. An exhale passed from my mouth and fluttered against his.

I gripped his shoulders, my fingers curling and digging into the solidness of him. The warmth of his body seeped into mine. His lips were everything. Heat and pressure and pure goodness slanting over my mouth. The kiss grew hotter: open-mouthed, hungry, starving. A shudder racked me. He had to feel it. My entire body was crumpled against him. We were fused together.

I forced myself to stop, coming up for air, releasing a shaky breath because it was all *so* much. I wasn't going to say *too* much because that wasn't true. Not when I wanted more. I stared at him wide-eyed.

"Night," he whispered, his heated gaze traveling over my face. "See you at school."

"Good night," I returned. "Yes. See you at school."

I wasn't going to hide the fact that I was into this guy. We might be the most unexpected thing to come out of Madison High School in the history of ever, but that was fine by me. I'd always done the expected, and where had it gotten me?

He backed away, watching me for a few moments before turning and exiting through the gate and disappearing down my driveway.

I went back inside my house, feeling lighter and happier than I had in months. I hadn't felt like this even when Mom lived here. Even when things had been good with Zach. I wore a stupid grin on my face as I walked through the living room, Rowdy trotting at my side.

"Ah, Flor. Could we have a word with you?"

I froze, the lightness slipping away like smoke fading on air.

Dad and Dana entered the living room together from the hall that led to the master bedroom—the room they now shared.

"Uh, sure."

Dad motioned to one of the couches. "Have a seat."

Uh-oh. I had a sinking sensation in my chest as I lowered down onto one of the couches. They sat together, side by side, very much a uniformed front. A team. Why did it have to feel like me versus them?

I cleared my throat. "What did you want to talk about?"

"Well." He shared a look with Dana.

She smiled at him and gave an encouraging nod, and I knew this couldn't be good. Not if she was in support of it.

"I . . . we were thinking how you will be graduating from high school soon and going away to school. You're practically an adult now."

"Practically," I echoed. I had no idea where this was going, and that only made my uneasiness grow.

"Sure." Dad nodded. "Maybe it's time for you to go ahead and fly from the nest. Why wait until next fall when you can start learning how it is to function on your own now?"

I dropped my hands to the plush leather couch on either side of my legs. "What are you saying?" It almost sounded like they were kicking me out.

"Don't you think it would be fun to have your own place?" This from Dana. She leaned forward, her eyes bright.

I moistened dry lips. "You want me to live on my own?"

Dana nodded. "Wouldn't that be fun?"

I angled my head sharply and looked at my father. "I'm not even eighteen yet."

"The apartment above the garage is very nice. Full kitchen and bath. Small living area where you could entertain your own guests. I think the bathroom is even bigger than the one in your room now. And we can paint it any color you like."

I nodded slowly, feeling too nauseous to speak.

"How's that sound, sweetheart?" Dad stared at me hopefully.

He wanted this. He wanted me gone.

I'd lost my mother. She'd left. She didn't want me. And now my father didn't want me either. I was down two for two.

Why didn't they want to keep me around?

I had other friends with helicopter parents. They couldn't send a text without their mothers reading it. How was this my life?

I pushed up from the couch, broken, unwanted. "When do you want me to move out?" I stared steadily at my father as I asked this. It was his choice. His decision to get rid of me. He'd have to say it.

He looked uncertain for a moment, pinned beneath my stare. "Oh, I don't know—"

"You can move next weekend," Dana interjected.

Dad blinked, glanced at her, and then looked back at me, nodding. "Next weekend."

"I'll be out this time next week." Turning, I walked quickly from the living room to the stairs. Once free from their sight, I ran to my room, shut the door, and collapsed against it, sliding down its length to the floor as great sobs racked me.

I was an orphan.

GIRL CODE #27:

Don't let a pretty outer shell blind you to what's inside.

Willa

>>———————→

I was washing dishes at the sink when I heard a car in the drive-way. The dishes were mostly Mia's juice cups, which Chloe hadn't gotten around to washing. I rolled my eyes at the thought. As if Chloe ever would. I quickly told myself to think nicer thoughts about my sister. Since we'd had it out last night, things had been okay today. I had to give her a chance.

At least one relationship in my life didn't have to be a total mess. I cringed, thinking about my conversation with Flor tomor-row. I'd snuck my phone and risked calling her. Rumors thrived in this town, especially if they had to do with local football heroes. Maybe the full scale of what had happened last night wouldn't go public. She hadn't appeared to know anything when we talked. Tomorrow I would come clean. Better she hear it from me than from someone else.

I finished the last cup before turning to see who was here.

I moved to the front hallway and spotted him through the glass panel on the side of the front door and froze.

What was *he* doing here?

He moved with casual grace, his long denim-covered legs bringing him closer. The afternoon sun glinted off his thick head of hair. He was even better-looking in the light of day. It wasn't fair. Why did rotten things have to come in such pretty packages?

Shaking my head, I quickly opened the door and stepped out onto the porch before Mom or Chloe could hear the doorbell.

His steps slowed as his gaze landed on me. "Hey," he greeted me, his voice as easy and mild as his manner.

Hey?

He approached me like he was walking up to a friend and not a girl he had insulted just the other night.

I bristled. "What are you doing here?" I looked beyond his shoulder and then all around, up and down the driveway and even down the street, as though he might not be alone.

It was paranoia. What did I think? That he'd brought friends? To do what? Toilet-paper my house?

But then what was he doing here at all? I *should* be paranoid. This couldn't be good.

I glanced behind me, wondering if I should bolt back inside and lock the door on his too-pretty face.

"I wanted to see you after what happened the other night." He buried a hand in the front pocket of his jeans. The action stretched his T-shirt across his chest. A ridiculous chest. It was broad and muscled. Improbable for an eighteen-year-old, but then this whole scenario was improbable.

What were the odds that Travis's star quarterback would have singled me out at that party? That he would have kissed me? That he would now be standing on my front walk?

I crossed my arms over my chest, feeling suddenly cold and nervous. But, refusing to look like the coward I felt, I stepped down the porch steps toward him. "Why are you here?"

He shrugged like it was obvious. "I don't feel right about that night."

That was funny. I didn't feel right about that night either, but it didn't have anything to do with Beau Sanders. "How'd you even know where I live?"

"Not too hard to find out. I have friends that go to Madison." He held up his hands in the air in a nonthreatening gesture. "I promise I'm not stalking you."

I released a tight, breathless laugh. "Says every stalker who ever existed."

His mouth twisted in a semblance of a smile. "I forgot that you're funny."

"Yeah. Well . . . what do you want?" I didn't worry about sounding rude. He'd been a jerk the other night, and now he'd shown up here. I didn't owe him politeness.

"Well, I thought about what I said, what I called you . . ."

"Cock-tease?" I reminded.

"Yeah." He rubbed his nape, actually looking shamefaced. "I feel bad about saying that."

"Except you did say it. Friday night. You called me that." I held his stare, not so much as blinking.

He nodded. "I was in a bad place that night . . . and I took it out on you and Tucker." He exhaled. "Just because you walked out to the dock with me didn't entitle me to anything. Even though you kissed me—"

I held up a hand, wishing he would just stop now. I didn't want to think about that regrettable kiss. I'd let his pretty face blind me. I'd thought it could distract me from other stuff. Zach stuff. Zach-flirting-and-being-with-other-girls stuff.

"That kiss didn't entitle me to anything," he added again. "A girl decides. I've always known that. I guess I just . . ." His voice faded. He looked at me. "I was just a dick and I'm sorry, Willa. I deserved that slap."

I stared back at him, then away and back at him again. "You tracked me down to tell me that?"

"Well, yeah. That guy isn't who I want to be." His hazel eyes took on an earnest light. "I'm not him." Clearly this mattered to him, and I couldn't help wondering what he meant when he said he'd been in a bad place. I guess all of us had our baggage, and I got the sense he was trying to shake his loose.

"I hope you believe that and accept my apology," he said.

I stared at his handsome face a moment longer, wondering what it was about star football players. Did they all have to look like they'd stepped off the set of some CW show? I mean, was it a requisite?

I sighed. Whatever the case, he wasn't the complete jerk I'd thought. He'd sought me out to admit that he had been a dick and apologize. It was decent of him.

"I see that." I uncrossed my arms, feeling less nervous now. "Thanks for telling me."

"Sure." He nodded and looked around. An awkward silence fell. "Okay, then," he said, and started to turn. A door slammed and drew our attention to the house next door.

Zach charged across his lawn. I blew out a breath, knowing this wouldn't be good. He must have spotted us out the window. Knowing what was coming, I stepped in his path, blocking him from reaching Beau.

He stretched an arm over my shoulder, pointing at Beau. "What are you doing here?"

"Zach," I said. "Calm down. It's fine. He just came over to apologize to me for the other night."

He shot me a quick glance, his lip curling in a sneer. "Are you kidding me?"

My hands sank against the soft cotton of his T-shirt, trying not to notice the firmness of his body underneath the fabric, trying not to think about last night and just how close in proximity I had been to this chest.

"Zach," I said in my best scolding tone. "Go home. This isn't anything you need to worry about."

"Leave you here with him?" His gaze shot back to Beau. "Not happening."

"Wait, wait, wait. Hold on." Beau's voice intruded. "You mean to tell me Tucker lives next door to you?" He pointed back and forth between us.

I sighed and tossed a glare over my shoulder at him. "Yeah. So what?" Beau shook his head and laughed, his expression full of amusement.

Zach's chest lifted on a hard breath under my hands.

"Man," Beau continued, "that explains a *lot*."

If my glare had the power to maim, Beau would never play football again.

"We're good now," I said tightly. "You can go, Beau."

"Sure." Still laughing lightly, he started down my walk. "I don't want to cause any trouble. You two clearly have a lot to work out."

No! I wanted to shout after him. *We don't have anything to work out!* But of course we did. We had everything to work out.

Zach continued to press his weight into my palms, clearly still eager to tear into Beau. And this wasn't like him. He might have played football and hung out with guys that enjoyed aggression and violence even off the field, but he'd never been like that.

"Enough," I growled. "He's leaving." I looked up at his face. His eyes followed Beau as he walked toward his truck.

Finally, he eased against my hands.

"What's wrong with you?" I demanded.

His gaze snapped to my face. "Sorry if I reacted to seeing the same guy you slapped the other night at your house."

I dropped my hands from his chest and stepped back. "I can take care of myself."

"Your ability to take care of yourself doesn't mean I just stop giving a damn about you."

"You're reacting like some . . . jealous boyfriend." Heat crawled up my face, and I wished I'd said anything other than that. The moment the statement was out, I regretted it. It brought to focus last night . . . and the question: What were we exactly?

I didn't want him to think I expected anything of him or was fishing for a declaration of love and undying fidelity.

I could be mature. People messed around for fun. That was normal. Healthy, to a degree. Our newfound intimacy did not mean he was obligated to be my boyfriend. I understood that.

He sucked in a breath that expanded his chest. "I'm not your boyfriend. Fine."

I held his gaze, feeling a little hurt and angry at myself for that.

I guess, admittedly, a part of me wanted him to insist he was my boyfriend now.

He waved toward the street. "But that guy wasn't here to apologize."

I crossed my arms. "I think he was."

Zach snorted. "Don't be naïve. I wouldn't trust that guy. He's looking to get in your pants."

I arched an eyebrow. "Kind of like you?"

Zach stared at me like I'd sucker-punched him. "Is that what you think? You think I'm like him? That you're just some hookup for me?" Zach pointed toward the street. He was furious.

"And you think I'd just let him in 'my pants'?" I curled my fingers into air quotes, refusing to let his anger surpass mine.

Heavy silence passed as our words swam around us like poison in the air.

The front door opened behind me. "Willa. What are you doing

out here? You're grounded." I looked over my shoulder at Mom on the porch. She didn't look happy, but then that had been her expression most of the day. Her gaze cut to Zach. "Go home, Zach."

He nodded, his hot-eyed stare still fixed on me even as he addressed Mom. "Yes, ma'am."

I didn't wait to watch him obey my mother. I turned and went back inside my house and tried not to think about him for the rest of the day.

GIRL CODE #28:

It's easier to be a friend than an enemy.

Flor

←————————«

AFTER a while I got up from the floor and took a shower. It helped. I felt a little better when I got out. At least a little less like crying.

I wiped my fogged mirror clean with a hand towel and stared at my reflection. My dark eyes stared back, shadows like bruises under my bloodshot eyes.

It was just one more thing. Another blow, but I'd handle it. My mind drifted to Grayson. I knew a boy shouldn't matter so much, but right now I was glad to have him. Seeing him tomorrow gave me something to look forward to, and I needed that.

Wrapped in a towel, I emerged from the bathroom, only to squeak when I spotted Dana on the edge of my bed, waiting for me.

"What do you want?" I didn't raise my voice. I hardly even glanced at her. My voice said it all. I was tired. Bone tired. Sleeping in late today hadn't done much good.

"Just thought you might want to . . . talk."

I gripped the edge of my towel tighter. "Talk? You want to talk to me?" I snorted. That would be a first. I glanced toward my door to see if Dad was lurking there. Was she doing this for his benefit? To impress him? She should wait for him to be present to witness her efforts.

"It might be nice if you and I got to know each other better."

I pointed at myself. "You want to get to know me?"

"Is that so surprising? I am in a relationship with your father."

And that reminder was a bitter pill to digest after an already eventful night.

"You don't need to get to know me, remember?" I snapped. "I'm moving to the apartment above the garage." How could she have forgotten? I was sure she'd had everything to do with getting rid of me.

She rolled her eyes and waved an arm in the direction of the garage. "You're right outside the house in your own apartment, which is more luxurious than anything I've ever lived in."

"Except now," I shot back. Now she had this house. "But you're right," I went on to add. "I will be right outside. Kind of silly, isn't it? You were so determined to boot me out of this house, and I'll still be so close. You could have just waited until I left for college next fall. Rather impatient of you."

She shook her head. "Don't do this."

"What am I doing?" I shrugged.

"Being difficult."

"Life is difficult, I'm learning."

She laughed. "Spare me the teen drama." She propped her

hands behind her and leaned back on the bed. "You have your looks. A father who loves you. You can go to any college you want. Oh, and you're a crazy talented athlete. I would have killed for even *one* of those things when I was eighteen."

I stared at her. Words eluded me. I never would have thought she thought any of those things about me. I was surprised to know she thought about me at all.

"You didn't have a father who loved you?" I finally asked.

"It was just my mother. My father wasn't in the picture. He left us when I was four. I don't even know if he's alive or dead."

I processed that. At least my mother called occasionally.

"Look, Flor. Your dad is important to me. This relationship . . ." She paused, crossing her legs and leaning forward. "He makes me happy and I want to make him happy, too. I guess asking you to move to the apartment is selfish of us."

"You think?" I snapped.

She nodded in acknowledgment. "I just want to make this thing work between us." Her gaze pinned me to the spot. "You said it. You'll be gone soon. You'll be at college and starting your own life. Don't you want your father with someone and happy?"

Staring at Dana, I finally saw her as something besides the jail-bait witch out to steal my dad. "Yeah. Maybe I can see that." And I guess I did. I guessed having me underfoot probably didn't give them much solitude either. I sighed.

She smiled then, looking relieved.

I fidgeted where I stood, adjusting my grip on my towel, wondering if we had just entered some manner of truce. It seemed impossible considering my earlier tears, but I didn't want to be mad or sad anymore, and she just seemed so *human* sitting here on my bed.

"So how's that hot tutor of yours?" Dana suddenly asked.

"Grayson?"

She laughed. "Who else?"

"Um. Fine." Better than fine. He was an amazing kisser and a kick-ass fighter. Part of me felt compelled to tell her that. To see her reaction. And maybe . . .

Maybe I just didn't want to hate her anymore. Hating someone was a lot of work. It was easier not to hate. It would be easier, I realized in that moment, to turn her into a friend.

I cleared my throat. "Why don't I get dressed and I'll meet you downstairs to try some of those black-bean brownies you made."

Her eyes widened. "Really?"

I shrugged. "You got Dad to eat them."

"He loves them!" She nodded.

"Er, he said they were okay . . ."

She moved excitedly for the door. "I'll pack some in your lunch, too. You can share with your friends."

I watched worriedly as she left the room, wondering if I wasn't going to regret this particular act of goodwill.

GIRL CODE #29:

If your ex likes another girl, don't treat the girl like it's her fault.

Willa

>>———————→

MOM dropped me off. She'd hardly talked to me since that brief exchange with Zach, but she wasn't about to let him take me to school.

I knew something was wrong the moment I stepped into the halls. My entire existence had been largely invisible at Madison. And now far too many people were looking at me. Whispering. Smirking. *Seeing* me. My shield of invisibility had lifted.

I turned down the hall for my locker and it was more of the same. Eyes on me.

I scanned the faces, searching for someone familiar. A friend among unfriendlies.

My heart leapt as I spotted Jenna and Farah. I waved and then stopped, my arm dropping to my side as they quickly looked away from me, not meeting my gaze. Their expressions were grim —somber, even. And then I couldn't see their faces at all because they turned, walked away as one, and ducked down an intersecting hall.

Oh. God. It was out.

Everyone knew about Saturday. Or at least they knew some semblance of the truth. The warning bell rang and I wasn't even at my locker yet. Great. I was going to be late. But I didn't care. I didn't care because it felt like I was dying inside.

"Hey, lookee, guys. It's Willa."

I whirled around as Hayden and two of Zach's other teammates stopped in front of me. These guys never talked to me, but they were in front of me now, looking me over like I had something on my face.

"Heard about your little escapade with Tucker on Saturday."

Mortification washed over me, scalding my face. I tightened my grip on the straps of my backpack. "Nothing happened."

"Public lewdness." Hayden chuckled. "Nice. I didn't know you were into doing it in public."

One of the other guys added, "I didn't know she was into doing it at all."

They all laughed then.

Disgusted, I tried to step around them, but Hayden blocked me. I glared up at him. "Get out of my way."

He tsked. "So rude. I heard you could be really friendly."

I fought the urge to slap him. That was a scene I didn't need. My face burned hotter. The tension in me twisted tighter. I couldn't believe this was happening. I felt the attention around us growing. Things were bad enough, and now I was stuck with these

Neanderthals, one step away from a scene. Didn't people have class to get to?

He reached out and toyed with a piece of hair draped over my shoulder. "If you're done with Tucker, maybe you can try out my back seat this weekend."

I sucked in a breath. "You're a pig."

"Aw, c'mon, Willa. The whole world knows you got a dirty little streak in you now. How about you and me see if—"

Suddenly he was shoved into the metal lockers with a crash. He spun around on his assailant and started to come up off the lockers. "What the fuck!"

Zach shoved him back into them. "You don't look at her and you certainly don't spout off your filth at her. Understand, Hayden?"

"Damn, Tucker! You don't have to get all worked up. I didn't touch her. I sure as hell didn't realize you and her were a thing—"

"Well, now you know. So show some respect or it's my boot permanently in your ass."

I couldn't breathe. My lungs were too tight. I felt a shift in the air. A ripple passed through the sudden silence swelling like a storm around us.

The tardy bell rang shrilly, and I jerked like it was a new sound to me. No one else seemed to move or even care. Everyone continued to gawk. They wouldn't dare leave and miss the drama. They smelled potential blood in the air, and they wanted to be present for the first drop.

I scanned the crowd and that was when I saw her.

Flor stood as still as a statue, her gaze shifting from Zach to me. Her mouth hung open, lips parting in a small O.

"Flor," I started to stay, stepping forward, holding a hand out to reach her. I had to get to her. Had to make her understand. "I—"

She didn't let me.

She turned and bolted into the crowd.

GIRL CODE #30:

Because sometimes even best friends fail you —
it's okay to break down.

Flor

I pushed through the hall, desperate to escape.

Willa and Zach . . . Zach and Willa.

I couldn't wrap my head around it. The betrayal cut deep through me.

How long had this been going on? My ears rang with a pealing, unremitting buzz.

I thought back to the two of them. All the times I had seen them together. How close they were. They'd always had a special friendship. Obviously closer and more special than I realized.

"Flor!"

I ignored the sound of my name, pushing through a set of side doors that led to the courtyard. I could escape to the parking lot from here. Escape Willa chasing after me, maybe escape the pain, too . . . the knife in my back that felt like it was digging and grinding into bone.

"Flor! Wait!" She was right behind me. Her hand came down on my arm and I turned around swiftly, shrugging off her touch like it was something that burned.

"How long?" I choked. "Is this why he broke up with me? Have you two been going around behind my back all this time?"

Her eyes widened. "No! God, no! It just happened."

"'Just happened'?" I sneered. "How very cliché."

"I didn't mean for it to happen. I tried to stop it. I tried—"

"Oh my God," I choked. "Aren't you so tragic?" I looked up at the sky, blinking against the morning sunlight. "You're Romeo and Juliet, fated lovers, unable to resist each other."

"Flor, please."

I looked back down at her. "Maybe you'll both eat poison."

She blinked like I'd slapped her. "Please, Flor."

For the briefest moment, I felt bad for saying such an ugly thing . . . until I remembered the pain. Until I felt it burn a fire through me.

I shook my head slowly side to side, blinking long and hard. "And that stupid girl code we've been writing?" I let out a harsh laugh. "Pretty ridiculous, right? You must have been laughing inside at that. Sisters before misters and all that bullshit."

"I would never! I didn't want this." Her lips worked a moment before she confessed, "I've had feelings for Zach all my life."

"Oh? Funny you never mentioned that to me before."

"I didn't think there was any point. I didn't think Zach and I would ever . . ." Her voice faded, and she dropped her head to stare down at her feet, and I knew then. She loved him. "There's still no point." She lifted her chin like a stoic soldier about to march to her death. "We're not a thing. We're not *dating*. We're just friends."

"I heard him, Willa. I saw his face. You're either lying to me or yourself. And you know what . . . I don't care. I don't care about either one of you anymore. Because really . . . who needs this?" I motioned between us.

"Please don't say that." Her face twisted and reddened. "I'm your friend."

"I don't need a friend like you."

"You have to believe me. I didn't want to hurt you. I would never hurt you—"

"No? Well, you did."

Willa reached for my arm. I flinched as her hand brushed my skin. Shaking my head, I yanked my arm away.

"Please, don't do this. We've been friends ever since elementary school. That's a long time. Don't throw *us* away."

"You're right. It has been a long time, but you did this." I stabbed an accusing finger at her. "Not me."

The sight of her was too much. Right now I needed to get away. I couldn't trust anyone. First my parents . . . now Zach and Willa. I had never felt so alone in my life. Never so lost. Just staring at her, my supposed *best* friend, made me sick.

"I can't look at you. I can't hear your voice right now or see your face." I sucked in a thick breath and pushed it past my lips, wondering when it had become so difficult to breathe. "I need you to stay away from me."

I turned and fled. Clutching the strap of my backpack, I escaped through the courtyard and into the parking lot, weaving through cars, not even caring that all the windows faced out to the lot and countless eyes watched me run from school like some scared little rabbit.

I was almost to my car when I heard the distant shout of my name. It was a guy's voice. I tensed and turned, convinced that if it was Zach, I might get in my car and run him over in my present mood.

It was one thing for him to break up with me, but then to hook up with Willa . . . to ruin that friendship for me. He deserved no less.

Grayson jogged toward me, stopping when he reached me. "You okay?"

"You heard?"

He winced. "It's the only thing anyone is talking about."

"People need to get a life."

"It's high school." He shrugged, his eyes moving over me in concern. "That won't happen until after graduation."

"I guess it's fitting. First my mother moves out, then my dad gets a girlfriend and wants me to move out—"

"Wait, your dad wants you to move out?"

I kept talking, tears burning my eyes. "And then I find out my best friend is hooking up with my ex behind my back. God knows how long that has been going on." I laughed brokenly. "That's probably why he dumped me." I waved my arms wide at my sides. "I'm pretty much the girl that keeps getting crapped on."

"Flor." He stepped forward and touched my face, his thumb

brushing my cheek in a tender motion. "Things will turn around for you. Good things will happen—"

I kissed him. Hard and hungry, willing him to be that good thing for me right then.

For a moment his lips didn't move under mine, so I slanted my mouth over his and licked the seam of his lips, needy, desperate for him to kiss me back. To want me.

For someone to want me.

He relented. His arms came around me and hauled me against him. Which was just as well. I was about to climb all over him. I leaned into him, throwing off our balance. We staggered, colliding into a car.

I didn't care. He leaned back on the hood and I practically crawled on top of him, kissing him deeper.

"Flor," he muttered against my mouth.

I made a sound and continued to kiss him, glad, *relieved* for the heat of his mouth, the texture of his hands against my skin. I didn't feel nearly so alone with our mouths fused together.

His hands circled my arms. "Flor, wait."

"Why?" I gasped, staring at him in a fog. "You want me. I know you do. I want you, too." Fortunately the pain was a dull throb now, replaced by my desire for Grayson. He could make me feel better. Make me hurt less. I went for his lips again.

"Flor, stop." He peeled my arms from around his neck.

I jerked at his firm tone, feeling like a scolded child. I scowled up at him.

His dark eyes moved over me, the morning sun glinting off his glasses. "You're right. I do want you. But not like this. Not right now. Right now you don't know what you really want—"

A bitter breath escaped me. "Are you kidding me? Do you know how insulting that is? Poor little me doesn't know her own mind!"

"That's not what I mean. I'm just saying you're in a bad place today."

I stared at him with wide eyes, unblinking. "For a smart guy, you're really stupid. I've been into you from the first time you showed up at my house." It occurred to me that for once I was having no problem opening up. Speaking my mind. That had been Zach's chief complaint about me, but then, it had always been like that with Grayson. I'd told him things I hadn't told anyone. With Grayson I said exactly what was on my mind.

He stared at me with an expression of complete bewilderment.

"Forget it." I whirled around.

He was rejecting me. Like everything else that was failing in my life.

Ten minutes ago I hadn't thought I could hurt any worse. I was in a bad place? Yeah, you could say that. I was in this awful, soul-sucking place where light couldn't thrive, stars didn't shine. I had thought, hoped, he might make it better for me. That he might pull me out of the darkness and be that light. But he wasn't. He made it all worse.

"Flor!"

I heard my name again but didn't stop, didn't look back at him. I didn't want to listen to him anymore. The pain was back, even more intense now.

There were hard footsteps behind me. A hand on my shoulder spun me around.

I hissed out a breath at the sight of his face. When had it become so beautiful to me? So necessary?

"I want us to happen," Grayson growled.

"You sure don't act like it." I looked away, searching for my car. Better that than looking at his face.

He reached for me and hauled me against him, kissing me . . . bewildering the hell out of me.

And yet I kissed him back, euphoria blossoming in my chest.

"Flor." He pulled back slightly to talk against my mouth, his breath falling raggedly. "I'm into you, too. So much." His hands framed my face and I swore I could feel the pulse of his heartbeat through his palms. "I just want to matter. I want *us* to matter—"

"You've mattered to me before today happened. I was so excited to come to school to see you."

His dark eyes roamed my face. "I'm an asshole. I'm sorry."

I choked on a laugh.

"I never date. It's school and work and fighting. This is new, and it's a scary thing," he added.

"What's a scary thing?" I whispered, needing to hear it from his lips.

"Trusting someone with your heart."

Didn't I know that? I'd just been burned by my best friend.

He continued, "My plan was to get out of here. Escape. I wasn't supposed to fall for a girl way out of my league."

I shook my head, hating that he thought that. It wasn't true. "I'm not."

His dark eyes fixed on me, hands flexing on my shoulders. "Flor."

My breath caught at the intense way he was looking at me, his dark eyes full of determination and something else. Something I'd never seen in any guy's eyes before. "Grayson," I whispered back.

I felt raw inside, open and exposed. But gazing at him, that wasn't all I felt.

There was hope.

GIRL CODE #31:

Love makes you do crazy things. Try not to judge.

Willa

»———————→

THE rest of the day went by in an agonizing blur. There were the stares and whispers. My friends gave me a wide berth.

Ava bumped into me in the hall. It wasn't accidental. Her shoulder collided with mine, knocking me into the lockers. She looked down at me with spite in her eyes. "And you told *me* not to fool around with Zach. Bitch."

I just wanted the day to be over.

If I wasn't already in trouble, I would have skipped school like Flor had done. Mom wouldn't forgive that, though.

As soon as school ended, I hopped on the bus for home. I hadn't taken the bus since sophomore year, but I didn't imagine any of my friends would give me a ride home today. I definitely wasn't going to get a ride with Zach, either. Even if I didn't mind being in an enclosed space with him right now, I wasn't about to wait around for an hour and a half for practice to let out.

When I got home, no one was there. Chloe and Mia were gone.

A note on the fridge said they'd gone to get groceries. That was a first. Chloe chipping in and doing a chore that usually fell to Mom or me.

I grabbed a Coke from the fridge and took refuge in my bedroom, glad for the solitude.

I opened my laptop and went straight to Netflix. I scrolled through my shows and then clicked on *Freaks and Geeks*. It seemed an appropriate show to lose myself in . . . the drama was slightly more than what was happening in my own life. Only slightly. But it wasn't *my* life, so there was that. Anything was better than my life right now.

Footsteps sounded on the stairs and I sighed. Chloe was already home. Great. I'd been hoping for a longer reprieve.

A knock sounded on my door. Maybe it was Mom. Chloe never knocked. "Come in."

Zach stepped inside.

I froze with my Coke can halfway to my lips. "Why aren't you at practice?"

He was wearing his athletic clothes, the hair at his temples damp with sweat. "Left early."

"I didn't think you could do that."

"I wanted to talk to you. You weren't at lunch."

"That would be because I was hiding. After your little scene this morning, I pretty much had to hide."

He closed his eyes in a pained blink. "I'm sorry. It shouldn't have happened that way. I shouldn't have blurted it out like that."

"That we're a *thing*? Yeah, you shouldn't have." I lifted my laptop off my lap and scooted off the bed. "How could you do that?"

He shrugged. "Because Hayden is a jackass and he needed to know that you and I are together."

I blinked, pretty certain that had never been established. "No. We're not."

He straightened. "No?" He pointed at himself. "Have I just been kidding myself, then?" He waved between us. "What do you call this? What do you call what we've been doing?"

"An experiment! Isn't that what you said?"

He sighed and shook his head. "Forget I said that, okay? I wish I never had! I said it just so I could kiss you again. I wanted to convince you, and I didn't think you'd be ready to hear that I might want something more from you than friendship."

Might.

He wasn't sure. He was still using words like *might* because he knew what was happening with us was nothing more than the experiment he first proposed.

"Friendship is enough for me." I crossed my arms. "It should be enough for you."

"Stop being so afraid, Willa."

I scoffed. "Afraid? Of what?"

"Of us. Afraid that you might want more. Afraid that you might actually be in love with me."

Panic squeezed my heart. That was a foregone conclusion. I'd always been in love with him. I just didn't want him to know it. He couldn't know it.

"I'm not," I lied. "That's not it at all. I have loyalty to Flor. I've already broken girl code—"

"Fuck girl code!"

I gasped.

He continued. "It's just an excuse. You hide behind it because you don't want to take a chance on us. This isn't about some stupid code that doesn't acknowledge things like real life and that gray areas exist. This isn't about Flor, either. Flor has nothing to do with this." He cut a hand fiercely through the air. "This is all *you* . . . and your insecurities keeping us apart."

I stared at him. Words failed me. I felt stripped bare, exposed, raw and bleeding in front of him, but he wouldn't stop. He kept going, hurling ugly truths at me that I couldn't escape or dodge.

He stalked forward. "What I feel for you I've never felt for anyone." His gaze flicked over my face. "I know you feel it too. It's just a shame we're both going to miss out on something good, something great, even, because you're too much of a coward."

I opened my mouth, working my lips to say something, anything, to prove him wrong.

He pointed to my window, where his house loomed just beyond. "I'll be waiting where I've always been. Right next door. Any time you want to start living, I'll be there. You have me, Willa, whether you want me or not." His gray eyes cut through me, brilliant and deep and sharp as glass. He saw everything. He knew me. "I'm yours."

He turned away then and walked from the room. I heard his footsteps fade on the stairs.

I moved to the window and parted the curtains to look outside, marveling at what my life had become. Flor hated me. Zach and I were . . . well, not friends. I was grounded indefinitely and my mother was treating me like I was her great shame.

I watched as Zach crossed the lawn to his driveway, his strides swift and sure. He was always so sure, so confident in everything. I envied that. Maybe if I were confident in my decisions I wouldn't be in this situation, and Zach wouldn't think I was a coward.

And I wouldn't be starting to think he was right about that.

I mulled that over all night and well into the next day. I drifted through all my classes, walking in a fog through the halls, lost in my thoughts.

I wasn't so unaware of my surroundings, though, that I did not notice the whispers were less, as were the stares. Jenna said hello to me in the hall with only sight hesitation. There was still wariness in her gaze, as though she did not quite know if she should be talking to me.

I spotted Flor once. Our gazes locked across the cafeteria. There was nothing in her stare. Cold blankness. She didn't smile or wave or try to approach me, and my heart sank. Was it really over, then? Had I lost her forever? And was I going to lose Zach, too?

Was I such a coward I would let that happen?

The answer came to me during the last period of the day. I was sitting in English. The classroom had a view of the football field, and the team had athletics that same period.

I easily identified Zach practicing on the field, kicking the ball. English class was the extent of my football watching. I didn't do the games, scrimmages, or practices. People, especially girlfriends, actually came out to watch the team and support them during practices. I always rolled my eyes at that. As though games weren't enough.

The bell rang and I gathered my things. I exited the building but didn't head to the buses. I marched straight to the football field.

I hesitated at the fence, flexing a sweating hand around the strap of my backpack. Shouts and grunts and padded bodies crashed into each other on the turf, the sounds congesting the air. Coaches shouted and whistles blew.

I sucked in a breath and headed for the bleachers. Girlfriends were filing in, many accompanied by friends. They took their spots. Several looked at me curiously. They were clearly regulars and they knew I wasn't. The ones who knew the rumors were easy to mark. They pointed at me and then quickly leaned in to whisper among their friends.

I took a seat at the bottom of the bleachers and picked out Zach on the field. He was practicing a drill with two other players.

He kicked the ball, and it must have been good because it got him high-fives. I clapped and cheered his name. That seemed to be the thing to do. The other onlookers were doing it . . . showing their support.

That's what I wanted to do for him. Show my support. Be there for him. Stop being so afraid to show him how I felt.

I wanted to start living, just as he had challenged me to do.

He must have heard my voice. His head swung around and his gaze found me. He grabbed his helmet and pulled it off his head as though to see more clearly. Even across the distance I felt the intensity of his stare. Heat slapped my cheeks and I knew I must be red-faced.

Suddenly he dropped his helmet to the turf. He was moving, jogging across the field toward the bleachers. Heading right for me.

A coach blew the whistle and shouted, "Tucker! Where the hell are you going? Get back here!"

Zach ignored him. Everyone was watching. The entire team and coaching staff. The people in the stands.

I didn't care.

They could stare.

He crossed the field and pulled himself up over the bleachers stand like it was nothing. My stomach went wild, invaded by a thousand butterflies as he landed heavily on his cleats on the steel floor in front of me.

"Tucker!" his coach shouted again.

"What are you doing here?" He was slightly out of breath.

I smiled and shrugged lightly. "I came to watch your practice."

"You hate football."

"But I love you."

There.

I'd said it.

The words dropped like immense stones into the thick space between us.

He stared at me for a long moment, unsmiling, his eyes deep, devouring me where I sat. I pointed at the field. "They're calling you. You might get in trouble."

"I don't care." He stepped forward and grabbed me, hauling me up against his big, sweaty, pad-protected body.

He kissed me. At school. In full daylight. With the whole world watching.

In the distance, I heard a whistle blowing madly. We were probably both going to get detention. PDA alone guaranteed it.

He pulled back to look at me. "You're not scared anymore?"

"Are you kidding? I'm terrified." I was in love with this beautiful boy and life was scary. Every risk exposed you to possible pain.

He laughed softly. "Brave girl." He brushed his fingers down my cheek. "We can be scared together."

"Tuckerrrr!" Several curses from the coach followed this shout.

"I think your coach is about to have a coronary."

"Right." He nodded swiftly. "You'll be here?" He pointed where I sat. "We'll go home together?"

"You're my ride." I grinned. "I'm not going anywhere."

He smiled widely and nodded. After pressing a quick kiss on my lips, he jumped off the bleachers. Running backwards over the field, he spread his arms wide and shouted at me, "I love you, Willa Evans."

GIRL CODE #32:

When your friends let you down, it's up to you to decide what hurts less: forgiving them or living without them.

Flor

I opened the door to my apartment, expecting to see Dana. She'd bought a bunch of questionable wall décor, but she had insisted that it was fabulous and that I should hang it on my walls.

Only Dana didn't stand there.

Grayson grinned at me and held up two brown paper bags sporting grease stains that promised all kinds of unhealthy goodness.

I leaned against the doorjamb and smiled. I couldn't help myself. The sight of him lit me up like a tiki torch. Despite everything, I was happy. "Oh, um. Sorry. I didn't order a heart attack in a bag."

"Oh, this?" He glanced inside one bag. "You didn't want a cheeseburger with two sides of French fries and onion rings?" He blinked in mock innocence, his lashes lush behind the lenses of his glasses.

I half snorted, half laughed. "Oh, is that all? You better get inside here before Dana catches wind of what you brought. She'll force kale down me all week as penance." I opened the door wide so he could enter.

"Place is looking nice," he remarked, setting the bags on my coffee table. He'd helped me move most of my stuff in yesterday.

"I'm mostly settled."

His gaze went to the TV. "*House Hunters*?" he asked.

"Better than that. *House Hunters International*."

We settled onto my rug in front of the coffee table and pulled our food out of the bags. For the next half hour we pigged out and watched a couple debate whether they wanted a tiny flat on a fifth floor (no elevator!) or a place with a nonexistent kitchen forty minutes away from where the husband had to work.

"I'd pick the place in the country."

"Course," Grayson replied. "I bet you could see lots of stars out there."

I looked at him, my heart fluttering. He remembered that conversation we'd had that night in his car.

I took another bite of my cheeseburger and moaned. "This is so good. Where did you get this? I've got to tell Willa about—" I stopped abruptly, mentally cursing myself. We might not have talked all week, but she still kept creeping into my thoughts.

"Why don't you call her?"

"Who?" I asked.

Grayson gave me a disappointed look. "You know who."

I shrugged and turned my attention back to the TV. The wife was complaining about the lack of closet space.

"It's Amsterdam!" Grayson addressed the wife on TV, waving his burger in the air. "Don't worry about closet space."

I smiled. "You know she can't hear you, right?"

He stared somberly back at me. "I believe I have the power to influence the outcome of this."

"Really? It's a rerun, you know."

He threw an onion ring at me. It went down the front of my hoodie. I shrieked as he dove after it. We ended up wrestling and laughing.

Then we ended up making out until we were hot and breathless and our mouths were too busy to laugh.

I'm not sure what apartment the couple ended up choosing.

GIRL CODE #33:

Remember true friends are forever.

←——————→

It was dusk when Flor pulled into the deserted parking lot.

She told herself she'd stopped because it was on her way home from soccer practice. But that wasn't true. She'd stopped because she wanted to. Because this place called to her. Because she'd been thinking about a lot of things this past week—about all the things that were wrong in her life and all the things that were right.

Things like the A she'd gotten on her math test. Things like soccer. Things like Grayson. A soft smile curled her lips. He was an unexpected gift. She'd decided it was up to her if she wanted more gifts in her life. She had to make room for them and let them in.

The sun had almost descended below the rooflines of the nearby houses. The air was an orangey pink. She stared at the Fielding Elementary playground for several moments. It felt both familiar and oddly foreign.

It was like looking at a photo of yourself from years ago, when you didn't remember the shirt you had on or even where you were in the snapshot . . . but you knew it was you.

The playground seemed smaller. The slides, the swings, the rock wall where she'd lost her foothold and slipped and chipped her tooth in fifth grade. The yellow monkey bars were not nearly as daunting as when she was eight, when she was always falling off them and scraping her knees. Now she could climb them without falling.

Her gaze drifted to the faded purple bench. She almost expected to see Mrs. Grossman standing over it, glowering at her as she held out another worksheet for Flor to do while all the other kids played.

She wasn't there, of course. But someone else was.

A shadowy figure sat on the bench.

Flor squinted through the windshield, studying the figure, recognizing the shape of her head, the angle to her shoulders. She didn't need to see her face to know.

Of course she's here.

She studied her for a long moment, a dull ache starting in her chest.

Flor shut off the car, pocketed her keys, and stepped out. Her cleats clattered over the concrete as she walked to the playground. Her coach would hate that. Cleats were supposed to be for the field only. She came up on the faded purple bench and rounded it to sink down beside her.

Willa surveyed Flor, grass-stained and rumpled, and then went back to staring at the playground, suddenly nervous. She had been imagining this playground full of kids, running and playing, not worried about anything except the moment and what was for lunch.

Flor stretched her legs out in front of her, crossing her ankles as she, too, stared out at the playground.

Willa looked down at Flor's legs. "You need to bleach your socks. You're never going to get those grass stains outs."

"They're just my practice socks."

Willa nodded.

Silence swam between them in the fading day. Acorns broke loose and popped to the ground around them.

Flor flexed her fingers around the edge of the wood bench. "So you're with Zach now?" She asked even though she knew. It was all over school that they were together. Flor had seen them in the halls, too. Holding hands.

Everyone at school watched Flor wherever she went like they expected her to go all Carrie. They did this even though she wasn't walking the halls alone either. She had Grayson at her side, his hand in her hand.

But Flor had to ask. Had to hear it from Willa.

Willa turned and looked at her. Flor met her gaze.

Their faces were as familiar to each other as their own. Maybe more. Every line and hollow. Every curve and freckle.

"Yeah. We are," Willa answered. No point lying or denying. Apologizing felt too late . . . and somehow insincere. "We are."

Nodding, Flor looked out at the playground again. "You need to let me do your eyebrows. They're out of control."

It wasn't meanness. Flor always let her know when she thought her eyebrows had gone jungle. This was comfortingly normal.

Willa let loose a single laugh. "Okay."

More silence. More acorns fell. The air had turned murky, the sun lost behind trees and houses.

"So did I mention that my father kicked me out? He had me move into the apartment over the garage."

Willa gasped, her heart twisting. "No!"

"Yep. Lovebirds need their space, I guess." Flor shrugged like it was just one of those things that happened in life.

"Asshole," Willa muttered. It had to have hurt. And it hurt Willa if it hurt Flor. That would never change.

Flor chuckled. She hardly ever heard Willa curse. "It's okay now. I mean . . . I wasn't okay with it at first, but I'm okay with it now. Dana and I talked. She's not a total witch, I guess. Just wants her space with my father. The apartment is pretty big. I got to pick out new furniture for it. They even offered me an entertainment center."

"Oh. Well then." Willa blinked like she wasn't entirely convinced. Something like that would have crushed her, but if Flor claimed it was okay, the last thing she wanted to do was make her feel bad about it.

There had been enough feeling bad lately.

"I plan on buying the most expensive entertainment center I can find."

"Of course," Willa agreed. "As you do." A whimsical smile brushed her lips. She stared down at her fingers wrapped tightly around the edge of the purple bench. The wood was dry and cracked, in some spots not purple at all anymore. Just a weathered gray-brown in those places where there had once been color. Everything changes. Adjusts and becomes something else. This bench had been in this spot for a long time. She imagined it would be here for many years more, even if it looked different from when it had been fresh and new.

"You walk here?" Flor asked.

Willa nodded.

"Want a ride home?" Flor offered.

Willa looked at her, hesitating only a moment before answering, "Sure."

Flor nodded once. "C'mon."

They stood and left the bench, their arms brushing as they walked side by side, leaving the playground behind.

Acknowledgments

Acknowledgments are a tricky thing. There are always people you worry about leaving out, but here goes:

Thank you to my agent, Maura Kye-Casella, for never giving up on me or any book idea I have—especially this one! Thank you for the trust. You're a dream agent.

No book writes itself. Yes, there's me in the chair typing away, but also all my wonderful and supportive friends right alongside me: Sarah MacLean, Ally Carter, Kimberly Derting, Lark Brennan, Lindsay Marsh, Shana Galen, Lily Dalton, Nicole Flockton, Mary Lindsey, and Tera Lynn Childs.

Of course, this book would never have happened without my team at HMH: Elizabeth Bewley, who first read the proposal for *The Me I Meant to Be* and said the all-important YES. For my editor extraordinaire, Lily Kessinger, who has seen this book through every stage and variation—I'm so awed and humbled by the attention you gave to this book. THANK YOU! For Tara Shanahan, thank you for helping bring this book to the public—and for making me blush with your praise of that first draft! And thank you to Opal Roengchai for coming up with the perfect packaging for Flor's and Willa's stories.

And last—but first in my heart—love and gratitude goes to my family for putting up with me through all my deadline panics. You might not know which book I'm working on, but you know me and my quirks, and you let me do my thing.